I0772062

UNBREAKABLE VOWS

UNBREAKABLE VOWS

VOWS IN MAGIC AND STEEL™
BOOK THREE

RIVER TATUM

MICHAEL ANDERLE

DON'T MISS OUR NEW RELEASES

Join the Florid Romance email list to be notified of new releases and special promotions (which happen often) by following this link:

https://floridromance.lmbpn.com/about/sign-up-for-our-newsletter/

This book is a work of fiction. All of the characters, organizations, and events portrayed in this novel are either products of the author's imagination or are used fictitiously. Sometimes both.

Copyright © 2025 River Tatum
Cover copyright © Florid Romance

Florid Romance supports the right to free expression and the value of copyright. The purpose of copyright is to encourage writers and artists to produce the creative works that enrich our culture.

No part of this book may be reproduced, or stored in a retrieval system, or transmitted in any form or by any means, electronic, mechanical, photocopying, recording, or otherwise, without express written permission of the publisher.

Published by Florid Romance
an imprint of LMBPN Publishing
2375 E. Tropicana Avenue, Suite 8-305
Las Vegas, Nevada 89119 USA

Version 1.00, March 2025
eBook ISBN:979-8-89354-548-7
Print ISBN: 979-8-89354-549-4

CHAPTER

ONE

Elysia's hands trembled faintly as she lifted them from the guard's chest, letting the last threads of healing magic dissipate back into her palms. The swirl of golden light winked out, leaving only the flickering orange glow from the festival torches. She sucked in a ragged breath, willing her own racing pulse to slow. The entire crowd around her stood stunned: some wore expressions of naked fear and superstition, others an uneasy curiosity.

The guard on the ground—big, broad-shouldered, wearing the baron's colors—drew a shaky inhale and braced himself on one elbow. Elysia gently pressed his arm, urging him not to lurch upright too quickly. "Give yourself a moment," she said, voice hushed but firm. A wave of guarded relief spread outward. The man's face was gray with shock, but his color began returning. His heartbeat steadied beneath her palm. In the swirl of so many stares, that small triumph felt precious and fragile.

Above her, Lorand's voice was already booming. "All of

you, step back—make room!" he commanded. She real- ized he'd climbed onto a nearby crate to address the crowd. In the uncertain lamplight, the Valecrest heir looked every inch the commander, one hand raised to still the rising panic. His authority sliced through the disarray that had seized the courtyard.

Across the circle, tension was tangible—a knot of festival-goers in bright tunics, half-eaten pastries still clutched in their hands, all jostling for a glimpse of the guard's condition. She heard bits of frantic whispers: "The witch's done something." "He fainted from her powers?" "No, I saw a hooded figure—" "He took a vile brew, that's what!" Rumor bled from mouth to mouth in the half-darkness.

Heedless of the onlookers, Elysia passed her hand a final time across the guard's forehead, checking for any lingering residue of the tainted substance that had nearly felled him. Faint traces of it curled through him like a venomous thread, but she'd managed to isolate the worst of it. Her stomach knotted. A purposeful sabotage, timed to look like her healing or wards might be at fault. She'd recognized the swirl of suspicious fluid as soon as she saw that hooded figure press the tiny vial into his hand. Kester's minions, no doubt, or some lesser conspirator hoping to stir panic.

At that moment, she felt Lorand's presence behind her —suddenly close, a warm shadow. He hopped down from the crate and laid a hand on her shoulder. "Is he stable?" he asked, the low timbre of his voice carrying only to her ears. Tension coiled in every syllable. She recognized the concern in it—concern for a random guard's health, but also for her. She was all too aware that members of her own house would cynically call that impossible, that a Valecrest heir wouldn't drop everything to see how a Kallendore mage fared. But she felt Lorand's sincerity in the subtle press of his palm, nonetheless.

"He'll recover," she said softly, glancing over her shoulder. "The poison was faint. Enough to knock him unconscious, nothing more, as long as it's treated." She swallowed. "We need to stop these rumors before they take root."

Lorand nodded, turning back to the onlookers without relinquishing his proximity to her. "Hear me!" he bellowed, scanning the crowd. "Lady Elysia has healed this guard from a staged ailment—someone planted a toxic substance on him. We have no reason to believe it was any Kallendore trick or so-called 'witch' act." His grey eyes roamed across the throng. "These insinuations that Kallendore wards bewitch the land are pure nonsense. Keep your heads."

At that, an uneasy ripple traveled among the towns-folk. Several Valecrest knights, posted near the orchard's edge, exchanged uncertain glances. Farther back, Elysia could see a few Kallendore cousins bristle—perhaps they, too, were suspicious that Valecrest might have orches-trated this fiasco. The baron's efforts at forging unity were unraveling by the minute.

Just then, the baron himself—broad shoulders in a serviceable cloak—pushed forward through the throng, flushed with urgency. "What is all this ruckus?" he demanded, voice pitched with alarm. "We have hours yet of festival events, and the courtyard has erupted into chaos!"

Elysia rose to her feet, offering the guard a final supportive hand as two other watchmen stepped in to escort him away. She forced her shoulders back, voice carrying above the band's half-forgotten fiddles. "My lord, a hooded figure slipped the guard a strange vial. The man collapsed—likely part of some sabotage to stoke fear of magic." She flicked her gaze around. "It's precisely the sort of rumor-laced trick Kester or his allies might use."

At the name Kester, a rustle of anxiety fanned through the crowd. The baron's face darkened. He'd suspected sabotage for days but had hoped to avoid an open spectacle. Now, with so many onlookers, the tension threatened to bubble over. He cleared his throat, raising a hand. "Enough," he declared loudly. "We will not let vague rumors overshadow the festival. I want no more talk of curses or illusions run amok. Soldiers and knights, help maintain order. Let us all keep calm—and if any of you see unknown prowlers or suspicious behavior, report it at once!"

A man wearing a Valecrest surcoat muttered from the side, "We saw a robed figure heading that way." He pointed, but the alley he indicated lay in near darkness, flanked by torch stubs that had long since guttered. Immediately, Darius—Lorand's longtime companion— stepped forward, beckoning two other knights. "Come on," he said tersely, voice clipped with readiness. "We'll see if that scoundrel is lurking." With that, they rushed off.

Elysia exhaled. Her heart still hammered from the abrupt swirl of it all. She'd known the sabotage would escalate, but not so brazenly in the middle of the festival's largest courtyard. The scuffle by the open fire cook stall had been so swift that if she hadn't glimpsed that hooded shape pressing the vial into the guard's hand, she might have been as perplexed as everyone else. Now the crowd's fear was pointed squarely at her.

She wiped a stray bead of sweat from her temple. The faint tang of rosin and bread lingered in the air—festive scents turned sour by tension. As the baron directed watchers to disperse and keep an eye out, Lorand jumped down from the crate entirely, moved to Elysia's side, and lowered his voice. "You saw the figure. Did you catch any detail that might help us?"

She pressed her lips together, scanning her memory. "They were too quick. I only saw a partial silhouette. Medium height, possibly slight build, wearing a plain hood. But the second they released that vial into his hand, they vanished into the crowd." She frowned. "The only surety: They intended to sow the rumor that my healing or wards backfired. The timing was perfect, right as that poor guard stumbled. People are all too willing to believe Kallendore magic is dangerous."

Lorand's jaw flexed. "Well, let them talk. We'll counter those rumors by showing them what's truly happening." He hesitated, eyes drifting to the ring on his finger—his Valecrest signet. The crowd had begun to break apart into smaller clusters of worried discussion, but still, Elysia felt multiple gazes pinned on her from across the courtyard.

She inhaled, clinging to Lorand's calm, forcibly assured presence.

A heavy step interrupted them as the baron strode closer. "We must keep the festival from dissolving into a riot," he said, voice low. "I'll post extra watchers around the cook stalls, though we're short on men. Everyone's scattered preparing for tomorrow's major events." He rubbed the bridge of his nose. "And tomorrow... We can't afford more of these stunts during the official dance or final speeches. The monarchy's envoy is watching. One rumor of supposed 'curse magic' could ruin everything."

Elysia bowed her head in agreement. Sir Remine, the king's examiner, had arrived that very morning, calmly awaiting a demonstration of unity. Now, if he saw the barony teeter on the edge of open panic over witchcraft claims, it would reflect poorly on the forced union they'd fought so hard to protect.

"We'll investigate," Lorand said firmly. "Darius might catch the culprit. If not... we'll keep searching. We cannot let them strike again unseen." He paused, glancing at Elysia. "But we also need you safe." His voice dipped quieter. "No telling if another saboteur tries to paint your healing as malicious."

She tensed, bristling at the notion of stepping away from the fight. "I won't hide, Lorand," she said, ignoring the flicker of warmth at his concern. "If the sabotage escalates, I'd rather be close at hand to heal or quell illusions than stand idle."

He didn't argue. The baron nodded curtly to them both. "I'll judge the guard's condition personally, then speak with a handful of my staff. Meanwhile, you two—" He gestured around the courtyard. "Try to calm the townsfolk. Be visible, show them the betrothed pair stands firm together. Because, by my guess, that's exactly what these saboteurs fear: that you might truly unify your houses."

Elysia inhaled slowly, her pulse still thrumming. The baron was right. Kester's entire strategy hinged on stoking fear and dividing Kallendore from Valecrest. If Elysia and Lorand paraded a stable front, it could disarm some of the rumors that incited panic. Her gaze snagged on Lorand's, and for an instant, she found reassurance in the faint lift of his brow—an acceptance that, right now, they had no choice but to keep forging forward.

"Very well," she said. "We'll do what we can."

The baron didn't waste a moment. He pivoted away, beckoning staff to come aid the guard. Elysia watched him go, then allowed Lorand to guide her gently with a hand at her elbow. He angled them toward a cluster of gawking villagers near the cookfires, some wearing expressions of naked suspicion. She steeled herself, determined to quell misguided talk of curses, even if half the barony was ready to blame her for everything.

A hush fell as they stepped closer to that cluster. Elysia recognized a traveling cobbler she'd briefly spoken with earlier in the day, as well as two older women. The cobbler drew back, shoving his hands into his pockets as though fearing a hex. Elysia bit down feelings of hurt. She took a measured breath. "No curse has afflicted that guard," she said in a steady voice, loud enough for them all to hear. "He was poisoned with a small dose of something, presumably by that hooded figure. My magic only counteracted that substance. I'd be happy to show you how if it would ease your minds."

She half-expected them to recoil, but one older woman blinked, uncertain. "But… I heard you witches could craft illusions that look just like healing." Another woman elbowed her lightly. "Oh, hush—you saw her clean that farmland a few weeks ago near the orchard. Or did you forget your sister was part of that rescue?"

Elysia's chest eased at hearing someone defend her. She offered the older woman a small nod of gratitude. "I promise, my spells can't force a healthy man to collapse," she said, voice calm. "No one wants more chaos tonight. I only want to help keep people safe."

Lorand stepped forward, his presence like a protective shield. "My knights and I have fought alongside Lady Elysia for weeks now. She has revived the injured from real attacks. She has no reason to stage harm in the middle of the baron's festival. In fact, we suspect a certain noble— likely Lord Kester—hopes to pit us against one another." He glanced over the group with an earnest, almost fierce resolve. "Don't let rumor outrun reason."

At that, the onlookers shifted. One man sighed deeply. Another rubbed his chin, eyeing Elysia's slight frame in her green embroidered dress. "I… guess no sense in blaming you," he muttered. "We'd all be fools to tear at each other's throats. I'm no fan of forced unions, but you've done a fair bit of good, from what I've seen."

It wasn't entirely an endorsement, but it was better

than fear. Elysia let a tiny flicker of relief pass her features. She murmured a thanks, extending her hand in a gesture that—just maybe—might open a shred of trust. The small group parted, allowing Elysia and Lorand to continue weaving through the courtyard.

The festival music had resumed in a half-hearted manner, as though the fiddlers were trying desperately to salvage the evening. Torches flickered in every corner, illuminating clusters of dancers in bright ribbons who now moved with forced cheer. Elysia's shoulders ached with tension; the entire atmosphere lacked the carefree spirit the baron must have envisioned.

Still, she and Lorand pressed on, pausing at intervals to reassure any pockets of citizens that the situation was under control. She forced herself to project calm, ignoring how fatigue tugged at her from the quick burst of magic she'd used on the fallen guard. Normally, she could handle healing easily, but anxiety weighed heavily on her reserves. Each time Lorand's gaze swung her way, she felt an odd, comforting warmth that cut through her exhaustion.

They nearly reached the courtyard's far side when Darius returned, stepping out of the shadows. A sheen of sweat glistened on his forehead, his Valecrest surcoat slightly dusty. He shook his head, the lines around his mouth tight. "We lost the hooded figure. They must've known the side alleys well because they vanished." He paused, glancing around for eavesdroppers, then lowered his voice. "A few of us found footprints in a narrow lane behind the inn. They're skilled at evading. No telling if they're one of Kester's direct hirelings."

Elysia's stomach sank. She'd hoped they might catch the saboteur quickly. "All right," she said quietly, "we'll remain on watch. They might attempt something else." She could feel Lorand's frustration radiating next to her. The tension coiling in his shoulders matched hers.

Darius pursed his lips. "I'll station some knights near the orchard. Others will roam the perimeter. We'll keep a lookout for any trouble. Tomorrow's going to be a bigger crowd." He paused, glancing warily at Elysia. "And more risk to you."

She dipped her head in gratitude. "Thank you, Darius. Just keep your men vigilant."

With that, Darius hurried off again, likely to confer with the baron's staff about additional patrols. Elysia and Lorand lingered in the courtyard's corner, the torchlight dancing over the high stone walls that framed the festival. The hum of anxious chatter seeped across the open space. Elysia exhaled and turned to Lorand. "You called this sabotage a 'stunt.' It might be more than that. A spark could catch and cause a wildfire of mistrust. If people truly believe I inflicted a curse…"

Lorand's expression hardened. "Then Kallendore's entire victory—every step you took showing your healing was beneficial—becomes suspect." He exhaled, glancing upward at the line of pennants overhead. "It's precisely the wedge Kester wants."

The idea made her chest twist. She willed herself not to let fear rule. "We can't allow them to sow suspicion.

That means I can't recoil from using my magic openly. If someone else collapses or we have another fiasco, I need to help, not hide."

A faint flicker of admiration lit Lorand's eyes, though he kept his voice measured. "Agreed. I'll stand by you if that occurs." He paused as though debating whether to say more, then continued softly, "Let them see that Valecrest stands with Kallendore. Even if it's a forced alliance, we'll show them it's working."

Her breath caught. She hoped it wasn't only feigned cooperation. They had come so far in trusting each other—she recalled the night he nearly died from mercenary ambush, the bitter swirl of fear when she'd used taboo healing to save him. They had grown beyond simple tolerance. But in front of these watchful eyes, she couldn't voice that deeper truth, nor was it the time. She simply nodded.

"Let's circle back once more," she said, forcing her mind back to the present. "The festival's going to continue another hour or two, and we can't let the tension fester unaddressed."

They set off side by side, weaving through knots of festival-goers. In moments like these, Elysia was acutely aware of every small detail: the ring of metal tassels on Lorand's belt, the firm line of his shoulders as he gently guided her around children or swaying dancers. Now and then, a Valecrest knight or cousin pointed them out to an uncertain onlooker, as if to say: There, do you see? They're patrolling together. Maybe there's hope.

CHAPTER

TWO

At a far corner, a performance of a traveling minstrel tried to rekindle a sense of festivity, strumming a lively tune on a lute. The onlookers were subdued, though a few clapped politely. Elysia paused to let an old woman pass with a tray of spiced pastries. She smelled the sweet tang of honey drifting by, incongruous with the tension crackling in the air.

Eventually, she and Lorand circled to the place where the guard had collapsed. A wide berth was still left around the site, as if people didn't wish to stand where the "curse" had happened. Elysia knelt briefly, running her fingertips over the ground. She sensed a faint residue—a chemical tang. Probably a drop from that suspicious vial. The hooded figure must have thrown or spilled it, ensuring a convenient scene. Rising, she wiped her hands, ignoring the prickle of disgust.

A tired hush began settling over the festival. Some

families, uneasy, herded their children and left early. It was well past midnight; the baron's usual plan for dancing and feasting was overshadowed by the sabotage. Elysia wondered if that was precisely the saboteur's goal: to create unrest that would linger until morning. They have to be planning something bigger for tomorrow, she thought.

Before she could dwell on it further, the baron emerged from the direction of the keep's archway, carrying a dark lantern. The old tension lined his face deeply. He beckoned them with short, brisk gestures, and they followed him to a quieter alcove near the keep's entrance. Once there, he lowered his voice. "The guard recovered well enough to speak. He recalled feeling a jostle, then someone pressed that vial into his hand. He had no chance to see who it was. The moment he tried to protest, the figure vanished. Then his head spun."

Elysia nodded grimly. "That's consistent with what we saw."

The baron's jaw clenched. "This fiasco is all the talk. People keep repeating half-baked theories: that your magic got away from you, or that some Kallendore curse was unleashed, or that Valecrest knights orchestrated it to discredit your house. Or that you and Lorand plotted it to look like sabotage. Idle minds spin endless webs." He sighed, tension evident in every line of his posture. "I brought up the idea of new patrol shifts for the night. That might deter further robed agitators."

Lorand crossed his arms. "We'll help arrange them,"

he said. "Darius is already setting watch. If any suspicious figure tries to slip around again, we'll be ready."

Elysia exchanged a look with the baron. "We have to be prepared for tomorrow. The main ceremony, the final speeches, the dance in front of Sir Remine... If there is a grand sabotage, that's when it'll erupt."

The baron gave a grim nod. "Precisely. The monarchy's envoy is expecting a show of unity. If something dramatic disrupts that event, the monarchy might suspect the alliance is a sham. Or the townsfolk might descend into open hostility." He pressed a hand to his temple. "Which is precisely what Kester wants—to prove Kallendore and Valecrest can't keep the peace. So be on your guard."

Elysia's muscles tensed. "Understood, my lord." She cast a quick sideways glance at Lorand, who gave her a solemn nod. They'd have to remain vigilant indeed. Tonight was but the first wave of sabotage. The real blow would come tomorrow, when the crowd was even larger.

A hush settled between them. Torches in the keep's courtyard guttered and hiss. The baron flicked a glance toward the scattering festival-goers. "We'll handle what remains of the night. I'll see you both in the morning, well before the official events start. Rest, if you can." His voice was laced with the skepticism that either of them would find restful sleep.

He departed with a swirl of his cloak, heading off to instruct more staff. Elysia stood there in the half-lit alcove, the tension in her limbs refusing to let go.

Lorand watched her, silent, for a long moment. At last, he stepped closer. "You've pushed yourself tonight," he said, quieter than before. "Healing that guard, keeping your composure in front of the crowd... I can feel your exhaustion."

She forced a small, taut smile. "I am a bit spent, yes, but I'll manage. The show of strength is necessary. We can't appear rattled." She paused, then inhaled, letting her shoulders fall. "But you're right that I shouldn't push too hard. If something bigger happens tomorrow and I've depleted my reserves, that would be worse."

The flicker of lantern light caught the silver threads in Lorand's embroidered tunic. She saw him weigh his words. "Then come," he said softly. "We'll walk back to the keep, away from the crowd. Have you eaten any supper? Or do you need to gather your satchel of herbs for tomorrow?"

Normally, she might bristle at someone fussing over her stamina. She was used to looking after others, not the other way around. But tonight, there was something comforting in Lorand's quiet vigilance, and in the knowledge that he, at least, truly believed in her magic's worth. "I should probably check my supplies," she admitted, voice gentler than she intended. "Then maybe find a moment to eat."

They set off, crossing the courtyard's wide cobblestones. The crowd had thinned significantly. A handful of Valecrest knights were posted at intervals, no doubt due to Darius's instructions. Elysia nodded to them as she passed. Some still bore haunted or suspicious looks, but no one openly challenged her. She even heard one say, "Don't' see that robed devil anywhere," to a companion, reinforcing the idea that the saboteur had likely vanished into the night.

A modest corridor led from the open square into the keep's interior. Elysia and Lorand slipped through it, leaving behind the drifting echoes of festival music. Inside, a hush folded around them, broken only by a few staff members lighting wall sconces. The stone passages seemed less austere than usual, perhaps because Elysia's nerves were so thoroughly rattled that even the cool walls felt like a reprieve from that swirling rumor outside.

Unconsciously, they fell into step side by side, a synchronized hush in their steps. Elysia noticed he'd slowed his pace to match hers, and her heart gave an unexpected flutter. The forced betrothal that had once made her furious no longer felt burdensome. Certainly not when he was so quick to stand by her in public. And certainly not now that she loved him. That thought made her cheeks heat. But recollecting the sabotage attempts, she forcibly steered her mind away from how comforting his presence felt.

A simple wooden door led to a small sitting room that the baron had offered them earlier in the festival—a spot where they could meet or rest in privacy if needed. They slipped inside, shutting the world out for a moment. The chamber was lit by a single, shielded lantern on a side table, and a tall wooden chair in the corner. There was a table with covered trays, too. A tapestry of Highdale's farmland lined one wall. Elysia stepped over to a small chest near the far side, kneeling to rummage inside for the pouch of healing herbs she'd stashed there.

She found it easily, retrieving a handful of fresh succulent leaves that could bolster her curative spells if she needed extra potency. Just as she started to tuck them away, her hand shook—ever so slightly—and one leaf slipped from her grip. She exhaled in frustration. The day had been long: from dealing with Sir Remine's scrutiny earlier to capping it off with this sabotage fiasco, always having to prove herself. She was drained.

Elysia placed her satchel of herbs on the table and turned to find Lorand uncovering the tray of food. The golden glow of the lantern softened the sharp lines of his face, and when he looked at her, his eyes held a warmth that made her breath catch for a moment.

"You should eat," he said gently, setting the cover aside. "You've been running on fumes all night."

"I know," she admitted, her voice softer than she intended. Her eyes flicked to the bread and cheese on the tray, the roasted vegetables and mutton on the table. The sight alone made her stomach twist with hunger. "I'm starving."

Lorand's lips curved into a small, knowing smile. "Then sit." He broke off a wedge of cheese, stepping closer as she pulled out a chair. "Try this first," he said, offering it to her. "It's sharp, but it pairs well with the wine."

Without hesitation, she leaned forward, letting him place the morsel into her mouth. The creamy, tangy flavor melted on her tongue, and she sighed, the tension in her shoulders easing as she chewed.

"You've been holding out on me," she said, swallowing. "That's delicious."

"I had a feeling you'd like it," he replied, a hint of amusement in his voice. He poured sweet wine into a goblet and set it in front of her, then filled his own. Before she could reach for the food, he tore off a piece of bread and added it to her plate, along with roasted vegetables and a slice of mutton.

"Are you planning to serve me the whole meal, or can I help myself at some point?" she asked, though her words held no real bite. She was too grateful to care.

"I'm not taking chances," he said, sitting down across from her. "If I leave you to it, you'll eat nothing but bread and say you're full."

"That's unfair," she countered, though she took a bite of the bread anyway. "I would've gone for the mutton eventually."

"Eventually," he echoed, smirking as he took a sip of his wine. "But you've earned a proper meal tonight."

They ate in a comfortable rhythm, the simple food satisfying in a way that reminded her of home. As the quiet stretched between them, she found herself glancing at Lorand more than once, drawn to the way his eyes softened when they met hers.

When she reached for her goblet, she caught him smiling faintly. "What?" she asked, tilting her head.

"You've got a bit of cheese," he said, gesturing vaguely toward her lip.

She brushed her mouth, frowning. "Gone?"

"Not quite." He leaned forward, his thumb grazing the corner of her lips with the barest touch. The gesture was so unhurried, so familiar, that her breath hitched. His hand lingered for a moment before he pulled away, brushing his thumb against his palm with quiet satisfaction.

"There. Now it's gone."

She picked up her goblet, taking a sip of the sweet wine to mask the flush rising to her cheeks. "You're awfully smug for someone who just fed me like a child."

"I'm content," he corrected, his smirk softening into something gentler. "There's a difference."

"You've been pushing yourself too hard lately," he murmured. "Let me see your hands?" His voice was gentle in a way that, once upon a time, she'd never have believed possible from a Valecrest knight.

She hesitated but found herself holding out her hands. He placed the leaf in her palm, then rested his own hands softly over hers. It wasn't just comforting; it sent a ripple of quiet electricity through her. She swallowed. "I'm fine," she insisted in a hushed tone that sounded far less certain than she'd hoped.

Lorand pressed his lips together, stepping fractionally closer. "Maybe so. But you shouldn't carry the fate of the entire barony on your shoulders alone. Let me help shoulder some burden." His words were intimately quiet, an echo in the small room.

She parted her lips to say that they were in this together, but for a moment, she couldn't find the words. Her heartbeat sped up, reminding her of how, in earlier times, any closeness between them felt forced. Now it felt... dangerously welcome. She forced a breath, carefully withdrawing her hands. "You're right," she managed softly. "We can't let each other burn out. Tomorrow might test us beyond measure."

He nodded, expression resolute. His presence filled the small room, the faint smell of leather and the tang of metal from his belt lingering. "We'll endure it," he said. "And after tomorrow, if we can quell these rumors, maybe the monarchy's envoy will see that Kallendore and Valecrest do stand united."

Elysia's chest tightened. "I hope so." She rose, stepping away to set the herbs into her pouch, focusing on something tangible. "We need a plan. The baron wants you and me to be the 'visible face' of unity. That means tomorrow, we can't shy away from the final dance or the speeches, no matter how many saboteurs lurk. We have to appear unwavering."

She heard him approach behind her—swift, quiet footsteps. "I'll stand with you." His words were a promise. "We'll watch for suspicious activity. Between my knights and your wards, we might prevent a worse disaster. So long as we remain... balanced."

That last word carried a double meaning. Balanced in magic and steel, sure, but also balanced in the precarious trust that had built between them. She turned, meeting his gaze. The low lamplight carved faint shadows over the sharp lines of his face. Her heart fluttered with a mixture of anxiety and... something else.

"You should rest," he said again, gently but with finality. "You've done enough tonight. I'll escort you to your chamber if you wish."

Heat threatened her cheeks. "I— Thank you." Her

voice nearly faltered. "What about you? You need rest too."

He half-smiled, a flicker that almost reached his eyes. "I suspect I'll check once more with Darius about the watch shifts, then perhaps get a few hours' sleep. If we both collapse from exhaustion tomorrow, Kester wins." He hesitated, then extended his arm in a polite, courtly gesture. "Shall we?"

She let out a half-laugh, half-exhale, accepting the crook of his elbow. Together, they exited the small sitting room into the hallway, footsteps echoing softly on polished stone. The corridor was empty, aside from a single sconce casting a warm glow. Elysia realized, with a pang, that their forced proximity had grown disconcertingly comfortable. The hush around them felt oddly intimate.

They navigated a short flight of steps leading to a corridor near the guest chambers used by Kallendore and Valecrest delegates. As they reached Elysia's door—unremarkable wood, but with a guard posted discreetly down the hall—she paused, hand on the iron latch.

"Thank you," she murmured, turning to Lorand, voice hushed. "For speaking out there tonight. For defending me. If you hadn't stepped in and explained that the guard was poisoned... I don't want to think of how quickly people's anger might have flared." She studied the faint flickers of torchlight dancing across his face. Soft lines of tension bracketed his eyes.

He let out a quiet breath. "I couldn't stand by. I've seen you heal too many times to believe any of this nonsense about curses." A pause. "And I—" He hesitated, searching her expression, then finished softly, "I won't let them twist your gifts into something vile. We've come too far."

Warmth spread through her chest. She parted her lips, uncertain what to say. The memory of earlier distrust between them flitted by—her father's lectures, Valecrest knights sneering at "witch powers." How far they'd traveled from that bitter standoff. She swallowed, stepping closer. "Then let's make sure they don't succeed," she whispered.

For a heartbeat, the hush between them brimmed with words unspoken. The corridor was too public, and yet Elysia felt a magnetic pull. The tension of the evening, the knowledge that tomorrow might bring an even fiercer storm, made her want—just for a fleeting moment—to rest her head against his shoulder, to draw strength from his unwavering calm. And from the flicker of something deeper she'd sensed in him.

She settled for pressing a hand to his forearm, letting the contact linger. "Goodnight, Lorand," she said at last. The torch's glow accentuated the faint color on his cheeks.

"Goodnight, Elysia." His voice was low, layered with things he didn't speak aloud. He inclined his head in a small, courteous gesture, breaking the connection to step back. A moment later, he turned and started down the corridor, quietly greeting the guard posted at the far end.

Lorand caught her hand as she began to turn away, his fingers curling gently around hers. "I hate this," he admitted, his words a quiet rumble. "Sleeping separately, pretending we're just... allies. I wish we could spend the night together. You, in my arms, where you belong."

Her heart thudded, and for a moment, she let herself imagine it—his warmth beside her, the safety and comfort of falling asleep together. She wanted it too, so much it ached. But reality reared its head, the weight of duty and appearances pressing down on her.

"I want that too," she whispered, her voice trembling with the truth of it. She stepped closer, her hand tightening on his. "But we shouldn't, not yet. There are too many eyes watching. Too many people eager to report us to my father... your mother. Until we're officially married, in a place that's ours, we can't arouse suspicion. It's too risky."

Lorand's jaw tightened, and for a moment, he looked as though he might argue. But then he exhaled, his shoulders softening. "You're right. As always." His lips quirked into a wry smile, though the longing in his eyes hadn't dimmed. "But it doesn't make this any easier."

"It doesn't," she agreed softly.

For a moment, neither moved. The flickering torchlight carved shadows across the stone walls, throwing their features into relief. Then, as if drawn by some invisible force, Lorand tilted his head down, brushing his lips softly against hers. It was a whisper of a kiss, tender and restrained, yet filled with everything they couldn't say aloud. Elysia's free hand rose, resting lightly against his chest, and for a fleeting moment, the world narrowed to just the two of them.

When he pulled back, his forehead rested briefly

against hers, his breath warm against her skin. "Goodnight, Elysia," he murmured, his voice like a caress.

Her chest ached with the effort it took to step back, to break the moment. "Goodnight, Lorand," she replied, her voice steady despite the swirl of emotions in her heart.

Elysia watched him retreat, her heart still hammering. Then she opened her chamber door and slipped inside. The latch clicked behind her, muffling the corridor's hush. Immediately, the fatigue weighed on her limbs like a physical burden. She dropped the herb pouch onto a small table, crossing to the narrow bed. Usually, she changed into something more comfortable and performed a short meditation to calm her mind. Tonight, she lacked the energy for the full routine.

Slumping onto the edge of the bed, she unlaced her gown's bodice enough to breathe more freely, letting her hair tumble loose from its partial pins. The quiet enveloped her. In the distance, she heard faint murmurs from beyond the thick walls—signs of festival stragglers, the baron's staff, knights finishing last checks. She closed her eyes, recalling the swirl of fear in the courtyard, the hooded figure's quick movement, and the collapsed guard with that vile glint in his hand. That single moment had nearly undone so much trust. And tomorrow, they would have even more to lose.

She drew in a long breath, then let it out slowly. She let herself replay the memory of Lorand's firm stance when he told the crowd that her magic was real and not to be feared. The memory warmed her more than she wanted to admit. She remembered the gentleness of his hand over hers in that small sitting room, the quiet vow in his eyes. If the monarchy or the baron had forced them together at sword point in the beginning, well... circumstances had changed. She felt it in how her heart fluttered around him and how she held her ground next to him, side by side.

Still, overshadowing all was the knowledge that sabotage lurked—Kester's plan was no doubt culminating. She had to be ready to face the worst tomorrow. For a moment, exhaustion threatened to swamp her, and she allowed herself to lay back on the bed, not even tugging off the dress or slippers. She'd rest for a few moments, then properly undress.

But as soon as her head touched the pillow, her thoughts spun. She pictured well-meaning villagers shrieking about curses, pictured a hidden figure in the crowd, pictured the monarchy's envoy scrawling harsh notes in a ledger... She forced herself to slow her breathing, counting each inhale. After moments that felt like an eternity, her pulse steadied.

Silently, she prayed the night would pass without further sabotage. She prayed that tomorrow, the official ceremony wouldn't collapse into chaos. Perhaps that was too much to hope for. Perhaps she was foolish. But a small iron thread of resolve wove through her: no matter what Kester or his hirelings hurled at them, she wouldn't cower. She'd face them—preferably with Lorand beside her—and she would prove that magic could heal more than just wounds, that unity meant more than forced compliance.

Sleep finally tugged at her. The faint lamplight blurred around the edges of her vision. She didn't even recall drifting off, only that at some point the tension in her limbs melted enough that she couldn't keep her eyes open. The last fleeting thought that occupied her mind was the memory of Lorand's voice promising to stand at her side, and the whisper of the possibility that maybe, despite the sabotage, a new bond was forming that no rumor or poison could destroy.

CHAPTER
THREE

E lysia jolted awake sometime later, uncertain of the hour. Her chamber had gone dark, the single candle on the side table burned low. Her heart raced as her gaze darted to the corners of the room, her mind insisting someone was there hidden, waiting. She almost screamed but didn't want to alarm Lorand and disturb those still sleeping.

A spike of dread knotted her stomach. Had she heard something? A crash? A shout from the corridor? She strained her ears, her pulse roaring in her head. But there was nothing—no sound except the soft whisper of the wind against the shutters and the faint creak of the old floorboards beneath her bed. The stillness pressed in, heavy and suffocating.

She exhaled shakily, pressing a hand to her chest as if to steady her pounding heart. It was just a dream, she told herself. A bad dream, clinging like cobwebs. The details were already fading, but the unease lingered, sharp and vivid. She remembered the flashes of chaos—the clash of steel, the shadows of enemies closing in, and the heavy weight of helplessness that the dream had pressed onto her.

Her fingers tightened against the bedclothes. The fight ahead loomed large in her mind, even now, invading her sleep. She let out a long, measured breath, trying to shake off the remnants of the nightmare. There was no one here. No threats in the room. Just her racing imagination and the ghosts of what might come.

Acute dryness in her throat reminded her that she'd never eaten or drunk water after her frantic evening. She stood, bleary, crossing to the washbasin to splash a bit of cool water on her face. The jolt helped. She forced a few mouthfuls of water from a nearby jug, wincing at how stale it tasted. At least it soothed her parched throat.

She mulled over whether to venture into the corridor to find something to eat. But it was likely the kitchens had long since closed. She rummaged in her pouch for a traveling biscuit—she usually kept something for emergencies—and nibbled it absentmindedly, wishing it tasted less like sawdust. Then she sank into the chair, pressing her hand to her temple.

The next big hurdle was only hours away. The baron had planned a midday feast, culminating in the final dance at dusk, with a speech from Sir Remine. The official demonstration of Kallendore-Valecrest unity. She pictured that dais in the courtyard, the orchard's trees with their bright ribbons, the elaborate swirl of too many watchers. Her entire body tensed at the memory that sabotage could strike them at any second. But her mind circled back to the steady presence of Lorand. A flicker of calm accompanied that thought.

She brushed her thumbs over the worn surface of the pouch's drawstring, letting the repetitive motion soothe her. This forced union had been a chain around her ankles once; now, it felt... different. Perhaps even fortifying. She tried to cling to that sense of solidarity rather than the fear that tomorrow's sabotage might—in one stroke—undo all their progress.

Finally, she roused herself enough to peel away her festival gown and slip into simpler nightclothes. Collapsing back onto the bed, she closed her eyes with a firm resolve: no matter what lurked in the morning, she would face it head-on. Beside Lorand. If their synergy over these past weeks meant anything, it meant they were not alone.

Slowly, the restless tension in her bones eased. This time, true sleep crept over her, deeper and unbroken by phantom crashes. Outside, in the corridors and courtyard, knights and watchers likely patrolled in hush. The baron might still be awake, roiled with worry. But for these hours, Elysia slept.

When morning broke across Highdale, it filtered in golden stripes through the tall windows of Elysia's chamber, stirring her from slumber. She blinked at the brightness, momentarily disoriented. Then the swirl of last night's events returned to her like a wave. The sabotage. The guard. The hooded figure. The final dance looming. She sat up quickly, the rumpled linens sliding to her waist. Cold dread still lay thick and unyielding in her stomach like stone dropped into deep, unmoving water, the ripples of her fear refusing to fade.

She dressed in a hurry, donning a green gown, bundling her hair into a half-twisted style that would allow for quick magical movements if necessary. She secured her pouch of herbs at her hip, checking she had the succulent leaves and a few measured flasks of restorative tonics. Sleep helped. She felt sharper. Good. She'd need all her wits.

A quick glance at a small timekeeping device told her the baron had likely summoned them to a preliminary meeting soon. She took the corridor steps in near silence, passing only a pair of conversing staff who nodded politely. Everyone seemed on edge, but outwardly the keep was calm. She found herself making for the baron's main hall, suspecting that was where the day's planning would commence.

Sure enough, the baron stood near the head of an oval table, poring over a half-unrolled scroll with one of his aides. Lorand stood across from him, arms folded, brow furrowed as he listened. Darius lingered a step behind, scanning the text of some note. At Elysia's approach, the group looked up.

The baron waved her in. "Good morning," he said,

though his tone lacked any cheer. "We were discussing how to organize the midday feast and the final dance. Sir Remine wants to see clear cooperation. We need to be certain no saboteur can slip in with something worse than a poison vial."

Elysia nodded, stepping to the table. She caught Lorand's quick glance—some mixture of relief and quiet reassurance. "Have there been any more sightings of suspicious persons?" she asked.

The baron's aide, a wiry clerk with a tired face, shook his head. "None. The night watch saw one figure skulk around but lost them behind a shuttered stable. Could have been the same saboteur. No confrontation occurred. We're all on high alert, but they didn't try anything further."

Lorand cleared his throat. "We'll have Valecrest knights posted at every major entrance. Darius will oversee the largest points of entry while a smaller group patrols the orchard. Meanwhile, we'll keep a few Kallendore watchers in the crowd—less obvious but ready to intercept or call out any masked agitator." He gave a quick look to Elysia. "That might help if someone tries to frame your magic again."

She inclined her head, appreciation swelling. The baron exhaled, pressing his palm to the scroll. "Yes. Let's finalize these plans quickly. The midday feast is in two hours. Elysia, you and Lorand must appear at the dais to greet Sir Remine and demonstrate that last night's fiasco hasn't shaken your partnership. Understood?"

Lorand nodded. "Understood. Where will our parents be seated?"

The baron glanced at the clerk, who quickly scanned a list and replied, "They will be at the front left, near the dais but not directly beside it. Sir Remine requested the head table remain limited to you two and a select few representatives."

Lorand's jaw tightened, but his voice was even as he spoke. "In that case, I'd like Elysia and I to be seated together, away from them. With tensions as they are, it's best we appear unified without the added... distractions."

The baron gave him a sharp look, one that almost questioned his nerve, but Lorand held his gaze with quiet determination. After a pause, the baron nodded. "Fine. That may be wise."

Elysia cast a sidelong glance at Lorand, catching the flicker of satisfaction in his expression, and felt a warmth bloom in her chest despite the morning's unease.

"And the final dance... you both realize that's the marquee event for the crown's envoy," the baron added, a flicker of tension in his stiff posture. "I want to see you two waltz in perfect unity. If sabotage threatens, it could be in that moment. Or right after."

Lorand's expression was grim but determined. "Then we'll be ready."

With that, the meeting concluded, each person heading off to their designated tasks. Elysia took a moment to catch Lorand's sleeve, quietly. "Thank you," she murmured. "For all of this." She didn't elaborate. She didn't need to.

His gaze lingered, warm despite the tension. He nodded. "Stay safe," he said softly, then strode away with Darius to finalize vantage points for the knights. Elysia inhaled, calling up her own reservoir of courage. The next time she saw him, it would be with the entire barony's eyes upon them, waiting for any sign of fracturing. She would not let that happen.

She turned and made for the orchard, where some of her own Kallendore aides were stationed. Anxiety twisted in her stomach, but so did a calm resolve. Whatever shape the sabotage took, she would meet it head-on. She wasn't alone; Lorand's vow echoed through her memory. And in that vow lay the flicker of hope that, even in a swirl of sabotage and centuries-old distrust, they could prove—once more—that Kallendore magic and Valecrest steel formed a shield no conspiracy could break.

Outside, the day had dawned crisp and bright, sunlight glancing off the orchard's dewy grass. So little time remained before the midday feast and the final dance that would define Highdale's future.

Elysia's heart still hammered with the knowledge that an unknown saboteur roamed free—and that behind them stood Kester, eager to unravel every fragile bond tying her and Lorand together. But an answering spark of determination flared in her chest. Let Kester watch in the shadows. She would not yield.

Pulling her shawl tight against a light breeze, Elysia headed deeper into the orchard, ready to coordinate her watchers. Her footsteps were steady, though her mind churned with the memory of last night's sabotage and the promise she and Lorand had forged. Tomorrow—today, truly—would decide if that promise could conquer the whispered lies and deadly cunning of those who refused to accept that healing and sword could stand side by side as one.

FOUR

Elysia's cheeks still carried the chill of dawn as she rubbed her hands together and slipped through the arched doorway into the side chamber of the baron's estate. Soft torchlight revealed the others already gathered —Mira, Darius, and Marcus—ringed around a rough-hewn wooden table strewn with creased parchments. A single brazier in the corner lent scant warmth to the otherwise cold room of stone. The hush that fell at her entrance carried equal measures of tension and weary resolve. Lorand joined her a half-step behind, boots striking the floor in practiced calm.

A thin, nervous servant stood at the table's edge; fingers twisted in a fidget that made Elysia's own pulse flutter. The man looked as though he had sprinted three flights of stairs—breath ragged, hair wild. But it was the letters clutched in his shaking hands that held the most ominous promise. Torn fragments, edges ragged, each scrawled with part of a seal Elysia recognized too well.

She drew a breath, forcing steadiness into her voice. "You... have more letters?" she asked quietly.

The servant bobbed a nod, stepping forward to set the scraps on the table. "These were found near the corridors of the keep's western wing, my lady," he explained, voice small. "Someone tried to discard them in a waste bin. But our steward recognized that half-familiar crest. He summoned me to bring them here."

Elysia leaned in, heart hammering. Even with the missing corners, the partial insignia was undeniably connected to Lord Kester. She reached for the largest piece, noting the carefully penned lines describing payments for "special tasks," the timing disturbingly synchronized with the exact days of her goodwill tour stops with Lorand. Her throat constricted. The evidence, while incomplete, aligned with the sabotage they had uncovered: the village ambushes, the spreading rumors of "witch curses," and the incident with a tainted vial at the festival.

Lorand stood close enough for her to feel the heat radiating off him, though he kept his arms folded behind his back. "Kester," he growled, glancing from one scrap of parchment to another. "So, he's doubling down—paying troublemakers to strike just when we appear, hoping each small crisis shatters the illusion of unity between us."

A wave of anger stung Elysia's chest. If she closed her eyes, she could still see the frightened faces of villagers felled by sabotage. She remembered how, more than once, Lorand's knights had risked their lives to fend off attackers, giving her enough time to shield the wounded or dispel illusions. All that anguish was orchestrated so Kester could ensure Kallendore and Valecrest never truly reconciled.

"This is sickening," she murmured. She lifted her gaze to the others. "Mira... Darius... we must do something more definitive. The festival's grand finale is tonight, with half the region expected to attend. If Kester has one last plan waiting—"

"He'll unleash it then," Darius finished, his tone heavy. Though a knight, he looked more scribe than soldier in that moment, deep circles beneath his eyes from sleepless vigilance. "The baron can only do so much. Kester is cunning enough to cloak his involvement unless we corner him with undeniable proof."

Marcus, warrior-straight even in a plain tunic, tapped the table with a gauntleted finger. "We do have a solid lead," he said. "Remember that mercenary the baron's men captured some days ago? He's been locked in the keep's cells. If he can be persuaded to speak on Kester's direct orders, that might give us a statement. Enough to brand Kester before everyone tonight."

Elysia nodded, a flicker of hope stirring. The baron's captivity of that mercenary was well known, but the fellow had refused to say a word—no doubt threatened by Kester or anticipating a bribe within the walls. "We must get him to testify—or at least confirm the link unequivocally." She placed the fragment gently on the table, her voice tightening. "I can't watch more innocent people hurt so Kester can stoke our families' bitterness."

A hush fell. Outside, the estate's corridor bustled

faintly—attendants transporting linens, kitchen staff calling for more supplies. Everywhere, the baron was preparing for the final night of festivities, and with the royal examiner, Sir Remine, still present, the tension soared. If the monarchy's envoy decided the alliance between Kallendore and Valecrest was a sham, both houses would lose their noble status. That was precisely what Kester wanted.

The nervous servant bowed. "My lord, my lady," he murmured, addressing Lorand and Elysia. "Shall I... remain or fetch the steward?"

Lorand exchanged a glance with Elysia. "Thank you for bringing these letters," he told the servant, voice tempered by concern. "We'll handle the next steps—I suggest you keep an eye on the corridors to ensure no further scraps surface unclaimed. And if you see anything suspicious..."

The servant's eyes widened. "I'll report it at once, my lord." Then he hurried out, leaving the group in the flicker of lamplight.

Mira inclined her head at Elysia. Her posture—usually so composed—looked tense, hands pinned behind her back. "So, the immediate question," she said in a low voice, "is how to coerce that prisoner to speak. We have no time for a drawn-out interrogation. The final festival events begin in mere hours."

Elysia's stomach twisted. She pressed her fingertips to her temple, recalling how exhausted she felt after healing the guard who collapsed last night. "Then we speak with him—together, if needed," she suggested, mustering resolve. "Perhaps he'll talk if we promise him some sort of protection from Kester's retribution."

"That might work," Marcus agreed, flicking a glance at Lorand. "But we need the baron's approval to approach the prisoner, or at least his guard's permission. We must handle this legally, so there's no chance for Kester's sympathizers to claim coercion."

Lorand exhaled, tension radiating from him. "Let's gather the baron, then. We can address this quickly. Darius...Marcus, can you speak to the baron's staff about opening the cells for a... direct conversation?"

They both nodded. Darius rubbed his tired eyes and said, "I'll alert the baron right away. Marcus, come with me." The two men turned, leaving the little side chamber with hurried strides.

That left Elysia, Lorand, and Mira alone. The brazier crackled, casting orange ripples over the table. Outside, footsteps echoed and tapered off. Elysia realized that for all her outward bravado, her heart was pounding a wild staccato in her throat. She bent toward the table, stacking the scraps of parchment more carefully, as if dogged organization might anchor her swirling thoughts.

Mira lifted her chin. "I'll check on a few Kallendore cousins," she said gently. "I want to see if they've heard any rumors of new sabotage among the staff or locals. Kester might have set more distractions." She paused, worry darkening her eyes. "Elysia, take care. If the prisoner does confirm Kester's guilt, I doubt Kester will hesitate to strike again."

Elysia reached to squeeze Mira's hand, grateful for her

calm sense of solidarity. "Thank you. Keep me updated if you hear anything." She watched as Mira slipped out of the chamber. Then they were gone—leaving Elysia and Lorand side by side in the hush.

For a long moment, neither spoke. The tension coiled around them like a physical thing. Elysia put a hand on the back of a chair, trying to steady the swirl of her emotions. Anger at Kester for orchestrating so much pain, fear for what might happen if they failed to prove his guilt, and an ever-deepening affection for the man standing a mere hand's breadth away.

Lorand shifted slightly. She felt his gaze drift over her—assessing, not in suspicion but in quiet concern. Finally, he broke the silence. "Are you holding up?" His tone was lower than usual, carrying a trace of husky warmth. "You've... done a lot of healing the past two days."

Her lips twitched into a half-smile. "I'm managing," she said softly. "But I'd be lying if I claimed not to feel it. My magic is still somewhat depleted." She remembered the faint tremor in her fingertips after she mended the guard's near-fatal collapse. "I'll be able to assist if something arises at the festival, just... not indefinite bursts of power."

The line of his jaw tightened. "Then we'll hope tonight demands more vigilance than raw magic. If we can subdue any trouble quickly, you won't need to push yourself." A brief pause. "I hate that you're forced to nurse these injuries while Kester stands safely hidden, pulling strings."

She let her gaze flick to his face. The stubble along his

jawline was more pronounced than usual—perhaps he'd been too busy to shave. It was a subtle change, but it hit her like a blow to the chest. The rugged shadow of it, combined with the firm set of his jaw and the quiet intensity in his eyes, made him utterly irresistible. She could practically feel the scrape of it against her fingertips, her lips, and the thought sent a delicious heat coursing through her.

He looked powerful and unyielding, the kind of man who could command a battlefield and then turn that same unwavering focus on her. Her pulse quickened at the image, her traitorous mind conjuring scenarios far too vivid for this early in the morning. She swallowed hard, forcing her gaze back to the table, but the memory of his stubble lingered, teasing her like a whisper of something forbidden yet entirely hers to have.

She forced herself to look away before that detail unsteadied her further. "We'll expose his manipulations," she vowed, voice taut. "If this mercenary in the cell can confirm those letters, we'll have enough to confront Kester publicly once and for all."

"Yes. And if Kester tries anything else…" Lorand's words trailed off, but the promise of action simmered in his eyes. He exhaled, tension crackling in the small space between them. "We should join the baron and see to the interrogation soon. But first, Elysia—"

Her stomach flipped as he gently put a hand on her arm, drawing her attention. The contact, so simple, sent a surge of warmth through her. The same peculiar resonance that had grown over these past weeks. She thought of how, at first, she had loathed the notion of even walking next to Lorand. Now, forced alliance had given way to something... far richer, more dangerous.

She swallowed, trying to keep her voice level. "Yes?"

His gaze lingered on her face with a rare openness. "No matter what happens tonight, I..." He hesitated—unusual for him, who so often commanded entire squads without blinking. "I want us to stand side by side. In public. If rumors flare or saboteurs strike, or if the monarchy's envoy doubts anything—let them see that we're not simply playing a part. I want them to see we mean this."

Her chest tightened. A swirl of longing, gratitude, and mild terror welled in her. The weight of House Kallendore's expectations pressed on her from one side, Valecrest's proud tradition from the other. Yet in this moment, the forced betrothal and all its bitterness melted away, overshadowed by the sincerity shining in Lorand's eyes.

A swirl of longing and gratitude settled over her, wrapping her like a blanket against the weight of House Kallendore's expectations pressing from one side and Valecrest's proud traditions from the other. In this moment, though, all of that melted away, overshadowed by the quiet sincerity in Lorand's eyes.

"I want that, too," she murmured, her voice soft, her heart pounding with an intensity she couldn't ignore.

The memory of how he'd defended her during the last banquet flickered through her mind—how his voice had been steady, unwavering, as he stood up for her healing powers against the murmurs of doubt. It wasn't just words, either. He'd proven his belief in her time and again, in the midst of battle and in moments like these, where his quiet support held her steady.

"This unity," she said, her voice growing stronger, "it's not just an outward show. It's real. We've proven it in battle. We've proven it in the healing tents. Let's prove it again tonight."

Lorand's lips quirked into the faintest smile, his gaze locked on hers. Though they couldn't touch here in the open, the space between them seemed to hum with unspoken warmth. His expression was as steady as always, but there was something in it now that made her feel anchored, safe—something she wanted to hold onto for the rest of her life.

"We will," he said softly, his voice like a promise. "Together."

Even without a touch, the moment felt intimate, wrapped in the quiet understanding they shared. Elysia let the warmth of it seep into her, holding onto it like a light in the dark.

His fingers squeezed her arm gently, then released her. An ache of yearning curled beneath her ribs at that small separation. She wondered—dizzily—how close they might have drawn if not for this public corridor, if not for the knowledge that the baron and others might summon them at any moment.

He cleared his throat, stepping back. "We... should go," he said, voice a fraction lighter. "Darius and Marcus will be waiting."

She nodded. "Right. Let's not keep them."

With that unspoken tension still humming, they left

the side chamber together, setting off down the corridor. The chill of stone walls seeped into her bones, but she felt the lingering warmth of Lorand's quiet presence.

It did not take long to find the baron. After ascending one winding staircase, they encountered a hustle of guards near the keep's hall. And there, in the center of the swirling staff, stood the baron—broad-shouldered, an air of perpetual exasperation in his deep-set eyes. Darius and Marcus flanked him, along with two lesser aides. The baron beckoned them over immediately.

"In here," he said, curt but not unkind. He led them into a small antechamber off the main hall. A single torch bracket flickered to life on the wall, lighting a stark, no-nonsense space that smelled faintly of old parchment and burnt wax. At the far end, a locked metal door presumably led to the keep's lower cells. The baron rubbed the bridge of his nose, mustache bristling.

"I'm told," the baron began, voice pitched low, "that you've uncovered more proof about Kester. Torn letters detailing payoffs. And that you plan to question the captured mercenary for a statement tying it all together."

Lorand inclined his head. "Precisely. We fear Kester's next move might strike during the festival's evening events. If we can confirm his direct involvement, we can present it to Sir Remine—and to everyone else—in time to thwart any sabotage. Possibly even forestall a riot if Kester tries to turn the crowd against us."

Elysia stepped closer, noticing how the baron's eyes slid from Lorand to her, checking if they were in agreement. "The monarchy's envoy wants tangible signs of unity," she added. "Proving Kester's sabotage does more than protect us. It shows we're not forging a simple charade in this betrothal; we're genuinely rooting out the forces that want our alliance to fail."

The baron let out a weary sigh, nodding. "Fine. My staff has the prisoner in the lower cells, under guard. He's remained stubbornly silent thus far, but if you can coax or corner him into a confession, so be it. I'll have two men accompany you, to ensure everything stays orderly. No one can claim you used... unscrupulous means." He cast Elysia a wry, cautionary look, as if he half-expected her to deploy some dark "witch method" of extracting truths.

Elysia stiffened slightly, swallowing an offended retort. Instead, she murmured, "I won't push him with magic. We just need to speak." She recognized the baron's reluctance was born from the precarious tension with Sir Remine's presence. One misstep could look like House Kallendore or Valecrest resorting to intimidation.

"Very well." The baron motioned two armed guards forward: men wearing the baron's neutral colors of brown and gold. Then he gestured to the locked door. "Down this way. I'll remain here to handle final festival preparations. Darius, Marcus—stay if you wish, or watch from the corridor. We mustn't crowd the cell. This prisoner may decide it's worthless to talk if he feels besieged."

Elysia and Lorand exchanged a quick glance. Darius looked at them both. "I'll remain near the baron," he said quietly, "in case something demands a quick response up here. But if you need me—"

Lorand nodded his thanks. Marcus murmured likewise, planning to linger just outside. Then, accompanied by the baron's two guards, Elysia and Lorand moved through the metal door and down a spiral staircase of worn stone steps that curved beneath the keep's main floor. Each footfall echoed in the cramped space, dust motes swirling under torchlight as they descended.

Elysia's heart beat faster. She had never enjoyed the feel of dungeons, their claustrophobic gloom always reminding her of stories about "witches" locked away. But she clenched her jaw, holding her healing pouch close at her side, just in case. She could sense Lorand's presence behind her, quiet and poised. One step after another until they reached a short corridor lined by stout iron-barred doors.

One of the baron's guards unlocked the last door on the left. "He's in here," the guard said quietly. "We've fed him, but he's refused to speak to anyone beyond hurling insults." He shot Lorand a measured glance. "Lord Lorand, I suggest we keep communications calm. He's edgy."

Lorand gave a curt nod. "Understood." Then he stood aside to let Elysia enter first, or at least peer in, which she did with braced breath.

The cell was surprisingly small—barely wide enough for a cot, a bucket, and a flickering lantern. The prisoner, a wiry man with matted hair and a stained tunic, lay sprawled on the cot, one foot tapping an uneven rhythm. When he spotted them at the threshold, he shot up, eyes narrowing, lips curved in half a sneer.

"So," he said in a rough voice, "the forced-lovers themselves. Heard you might show up." He spat at the floor—

an empty expression of defiance. "Come here to threaten me into compliance? Or maybe do some fancy sorcery, Lady Kallendore?"

Elysia forced her expression to remain neutral. Regulations demanded they keep some distance, so she hovered near the door, with Lorand just behind her. The bars made the conversation slightly awkward, but she could see the flicker of fear in the prisoner's eyes, laced with bravado. If he truly had no intention to talk, he wouldn't look so tense.

"No fancy sorcery," she said calmly. "We only want to know who pays you to cause trouble. We suspect you've been taking coin from Lord Kester to sabotage House Kallendore and House Valecrest's alliance."

"Lord Kester?" the man repeated with a forced laugh. "Tch, I don't know any Kester."

Lorand's jaw tightened. He rested a hand over the pommel of his sword, not in a threatening brandish but more in a firm stance of authority. "We have letters tying your group to him," he said. "We know about the payoffs. If you help us confirm them, the baron can petition for leniency on your sentence after the festival ends. Possibly reduce your time behind bars."

Leniency. That was their best card—protection from the harshest punishments. Elysia watched the prisoner's face twist at Lorand's words, eyes flicking around. A nerve twitched in the man's jaw, but he didn't speak. Silence stretched. Elysia decided to hazard a more direct approach:

"You've heard how Kester discards pawns," she said,

voice steady. "Are you so certain he won't do the same to you? If you languish here long enough, who's to say Kester won't ensure you never see the light of day again—or that something unfortunate might happen to you behind these bars? In exchange for your honesty, we can keep you safe."

The man's gaze jumped to her, hostility plain, but so was a seed of curiosity. He coughed, glancing sidelong at the flickering lantern. "What do you care? The baron or the monarchy will lock me up. You can promise all sorts of nonsense."

Lorand took a measured breath. "Men like you have more to lose if this sabotage continues. Kester won't want a captured mercenary singing. He might very well pay someone on the outside to... tie off loose ends. I understand your fear in talking. But if you remain silent, you become worthless to him. A minor threat, at best." He paused, voice dropping lower. "Join us. Offer a sworn statement detailing your orders: the day, the amount of coin, the instructions to attack or sow panic. In return, we'll push for protective custody."

The prisoner's foot tapped more rapidly. Elysia could almost hear his thoughts churning. "And if I do speak... I risk worse from him if your plan fails. If Kester escapes blame somehow, he'll come for me anyway."

"That's a fair worry," Elysia acknowledged, though her anger stirred at the man's whimpering tone. He had, after all, contributed to chaos in her barony. "But understand that we will not let him slip away. We have proof—letters, testimonies from other bandits who were captured." She glanced at Lorand, then pressed gently but firmly, "Your words could tip the balance. On the chance you speak, we can place you somewhere discreet under guard, out of Kester's reach."

She half-expected more denial or curses. Instead, the prisoner's foot stilled. He stared at the barred door, jaw working as if wrestling an inner debate. Then, after a moment, his shoulders sagged. An odd vulnerability flickered across his grimy features. "Kester," he muttered, voice barely audible. "I... might have heard of him."

Lorand drew closer to the bars, though still cautious, posture straight. "You'll confirm it in front of official witnesses?"

The man glanced at the guards by the door, likely recalling how they had overheard. Finally, with a defeated look, he spoke. "I can give names, times. Payment's supposed to pass from one of Kester's stewards, who meets us in certain places. I never saw Kester face-to-face, but the steward wore Kester's seal ring. We were told to keep your two houses on edge—attack caravans or slip potions to incite fear. The steward gave me a small sum and promised more if public chaos escalated."

Elysia's breath caught. Not just speculation: but direct mention of the steward, pay instructions. Enough that the baron would have a lead and the monarchy's envoy, Sir Remine, would see the truth. She felt a fierce jolt of triumph. "We'll need you to repeat that statement," she said quietly, "in front of the baron or his scribe, so it's official. Will you do that?"

The man's lips thinned almost to a line. "Yes. If it means I'm not hung out to dry. Kester could kill me if I block his route, and I have no illusions about how noble lords treat mercenaries." He glared. "But I'd rather rot in a cell under your baron's watch than be left for dead in a ditch."

Elysia let out a breath. Lorand's tension, too, eased slightly, though the anger in his eyes at Kester's cruelty still burned. "You have our word," Lorand said, "we'll see you safely into protective custody. We can't promise a comfortable cell, but we can ensure your survival."

The prisoner gave a jerky nod. Then he cast Elysia a half-suspicious glance. "Don't try your spells on me. I've had enough of magic meddling."

She met his stare, remembering the swirl of raw opinion so many people held of her healing. "I won't force anything on you," she said. "But if you're wounded or poisoned, you know who to call."

To that, the man made no reply. He sank back onto his cot, as if exhausted by the brief exchange. One of the baron's guards turned to Elysia and Lorand. "Shall I fetch the baron for an official deposition?"

"Yes," Elysia said. "Bring Darius and Marcus, too, so we have multiple witnesses." She glanced at Lorand. "When we bring this statement to Sir Remine, it might be enough to corner Kester publicly. We can present the letters, the prisoner's testimony, everything."

Lorand nodded, a subtle spark of grim satisfaction in his eyes. "We can do it before the final dance or speeches tonight," he murmured. "Right now, Kester likely thinks he still lurks in shadows. Let's see his reaction when we expose him to the entire barony."

The guard hurried upstairs. Meanwhile, Elysia and Lorand stepped back from the cell. She could scarcely breathe for the mixture of relief and fury swirling through her. Relief that they finally had what they needed, fury that so many had been harmed before this moment.

FIVE

Within the hour, the baron arrived with Darius, Marcus, and a clerk carrying an official ledger and quill. They convened in a small adjacent chamber to the cells, warmer and slightly more comfortable, allowing the prisoner to be brought up under guard to give his statement. Elysia lingered near the wall, watching as the clerk carefully documented the man's words, line by line. Everything the mercenary claimed matched the patterns they'd suspected: Kester's steward, the timed attacks, even the instructions to stage terrifying moments at the festival to cast doubt on Elysia's healing or Valecrest knights' competence.

The baron's face hardened as the testimony piled up, fury etched between his brows. Darius, stoic as ever, recorded each detail in a mental catalog. Finally, the clerk finished scrawling. The baron gave a clipped nod, turning to Elysia and Lorand. "It seems conclusive. Enough to force Kester's hand. I will assign extra watch around the prisoner, and we can proceed with an official confrontation tonight. He cannot slip away if I announce it publicly in front of the monarchy's envoy."

Elysia ran a hand over her forehead. "We must be strategic. If Kester senses he's cornered, he'll attempt one last sabotage. Possibly even a direct confrontation in the crowd. People might be in danger."

"We'll arrange double security," the baron promised. "I'll station some of my men near the dais and orchard. Valecrest knights and Kallendore watchers can mingle among the festival-goers. Once the main event starts and everyone's present, we'll unveil this testimony. With Sir Remine in attendance, Kester won't wriggle free. The monarchy will side with us."

Lorand exhaled, tension coiled in his shoulders. "And so, ends Kester's game. Provided we maintain caution." He glanced at Elysia. "Perhaps, after it's done, we might finally have an evening without sabotage or bloodshed."

She swallowed, trying to imagine that day of peace. The festival had once promised carefree dancing and unity, yet every step had been overshadowed by Kester's manipulations. Now, they stood on the cusp of exposing him.

The prisoner, after finishing his statement, was led away under heavy guard to a more private holding area. Elysia discreetly ensured the man's wrist-scuffs from manacles were cleaned—she refused to let him suffer infection, despite her anger at his part in the chaos. He no longer spat curses at her, either, apparently resigned to the reality that only her side of this conflict could guarantee his life.

When it was done and the baron retreated to arrange final details of the festival, Elysia and Lorand headed upstairs, quiet side by side. The keep humming with commotion: staff carrying trays of sweet pastries, servers rolling out barrels of mead. Bright ribbons were being re-hung in the corridors, hoping to recapture a veneer of celebration. It felt surreal, seeing such forced cheer in the midst of such tension.

Their footsteps echoed along a corridor that led toward the orchard exit. Low afternoon light streamed through narrow windows, illuminating dust motes in golden swirls. Elysia felt her heart flutter in uneven bursts, the day's events crackling in her mind. Tiny pulses of exhaustion tugged at her limbs, but also a fierce drive to see this through.

Lorand paused at the window, gaze drifting outward. She followed his line of sight. Beyond the orchard's edge, she could see a cluster of new torches being set up, presumably for the evening's culminating dance. Workers hammered a small platform stage into place. A dread-laced excitement stirred in her belly—tonight, everything coming to a head.

"You look pale," Lorand remarked softly, turning from the window. "Don't push yourself too hard. The final ceremony is still some hours away."

Elysia let out a shaky laugh. "It's a mix of nerves and draining magic. I'll manage." She braced a hand on the cool stone windowsill, glancing at him sidelong. "What about you? You've hardly left my side since last night, save to coordinate with Darius or Marcus."

He shrugged—an attempt at casualness, though she sensed the earnest concern beneath. "If Kester is indeed desperate, I'd rather be near enough to keep you safe if he tries something brash. I know you can defend yourself, but—"

"Thank you," she said softly, cutting him off—gratitude like a gentle flame in her chest. "Your presence... helps, more than I thought it would."

His lips curved in a faint smile. Silence stretched a second, laden with unspoken tension. She almost thought he might step closer, perhaps to brood over the orchard scenery with her, but a voice called from around the corridor bend—one of the baron's aides seeking Lorand's counsel about how Valecrest knights should be positioned for the festival. Lorand's expression flickered, frustration warring with duty, but he gave Elysia a regretful nod.

"Duty calls for a moment," he said. "Will you be all right?"

She lifted her chin. "I'll be fine. I might go rest or speak with Mira, check on the Kallendore side of security."

He nodded, stepping back. "I'll find you before the festival starts."

With that, he vanished down the hallway, leaving Elysia alone in the hush. She drew a slow breath, feeling the day's thick tension twist around her. Then she turned, forcing herself to find Mira or any other Kallendore folks who might need her input.

She spent the next hours in a haze of preparations.

Together with Mira, she updated certain Kallendore watchers, instructing them to roam the festival discreetly, looking for robed strangers or suspicious actions. Old lessons from her father—on how illusions might be used to sow hysteria—ran through her head. She refused to see that ploy succeed again.

Little by little, the keep bustled as dusk approached. Pale sunlight waned beyond the orchard trees, painting the sky pink and orange. Servants lit the courtyard torches, sending golden flickers dancing across the cobblestones. The air began to fill with the scents of roasted game, spiced cider, and fresh bread. In another world, Elysia thought, she might have welcomed such a festival with unguarded joy.

Instead, she found herself stepping aside from the swirling crowd, a hollow feeling in her gut. Something about the hush before a storm. She knew Kester lurked somewhere among these throngs; the question was whether he already suspected his doom.

Just then, a hand brushed her arm gently. She turned, breath catching, to see Lorand. His sword belt gleamed, and he wore a formal Valecrest surcoat, the crimson fabric pressed and edged with discreet gold piping. She imagined he'd done so as a symbolic gesture, to emphasize that this festival was supposed to represent unity. She herself wore a green gown, more practical than ornately bejeweled, but still signifying Kallendore. House colors displayed side by side.

"It's nearly time," Lorand said, voice pitched low. His storm-gray eyes flicked over the milling guests—

hundreds by now, from lesser nobles to townsfolk excited for the final dance. He extended an arm. "Shall we stand near the dais? The baron will gather everyone soon, and we can deliver our proof about Kester."

Elysia took his arm, letting her fingers rest light against the crook of his elbow. The surprising solidity beneath that cloth sent a thrill through her. "Yes," she said, swallowing the dryness in her throat. "Let's go."

They wove through the crowd. Many parted to let them pass, some bowing respectfully or simply staring in fascination. Elysia caught muttered conversation—half in awe that the betrothed pair looked so composed, half uncertain whether the forced union was real. She felt her shoulders tense. Let them watch. Let them see that House Kallendore and House Valecrest no longer had any desire to spill each other's blood.

They reached the dais near the courtyard's center, where a shallow wooden platform had been erected. Lanterns strung on tall poles threw warm light across the space. The baron stood there, conferring with an aide. Darius and Marcus were posted to one side, arms folded. Several lesser nobles formed a cautious circle. The orchard beyond was dotted with more torches, a place for dancing and music once the speeches concluded.

As Elysia and Lorand approached, the baron looked up, relief edging his features. "Perfect timing," he said. "Sir Remine just arrived. He wants the official demonstration of your unity, and I suspect he also wants to see if any... disruptions occur. On the surface, we'll proceed with the festival dance. Then I'll publicly address the sabotage, calling Kester forward. That is your cue to present the proof."

Elysia felt her lungs tighten. Publicly addressing sabotage could be as risky as an open challenge. "And if Kester tries to cause a scene before then?" she asked. "Or tries to flee?"

The baron frowned. "My guards are stationed around the perimeter. Valecrest knights stand ready, too. If Kester runs, we'll have him seized. If he tries to incite panic, we'll quell it together. The mercenary's statement is documented. Kester cannot bluff once I name him before Sir Remine."

Lorand gave a grim nod. "Good."

At that moment, a small flourish of trumpets sounded from the far side of the courtyard. Sir Remine emerged—silver epaulettes and a calm, inscrutable expression—flanked by two scribes. He ascended the dais, acknowledging the baron with a short bow. Then, in a clipped voice that carried over the hush, he greeted the assembled crowd. Elysia's heart thudded. Tonight, the monarchy's examiner would watch their every move, ready to judge whether their alliance was genuine or ripe for condemnation.

Sir Remine's short speech praised the baron for orchestrating a festival that brought "both houses together," then announced his eagerness to witness a symbolic dance. The hush among the crowd was palpable, heightened by flickering torchlight, the swirl of lute music picking up from somewhere beyond the dais.

The baron cleared his throat and addressed the crowd

with a showman's flair. "Friends of Highdale, we gather at this festival to celebrate not only tradition but the forging of a new peace. Our heirs, Lady Elysia Kallendore and Lord Lorand Valecrest, will open tonight's dance as a testament to the monarchy's hopes for unity." He gestured to them, beckoning them forward onto the dais. Applause and murmurs rose in ripples, uncertain but intrigued.

Elysia drew a steadying breath. She turned to Lorand, who offered his hand. Their gazes locked, the swirl of tension between them more intense than any large crowd could conjure. She saw his silent reassurance: Should anything threaten you; I will be here.

She hesitated only a beat. Then she placed her hand in his, stepping onto the dais. The quiet expanded, all eyes riveted on them. The lute strings grew in gentle volume, joined by a soft drum—a slow, stately rhythm that beckoned them to begin.

So, they danced.

At first, Elysia tried to quell the tremor in her limbs. They had practiced steps once, in a tight side chamber with only a flickering lantern to witness. Now, in front of an entire barony, she had to let go of all that fear. She and Lorand moved together, turning in careful circles across the dais's wooden boards. His palm pressed lightly at her waist, guiding her with quiet confidence. She matched his rhythm, focusing on the one-two-three count, ignoring the fervent prickle of so many watchers.

The hush of the crowd slowly shifted into murmurs of awe. She glimpsed scowling older knights, reluctant but transfixed, and Kallendore cousins who had never believed a Valecrest heir could move with such grace or gentleness alongside a Kallendore mage. Yet here they were.

She let herself breathe, leaning into the swirl of each turn. The candlelit courtyard blurred around them, and for a charged moment, Elysia forgot everything but Lorand's nearness—the subtle brush of his surcoat, the warmth beneath her fingertips. She felt the slow burn of unspoken emotion, more powerful than forced unity or showy steps. Lorand's jaw was taut with concentration, yet when their eyes met, she saw flickers of something raw and deeply personal.

Applause rose, and it took her a heartbeat to realize the dance had ended. Lorand bowed slightly, and she curtsied, dipping her head. The crowd clapped in increasing waves. Even from the dais, Elysia could hear uncertain cheers, the sense that perhaps, just perhaps, Kallendore and Valecrest could stand as one.

Out of the corner of her eye, she spotted a tall figure in a dark cloak near the orchard's perimeter. Her heart jolted —Kester? She almost missed it, the cloak swirling behind a group of guests. But if it was him, the confrontation was almost upon them.

The baron stepped forward onto the dais, lifting his hands to signal silence. "Citizens of Highdale, I pray you've witnessed how these two heirs move in unison. But tonight's festival is about more than a dance. I have an announcement—one that concerns all, from the lowest stable hand to the monarchy's own envoy."

A ripple of confusion passed through the crowd. Elysia

caught Lorand's fleeting glance—this was the moment. She steeled herself, heart pounding like a war drum.

"Of late," the baron continued, "there have been disruptions. Sabotage. Some have tried to pit House Kallendore and House Valecrest against each other. But these acts of violence and rumor are not random. They have a single source." He paused, scanning the crowd. "I have in my possession statements and written proof that directly implicate Lord Kester in orchestrating these disruptions."

Gasps flooded the courtyard. Elysia felt a wave of tension surge. She spotted movement near the orchard lights—a swirl of cloaks, some exclamation. Sir Remine, standing discreetly to one side, lifted his brow.

The baron pressed on. "Lord Kester, if you are present —and we know you are—I urge you to step forward."

For a breath, no one moved. Then, from the orchard's edge, a voice rang out—filled with anger, edged with desperation. "This is slander! You conjure lies to mask Kallendore's dark magic or Valecrest's bribes!" A figure emerged, face partially in shadow behind his fine cloak, but the shape of his auburn hair and the glint of a signet ring gave him away. Kester indeed.

Lorand tensed at Elysia's side. She could feel his muscles cord, ready to stop Kester if he bolted. But Kester did not flee. He stalked nearer; face twisted. "I stand by my innocence," he spat, voice carrying over the hush. "This forced union was doomed from the start, and your so-called evidence is contrived."

Elysia, heart pounding, moved forward as well. She

drew from the inner pocket of her cloak the scraps of letters discovered earlier in the day. Darius, who stood at the dais steps, stepped up with the clerk's official documentation. Lorand had his hand on his sword hilt, not drawn, yet menacing enough to warn Kester.

"I can show you these letters," Elysia said in a clear, ringing voice, ignoring the dryness in her throat. "Along with the testimony of a captured mercenary. They match details and times of sabotage that coincide exactly with the moments you sought to discredit our alliance."

A hush, thick with tension, spread across the courtyard. Kester's eyes flickered in alarm, but he tried again. "Hearsay. I want no part of your illusions. You—a Kallendore witch—easily forge letters or enchant men to say what you want." He turned a desperate glare on Lorand. "And you, Valecrest boy, too naive to see you're being used."

Hatred coiled in Elysia's chest, but she held her composure. This was exactly how Kester stirred doubt. "We want the monarchy's envoy to see these documents," she said, turning to Sir Remine, who advanced with quiet authority. "No illusions, no trickery. The baron's clerk recorded them, witnessed by multiple men, including Valecrest knights."

Kester's mouth pinched. The gathered crowd watched with bated breath. Sir Remine gave a single sharp nod, one of his scribes stepping to Elysia's side to inspect the papers. Meanwhile, the baron spoke again, voice hard as iron. "My men hold a prisoner who collaborated with your steward. He's prepared to speak publicly if needed. Are you going to deny that Kester?"

Kester's gloved hand twitched, perhaps longing to reach for a weapon, but he was outnumbered. He flung his cloak aside in a grand gesture. "I deny everything," he barked. But the tremor in his tone betrayed fear more than righteous fury.

Sir Remine's scribe raised his voice: "These letters are indeed sealed with your signet, Lord Kester. The references to payment match the prisoner's claim. I see no illusions upon them."

The color bled from Kester's face. A swirl of whispers ran through the watching crowd. Elysia's pulse hammered, tension thrumming like a taut bowstring. One final push, she told herself. Let Kester see he cannot wiggle free.

"Kester." Lorand's voice cut across the tumult with unexpected calm. He stepped forward, level sword-gray gaze locked on the lesser lord. "If you had spent half the energy forging peace instead of sabotage, think of what you might have achieved for Highdale. Instead, you used fear to line your pockets and feed an old feud. That ends tonight."

A flicker of mania danced across Kester's features. "You... insolent whelp," he hissed. He made a half-lunge, as if intending to tear the papers from the scribe's hands, but Lorand intercepted him in a single practiced movement. A swirl of the Valecrest heir's cloak, the glint of steel, and Kester was seized by the baron's guards, pinned by the arms. Gasps erupted from the crowd.

Volume rose. Some shouted in confusion; others demanded to hear more. Elysia, shaking with triumph and nerves, turned to face the courtyard. This was it. They had laid it all out.

Sir Remine stepped fully onto the dais, commanding silence with a raised palm. "I have seen the documents," he said, voice carrying with a crisp authority that reminded everyone of the monarchy's power. "And I intend to question this prisoner further. But it is apparent that Lord Kester stands accused of grave sabotage. He will be taken into custody, pending royal judgment."

At the envoy's words, Kester cursed, wrestling the guards. But they jerked him back, ignoring his sputters. The orchard flickered with torchlight, revealing the uncertain faces of townsfolk who had once suspected Elysia's magic. Now, they saw Kester, the real manipulator, exposed—caught in the open by the heirs he tried to tear apart.

SIX

A wave of applause and shouts rippled. Some from Valecrest knights, some from Kallendore mages, a few from relieved villagers. The baron, though exhausted, offered Elysia and Lorand a stiff nod of respect. And in that moment, Elysia's chest felt impossibly light. It was done. The sabotage that threatened to break them was extinguished... at least, the core behind it.

Sir Remine turned with that same unwavering stare. "It appears you two have done the monarchy's work," he said, flipping open his small leather-bound notebook. "If your testimony, corroborated by the baron's captive mercenary, stands—then the Crown will see your union as more than forced convenience. I will personally attest to the sincerity of your combined effort to preserve peace."

Elysia's eyes stung, relief pouring in. She felt Lorand's hand find hers, a subtle squeeze that helped anchor her in this swirl of emotion. She was too stunned to speak for a beat, heat rushing to her cheeks as onlookers stared at their joined hands.

The baron, wanting to salvage the festival's warm note, lifted his arms. "Let us not drown in rancor!" he called, recapturing the crowd's attention. "Kester will face the monarchy's justice, but the rest of us may celebrate the dawn of a new chapter—where Kallendore's healing and Valecrest's steel stand side by side, as we have witnessed tonight."

Cheers rose anew, loud and resonant. The tension in the courtyard shifted from uneasy to celebratory, swirling around Elysia like a gentle storm. She drew in a trembling breath and turned to Lorand, half expecting him to release her hand for decorum's sake. Instead, he kept it, guiding her off the dais as the baron signaled the dancers to reconvene.

Lorand led her toward the edge of the orchard, past rows of apple trees glowing faintly under the lantern light. His pace was steady but purposeful, his hand firm around hers. They slipped away from the hum of the celebration and approached a small stone folly tucked against the garden's outer edge. The circular structure, weathered with age, boasted low walls that rose just high enough to shield them from the view of the dais and any curious onlookers.

As they stepped inside, Elysia felt a sense of seclusion wrap around them. The air here was quieter, stiller, carrying the faintest hint of the orchard's sweet fragrance. Lorand turned toward her, and without a word, he reached for the heavy ivy-strewn drapes that hung across the folly's arched entrance. With a gentle pull, he drew them closed, the soft swish of fabric sealing them into their hidden haven.

The lantern light outside barely filtered through, casting them in soft shadows. Elysia's breath quickened as Lorand's gaze locked on hers, the weight of it sending a shiver down her spine. Here, within the stone walls and under the cover of night, the tension and restraint that had bound them in public melted away, leaving only the raw, unspoken connection simmering between them.

Hoarse with emotion, she murmured, "We did it."

"We did," Lorand agreed, voice thick with feeling. His gaze lingered on her face, as if words hovered on his lips—words deeper than triumph.

Around them, music resumed, the crowd's attention drifting to conversation and relief. Some officials hustled Kester away to an improvised holding area, and Sir Remine stepped aside to confide in his scribes. The orchard behind the dais glowed with torches, inviting more dances.

Elysia's pulse pounded. Before she fully realized what she was doing, she let Lorand draw her toward the orchard's more secluded nook. Lanterns hung among the apple branches, filling the air with a sweet fragrance. The hum of celebration drifted behind them, leaving them in a hush that felt intimately separate.

Her heart hammered as Lorand paused, turning to face her. The soft glow from the orchard lantern played over the lines of his face, revealing exhaustion, relief, and something tender. Gently, he reached up to brush a stray curl from her cheek. That light, fleeting contact sent a current of sensation along her skin.

She swallowed, tears threatening. "Thank you," she whispered, "for standing by me. For... for trusting in my magic, believing in this alliance, even when it was forced."

He shook his head slightly. His thumb traced her cheek in a slow, reverent motion. "I was so certain we could never truly unify. But... you showed me hope."

She pressed her lips together, breath catching. The orchard's hush wrapped them in a cocoon of flickering lamplight. "I never asked for this betrothal," she said softly, voice trembling, "but... I've come to realize I wouldn't trade what we've built. Your house and mine... maybe we can reshape Highdale."

He opened his mouth to say something but thought better of it, allowing his lips claiming hers to, firm yet tender, as though the kiss could convey all the emotions words couldn't. Her hands gripped to his shoulders, clutching the fabric of his surcoat as his mouth moved against hers, stealing her breath and igniting a fire in her chest.

She leaned against the wall for support as Lorand deepened the kiss, his tongue teasing hers with a heat that sent shivers cascading down her spine. Her legs trembled beneath her, and his hand slid to her lower back, steadying her as though he could sense her surrender.

When he finally broke the kiss, they were both breathing heavily, foreheads pressed together. But he didn't stop. His lips trailed to her jaw, then her neck, placing reverent kisses along her skin that made her gasp softly. His hand slipped under the hem of her skirt, the roughness of his fingers against her thigh sending a shock of pleasure through her.

"Lorand," she whispered, half a plea, half a warning, though she didn't stop him. Her fingers tangled in his hair as his hand moved higher, brushing over her most sensitive skin. The sensation overwhelmed her, her head tipping back against the wall as a soft moan escaped her lips.

His gaze lifted to hers, dark and filled with desire, and the sight of him watching her—seeing her come undone for him—made her ache even more. He leaned in, kissing her deeply as his fingers moved in deliberate, teasing circles that unraveled her completely. Her breath hitched, her nails digging into his shoulders as her body tensed with pleasure.

Just when she thought she couldn't take any more, he dropped to his knees before her, pushing her skirts higher as his lips replaced his fingers. The sensation of his mouth —warm, insistent, devastatingly skilled—shattered what little composure she had left. Her fingers curled into the stone behind her, her cries muffled by the drapes as he worked her with unrelenting precision.

When the climax hit, it was like a flood breaking through a dam. Her body shuddered as wave after wave of ecstasy washed over her, leaving her breathless and trembling. Lorand held her thighs steady, his grip firm and grounding as he coaxed every last tremor from her.

When her breathing slowed, he rose, brushing a strand of hair from her damp forehead. His lips, slightly swollen, curved into a soft smile as he leaned in to kiss her once more—gentler now, as though savoring the moment.

"I love you," he murmured against her lips, the words so quiet they felt like a secret meant only for her.

She smiled, her heart full and steady. "I love you, too," she whispered, the weight of the night forgotten in the warmth of his arms.

Lorand rested his forehead against hers, voice barely above a whisper. "No more forced illusions. Whatever happens next... it's real, Elysia."

She clutched the fabric at his shoulder, nodding, tears prickling. "Real," she echoed. "No matter how many try to break us."

In the distance, the crowd cheered anew—likely another flourish of music. Elysia and Lorand lingered in that orchard bower, hearts hammering, each grounded by the other's nearness. For the first time since that dreaded royal edict, she felt... at peace. The barony's future might still hold challenges, but they would face them together. Kester's downfall, exposed in the most public manner possible, was proof enough that when they truly united, no sabotage could triumph.

Eventually, they pulled apart, smoothing their clothes with abashed smiles. She realized they should return to the central celebration, where the baron and Sir Remine would be waiting to confirm Kester's removal. But there would be time enough for formalities. In these breaths, she and Lorand had granted themselves permission to hope.

She tucked her arm in his again, walking side by side

back toward the dais. The orchard path glowed with lamplight, and the festival's hum enveloped them. As they approached, a few onlookers cast knowing glances, but Elysia only lifted her chin, refusing to let embarrassment overshadow the quiet elation in her chest.

The baron spotted them returning, relief etched on his face. Darius and Mira exchanged subtle smiles from the crowd's edge. Even Lady Devia, glimpsed among the Valecrest contingent, wore a tentative acceptance in her posture. And from the Kallendore side, Lord Daryon offered a faint nod, the tension in his jaw easing.

Amid this swirl of movement, Elysia squeezed Lorand's hand, leaning closer to whisper. "Shall we see to the rest of the festivities, then? We might actually enjoy them now."

He turned his head, a tiny grin curving his mouth. "Yes," he said softly. "I think we've earned a night of dancing... without sabotage for once."

So, they stepped forward to join the swirl of the festival, hearts lighter than they had been in weeks. Kester's attempts to exploit old hatred had failed, undone by the strength of their partnership. Elysia felt sure that no forced decree from a distant king could have orchestrated what she and Lorand now shared.

CHAPTER

SEVEN

A hush fell over the torchlit expanse of the baron's courtyard, as if all of Highdale held its breath in the moments before triumph or disaster. Elysia stood near the center dais, her festival gown catching stray lantern light that danced across the embroidered leaves and vines along the hem. She could feel her heart racing against her ribcage, masked only by her measured posture to signify the crowning unity of House Kallendore and House Valecrest. And in a matter of seconds, this evening might descend into utter chaos—or, just possibly, bring Highdale's greatest hope.

She could sense Lorand at her side, standing so close she caught the faint tang of the polished metal on his armor. Together, they had traveled the length and breadth of these lands, healing farmland blight and driving off raiders meant to sabotage their forced union. Tonight was meant to be a victorious showcase—that they and their two houses truly stood together. Sir Remine, the royal envoy who had arrived to scrutinize their betrothal, looked on from behind a small podium. The baron, broad-shouldered and in a dark cloak, was posted near the dais steps, his arms crossed over his chest as he surveyed the mass of festival-goers.

It was hardly the joyous celebration Elysia might have imagined for a peace festival. Though the courtyards and orchard behind the keep had been transformed into a swirl of color—lanterns, ribbons, and stalls featuring sweet pastries—and lively music drifted from fiddlers near the gate, she sensed an undercurrent of tension in the crowd. Rumors of sabotage had flared after the fiasco the previous night. The baron's knights were stationed in careful clusters, while Valecrest men and Kallendore aides intermingled on the periphery. More than once, Elysia had glimpsed suspicious shapes moving behind the throng, only for them to vanish into torchlit gloom.

She inhaled, steadying herself. The dais under her feet was a makeshift wooden platform adorned with both Valecrest crimson and Kallendore green banners. This was where they would address the assembled townsfolk, reaffirm the monarchy's demand that their marriage quell the ancient feud, and—if all went as planned—publicly thwart Kester's sabotage once and for all. Elysia glanced toward Lorand, who caught her eye. In that moment of shared tension, she discerned the same swirl of resolve and quiet dread in his gaze. Their dynamic had changed so much from the day they were shoved unwillingly into a carriage together. Now, the memory of how she once called him a "glorified swordsman" felt almost laughable.

She exhaled slowly and leaned imperceptibly closer, letting the corner of the dais hide her. "Are we ready?" she asked under her breath.

He dipped his chin. "We're as ready as we'll ever be. Darius and Marcus have men stationed around every entrance. No robed stranger should be able to sneak close again." Then, as if reading her apprehension, Lorand's hand closed gently around her elbow. "Stay alert," he murmured. "If anything happens, we move quickly."

Elysia's stomach roiled with both nerves and a faint, stirring warmth at his nearness. "We'll handle it," she said, drawing a steadiness from the set of his shoulders. "Kester won't catch us off guard."

Echoing footsteps on the dais made her stiffen. The baron stepped forward. His gaze flicked from Elysia to Lorand, then out to the anxious crowd. He raised his arms with a commanding gesture, and a hush descended. "People of Highdale," he began, voice carrying across the courtyard, "we gather here beneath the watch of our barony's keep, under the monarchy's eye, to celebrate cessation of old feuds." His tone, though practiced, bore an edge of nerves. "We have endured sabotage and rumor, but House Kallendore and House Valecrest remain aligned."

A ripple of uncertain applause. Elysia swallowed and hoped no one had noticed her trembling hands. Spotting Lady Devia—Lorand's mother—standing near the front ranks with a guarded expression, Elysia offered a faint nod. Even Lady Devia, typically scornful toward Kallendore ways, seemed unsettled by the swirling anxiety. And behind her, Elysia glimpsed her own father, Lord Daryon, jaw clenched tight.

The baron continued, "Tonight, to demonstrate this union, Lady Elysia Kallendore and Lord Lorand Valecrest shall address you, so that all may witness they stand united. Sir Remine, the royal envoy, is here to evaluate the sincerity of their bond." At that, Sir Remine gave a short nod, arms folded behind his back, his neutral expression offering no hint of approval—or condemnation.

When the baron gestured invitingly toward them, Elysia squared her shoulders. Beneath her festival gown, she wore small pouches of herbs. Just in case. She stepped forward, and Lorand mirrored her. The noise in the courtyard subsided, leaving only a pregnant hush.

She cleared her throat, summoning the composure she had honed during countless visits to farmland gatherings. "Good people of Highdale," she began softly, yet loud enough to carry. "We come to you this evening not only under the monarchy's edict, but out of a shared desire to see peace and prosperity return to these lands. My magic has healed your blighted fields, and Valecrest knights have fought to keep bandits at bay." She paused, letting her gaze sweep the crowd. "I know many of you still doubt. You have cause—fear can linger for generations. But I ask that you see how we stand together here, no longer as enemies."

An uncertain murmur ran through the crowd. Some faces softened, while others remained stony. Elysia felt Lorand shift. His voice, deeper and resonant, followed hers in a seamless continuum: "Our houses cannot thrive if we remain at each other's throats. It's time to unite. For every moment that Kallendore's wards have protected our farmland, Valecrest knights have stood guard to defend it. We may not have chosen this betrothal, but we have recognized its value."

A breath threaded through Elysia's lungs. A prickle of awareness traversed her spine, that tense moment of waiting. She half expected the courtyard to erupt in dissent. But to her relief, a wave of applause—perhaps a bit hesitant—rose, especially from townsfolk who had witnessed their combined efforts in recent weeks. A flicker of hope warmed her. Maybe, after everything, the night would pass...

Suddenly, a thunderous crack echoed across the yard. She jumped, her stomach dropping. The next instant, a screech of metallic clangs and bright sparks erupted to the eastern edge of the courtyard, swirling near some festival stalls. Instantly, the applause collapsed into shouts and shrieks.

She recognized the sign of a sabotage trick: twin blasts of some powdery substance, releasing choking smoke. People scattered as a haze billowed outward. Through the shifting wave of festival banners, Elysia glimpsed hooded shapes. Four, no—five of them, darting forward, small canisters in hand. She realized at once this had to be Kester's last stand. The infiltrators had planned to disrupt tonight's gathering in the most public way possible.

"Guards!" the baron bellowed. A wave of Valecrest knights and Kallendore watchers rushed toward the robed figures. The masked agitators hurled another pair of canisters, unleashing a second thunderous crack.

Elysia's heart hammered as villagers screamed. Smoke rolled in, stinging her eyes. She coughed, feeling Lorand move swiftly at her side. "Stay close," he whispered. She nodded, fighting through the swirl of acrid air. At the dais steps, she spotted a cowering child, separated from his family by the sudden panic. Without a second's hesitation, Elysia lunged forward, skirting around beams of the stage, reaching for the child just as another pop of smoke flared.

Her body flared with adrenaline. She crouched protectively over the trembling boy, ignoring the swirl of chaos around her. Summoning her magic, she beckoned a shimmering ward, shaped like a partial dome, to contain some of the drifting smoke. She pressed her free hand to the child's shoulder. "It's all right," she managed, voice calm despite the panic clawing at her throat. "Follow me, we'll get you safe."

The child nodded, tears streaking his soot-stained cheeks. With one gesture, Elysia led him away from the dais, half-running toward a cluster of watchers who waved them to safety. She shoved him gently into their arms, murmuring, "Help him find his family," before spinning back toward the epicenter of the disruption.

The robed figures were spreading out, creating pockets of confusion. Elysia caught sight of two men in Valecrest surcoats toppling beneath an attacker's blow. Another masked saboteur brandished a short blade, lunging at a Kallendore retainer. Anger seared through her—these were not random criminals. They moved with coordinated precision. Kester must have paid them to stoke maximum fear and pit the watchers against each other. A perfect festival fiasco, she thought bitterly, fury roiling in her stomach.

She glimpsed a swirl of movement behind them. Lorand, cutting through the haze with Darius at his side, had drawn his heirloom sword. Despite the madness, Elysia felt a surge of relief at the sight of him, tall and steady amid swirling colors of smoke. He beckoned to a cluster of knights, pointing them to subdue one saboteur. Darius rushed another, tackling the robed figure to the cobblestones with a crash. A cheer from nearby watchers rose and then dissolved into frantic scattering as two more canisters detonated in the midst of terrified onlookers.

Chest tight, Elysia darted to a vantage point near the dais. She pressed one palm outward, conjuring a shimmering barrier of golden wards. The magic coalesced above the tumult in a protective arc, deflecting flying shards from the blasts. She heard scattered gasps from villagers who had cowered behind overturned tables. A wave of draining fatigue tugged at her, but she pushed deeper into her reserves, determined to keep the shield in place until the worst of the whirling powder cleared.

As she maintained the ward, shapes emerged from the thinning smoke. One robed saboteur had pinned a Kallendore retainer, forcing him to kneel in front of the crowd. "See how their magic fails you!" the saboteur yelled; voice distorted by a cloth mask. "This is what Kallendore's so-called healing leads to—curses and illusions!"

Elysia's blood boiled. That's exactly what Kester wanted: sowing the rumor that her wards were to blame for these blasts. She locked eyes with the pinned retainer, who silently pleaded, but her vantage point behind the dais was too far. She needed to get closer to help.

Suddenly, another figure dashed from the swirl of onlookers—a man gripping the retainer's collar. Elysia's heart seized at the realization: that was Kester himself, auburn hair straggling out from beneath his hood. She recognized his face, contorted in a sneer. He dragged the retainer into a staged scuffle, brandishing a short staff or rod. He roared, "Observe how Valecrest knights stand idle —caught attacking a Kallendore man!" The pot of confusion thickened, exactly as Kester must have planned.

She lifted her ward hand higher, meeting Kester's eyes. His expression flickered with triumphant malice. She wanted to lash out, but if she dropped the shield, the unprotected crowd behind her might be vulnerable to more shrapnel blasts. For a moment, helplessness gnawed at her chest.

Then, from nowhere, Lorand plowed past the dais. "Stand back!" he shouted to the nearest cluster of villagers. He turned, scanning the scene, then zeroed in on Kester's shape. Elysia drew a sharp breath of relief. Thank heavens. She would hold her wards a little longer—just enough to let Lorand break Kester's staging.

Pivoting on her heel, Elysia rotated her protective magic, intending to shift the arc of the shield to shield the pinned retainer. She grit her teeth, focusing on the swirling filaments of golden energy. Her arms ached from channeling so continuously. Over the past weeks, she had become better at sustaining wards, but this was far more than an ordinary festival demonstration. She could feel her pulse drumming in her wrists, a sign that her magic wouldn't last forever.

A strangled cry grabbed her attention. Kester was now forcibly hauling the retainer forward, while some of Kester's minions rushed at Lorand from behind. Fierce rage lit Elysia's veins. She must do more than stand behind a static shield. Summoning the last bit of raw power, she angled her free hand and conjured a band of shimmering light across Kester's path. Not a full barrier, but enough to hamper him from dragging the retainer any further. She sensed it collide with his shins as he stumbled, shooting her a livid glare.

In that instant, Lorand sprang at Kester with a fluid motion, sword raised but not striking yet. "Kester!" Lorand's voice rang out. "Drop your weapon. This sabotage is over." It was a declaration that carried a resonant finality.

But Kester bared his teeth. "What do you know of sabotage?" he spat. "You're part of it—plotting with that witch to enthrall the barony." His words echoed across the courtyard, seeking to whip any bystanders into fresh panic.

Elysia watched, breath locked in her throat. The entire courtyard felt precarious, as if balanced on a single point of tension. If the villagers believed Kester's accusations, they might turn on her in fear. If they believed in her wards, then Kester would stand alone. She forced steadiness into her posture, letting magic pulse in a quieter rhythm. Summoning her voice with a controlled ring, she shouted, "He's lying—these blasts, these robed agitators, are part of his operation!" She let her ward flicker slightly, showing them, she was focusing on speech over direct illusions. "We have proof."

Some eyes wavered uncertainly. The figure pinned beneath Kester tried to squirm, but Kester tightened his hold. "You think you can outmaneuver me?" he snarled at Elysia. "I have more men. All it takes is one rumor—that your spells caused those blasts. This festival will riot against you."

Lorand sidestepped a lunging saboteur, parrying with an expert flourish. A grunt and the saboteur collapsed. Darius and the two knights tackled another robed figure. One masked minion dropped a small ledger with a clatter. The movement caught Elysia's eye like a flash of destiny. A ledger. Her heart soared—these pages might be the final piece of evidence they needed, if it was indeed one of Kester's incriminating logs.

"Get that ledger!" she called out. Across the swirling courtyard, a Valecrest knight stooped, lifting the small book. The crowd collectively strained to see. Kester hissed something under his breath, his mask of composure fracturing.

In the surge of confusion, Lorand found his opening. With a sharp pivot, he lunged forward, catching Kester's staff arm in one swift motion. Another Valecrest knight— Marcus, likely—darted in to yank the retainer free from Kester's grip. Kester let out a strangled curse, trying to tear away, but Lorand slammed him back with a controlled force, grappling him until Kester staggered to his knees.

Chaos broke across the courtyard as the barred saboteurs realized their plan was folding. The masked infiltrators spat curses, some trying to flee. Darius and the baron's watchers rushed to corner them, steel glinting. Elysia eased her wards, letting the golden dome fade now that more direct threats were subdued. Her entire body shuddered with the sudden letdown of tension, her vision pulsing at the edges. Carefully, she inhaled until her breath steadied, ignoring the weakness in her legs.

All around them, the crowd began to realize that the masked attackers were cornered. A wave of uncertain relief swept the courtyard. Elysia willed her trembling limbs not to buckle. She turned and saw Lorand still gripping Kester's collar. Kester's face was twisted in hatred, eyes darting wildly like a trapped fox. He spat again at Lorand. "This unity is a sham. Witchcraft, curses—once the monarchy sees the truth, you both will be stripped of your titles."

Lorand's jaw worked, controlled but furious. "No," he said quietly, a muscle ticking at his temple. "We have numerous witnesses, multiple scraps of letters—and now your own sabotage, displayed in front of an entire festival. This time, Kester, you cannot hide behind rumor." He wrenched Kester's staff away, letting it clatter to the cobblestones.

The hush broke as the baron's voice thundered: "Seize him!" The nearest watchers sprang in, forcibly restraining Kester's arms, wrestling him to stand. The masked saboteurs who had not fled were likewise held at sword point by knights and watchers, back by the orchard's edge. A subdued fracas lingered, but the main threat was contained.

Cautiously, Elysia stepped forward. The crowd parted for her as she moved toward Lorand and the detainees. She glanced at the ledger on the ground, now in the hands of one of the baron's men. Lifting her gaze, she locked eyes with Kester, her voice still thrumming with leftover adrenaline. "This ledger—" She pointed. "It contains payment records for mercenaries. We've seen scraps of it before. You paid them to sabotage our union, endangering villagers and guards alike." She saw the baron's aide leafing through the pages, scanning lines of scribbled sums. A hush hung over them. For a moment, Elysia allowed her swirling anger to filter into her words. "All those raids and illusions...all to incite fear that Kallendore's wards or Valecrest's knights were harming the barony. You caused every bruise, every burned stall, every collapsed guard."

Kester pressed his lips into a tight line, eyes darting to the watchers. He spat, "Lies. I maintain you are the culprit, bewitching us. That ledger could be forgery—"

"Enough." The baron's voice snapped through the night. He took the ledger from his aide, scanning it. Then he turned to Sir Remine. "My lord envoy..." He passed it over, those lines of proof now wholly visible. Elysia held her breath, watching Sir Remine's expression flicker from guarded to grim. The envoy nodded sharply.

Kester's face blanched. "Wait—" he began, but the

baron's watchers hauled him back, ignoring his protests. Gasps ran through the crowd as the baron gestured to the knights, indicating they should hold Kester for further questioning. Whispered voices rippled among the villagers, and Elysia caught repeated references to "Kester behind attacks" and "Kallendore was innocent."

A trembling relief coursed through her. This was it: the final move in the game Kester had played for weeks, maybe longer. She willed her breath to steady, pressing a hand against her drumming heart. Beside her, Lorand exhaled in a long, controlled sigh, lowering his sword. The swirl of tension between them sometimes felt more potent than any sabotage, but at this moment, it was purely a comfort to know she wasn't alone.

CHAPTER

EIGHT

For a moment, no one spoke—people were reeling in shock. Kester's sabotage had manifested openly in the most brazen way, but it had also been subverted in front of the baron, Sir Remine, and the entire population gathered. Then Sir Remine cleared his throat, stepping forward. The hush thickened.

"You there—guards, keep a firm hold on him. He'll face the monarchy's justice." Sir Remine's voice was unwavering, but somewhere in it, Elysia sensed both anger and satisfaction. He turned, surveying Elysia and Lorand with a cool, measuring eye. "You two—and your watchers—just thwarted a sabotage attempt that might have sent Highdale into chaos. You worked in tandem, combining wards and steel." He paused, letting the significance sink in. "The monarchy demanded proof of your union's authenticity. Tonight, we have witnessed it plainly."

Elysia's cheeks warmed. She glanced toward Lorand,

who was still breathing hard, the flush of exertion across his face. He slid his sword back into its scabbard. In the flickering torches and the swirl of leftover smoke, he looked as though every ounce of tension had poured out of him. Some uncertain hush lingered among the crowd. Then the baron, sounding almost jubilant despite himself, shouted, "People of Highdale—do you see? Kester's final sabotage has failed. We have the evidence, and the monarchy's envoy stands witness. Kallendore and Valecrest are not the cause of your troubles. They have fought to protect us, side by side."

With that, a rustle of relief spread outward. Applause started in a few pockets. Others joined in. Elysia felt her shoulders sag. The moment felt surreal—like stepping out of a nightmare into dawn.

Then Lorand turned toward her, expression alight with fierce relief. A hundred unspoken thoughts flickered behind his eyes. Before she could fully parse the swirl of her own emotions—anger, triumph, gratitude, a stirring warmth—he moved, bridging the distance. His gauntlet found her hand, tugging her closer. A soundless question formed in her mind, and she saw the answer in his eyes. In front of the entire courtyard, in front of knights, watchers, and suspicious villagers, he stepped forward and pressed his lips to hers.

For a heartbeat, the world went silent. Elysia's pulse pummeled a dizzying staccato as she tasted the sweat and warmth of him, the faint tang of smoke still lingering in the air. This kiss was no polite formality for the monarchy's sake; it was raw relief, an overflowing of bond they'd forged through every sabotage, every healing, each shared night of watchful tension. She let out a trembling breath against his mouth, then returned the kiss, ignoring the scandalized gasps or startled cheers from the crowd. Her heart soared, and she felt the trembling final shards of fear dissolve in that contact.

When they finally parted, Elysia's cheeks burned. She heard the baron exhale loudly, perhaps in relief. The hush in the courtyard simmered, then broke into a rising roar of applause and cheers. Even those who had once eyed her with suspicion now clapped, uncertain but carried by the moment. She glanced at Lorand, who wore a small, uncharacteristically bright grin. She recognized in his gray eyes the same jolt of wonder she felt in her own chest.

She tried to regain her composure, turning toward Sir Remine—and found that the envoy was regarding them with an air that bordered on approval. A surprising warmth glowed behind his measured stare. "The monarchy tasked me with discerning the truth of this alliance," he said, letting the voices eddy. "I can see no better reinforcement than what's transpired: you have fought in union rather than for show. Highdale stands indebted to you both."

His words were formal, but Elysia heard the subtext. The monarchy's threat of dissolving their noble lines was receding. A wave of relief so strong it nearly buckled her knees washed through her. She reached out and touched Lorand's arm, still breathing hard. He curled his fingers around hers, a gesture of quiet, unspoken solidarity.

At the dais steps, the baron raised his hands again for

the crowd's attention. "Kester and his men will be taken into custody immediately. Sir Remine shall oversee an inquiry verifying these ledgers and statements. But from what we have already seen, House Kallendore and House Valecrest bear no guilt for this sabotage." He paused, surveying the many townsfolk. "Therefore, we will continue this festival—let it not be marred by fear. Instead, let it stand as a testament to what unity truly looks like."

A cheer rippled outward—less frantic, more genuine. Elysia felt an odd choking sensation in her throat, like relief was too big for her chest to contain. Over the last few weeks, she had faced everything from poison on a guard's lips to illusions meant to discredit her. She had poured her healing power into farmland, endured nights in cramped inns, wept for the injured in remote villages. And always, Lorand had been there, bristly and proud but unwavering in each crisis. This moment—the moment they had planned to confront Kester—had nearly collapsed into chaos. But now, they were standing in the aftermath, triumphant.

The baron hopped off the dais to handle details with his aides, instructing watchers to round up the saboteurs. Sir Remine moved toward the orchard's edge, likely planning how to formally record an immediate statement. Gathered near the dais, the rest of the courtyard's onlookers watched Elysia and Lorand with an expression that ranged from awe to curiosity. Some parted for them, others offered hesitant bows. Elysia exhaled, face still flushed from that very public kiss.

Lorand's hand remained atop hers, warm and steady. She couldn't quite meet his eyes for a moment, startled by the tenderness she felt there. It was too open, too raw. "I —" She began, her voice coming out too soft. "I can't believe it's done."

He drew closer, gaze flicking across her features. "We finished what we came for," he said. The faintest note of wonder hung in his tone as if he too couldn't believe it. "Kester's sabotage is out in the open. The monarchy sees it. The baron sees it. Possibly even the townsfolk see it now." His lips quirked in that half-smile she'd grown to both admire and fear, in the sense that it reminded her how far she had fallen for him.

She opened her mouth to respond, only for a pair of Valecrest knights to approach. "My lord," one said, voice brimming with excitement, "we've secured those robed men behind the orchard. Mars and Darius pinned them. Do you want us to bring them to the baron, or—"

"Take them straight to the baron's guard," Lorand instructed. "He'll want that entire group under lock until morning." The knight nodded swiftly and hurried off. Then Lorand turned back to Elysia, an apology in his gaze. "I expect we'll have little rest tonight—paperwork, statements. But at least it's not more sabotage."

She tried to smile. Instead, tears pricked the corners of her eyes. Expending so much magic for the shield had worn her down, and relief battered her composure. She glanced toward the orchard, where colorful lanterns still hung overhead, and heard faint scraps of the fiddlers attempting to resume festivity. "It was nearly a disaster," she whispered, "but we stopped it."

A fresh wave of applause from behind them made Elysia turn. A group of villagers—maybe orchard workers and a few traveling merchants—had begun to gather in a ring, eyeing Elysia with gratitude and Lorand with respect. One older man, hat in hand, called out, "You kept us safe from those blasts, m'lady. Your wards shielded my wife and daughter." Another voice chimed, "It was your knights who tackled that scoundrel, my lord." A third added, "Finally, these rumors are put to rest. Thank you both."

Heat rushed to Elysia's face. She tried to offer a modest nod, though her heart soared. She'd grown used to suspicious stares, or reluctant acceptance from people who might appreciate her healing but did not trust her "witch" lineage. This open gratitude was new. She realized now that seeing the sabotage with their own eyes had made the difference.

Lorand placed a comforting hand high on her back. "Let them see you," he murmured gently. "Let them see what you did. They'll never again mistake your powers for curses."

She nodded, swallowing thickly. Forcing a watery smile, she lifted her voice so the little knot of onlookers could hear her. "We are relieved you're safe. That's why we came, from the very start—to protect these lands, not harm them." Another round of applause swelled. Elysia felt her breath catch in her throat. This was everything she had wanted—to do the right thing, to heal, to see Kallendore and Valecrest working together. She recalled the early days of the "goodwill tour," how stifled and resentful she'd felt in her forced closeness to Lorand. Now, ironically, that closeness was the only thing she truly depended on.

As the group parted, leaving her with Lorand again, she pressed trembling fingers to her temple. "I might need a moment," she admitted quietly. "My wards have me drained."

He hesitated, glancing around. The dais was still partly ringed by watchers and villagers, but off to one side, near a modest archway leading to the orchard, the crowd had thinned. "Come," Lorand said, voice warm with concern. He gently guided her from the center of the chaos, weaving around an upturned bench and scattered lantern poles. She obeyed, letting him steer her out from the swirl of congratulatory chatter.

Within a few steps, they passed beneath the orchard's first rows of trees. Lanterns hung from the branches in pastel ribbons, the gentle glow casting dancing patterns on the grass. It was quieter here; the hum of the crowd behind them softened into a dull roar. Elysia sank onto a low wooden seat that had been placed for festival-goers to rest. She closed her eyes, inhaling the orchard's cooler night air. The sweet tang of apples replaced the acrid smoke from the blasts, and she let tension slip from her shoulders.

Lorand watched her, a mix of worry and admiration in his gaze. "You used a lot of magic," he remarked softly, stepping close enough that his hip brushed the bench.

"More than I've seen in a single burst since that time you cleansed those bigger farmland blights." He paused, his voice thickening with an undertone of awe. "I can't... I can't tell you how grateful I am you did it. That boy you shielded might have taken a direct hit otherwise."

She blinked, recalling the child in the moment of swirling chaos. "I couldn't let him be hurt," she said, her voice quivering. "Or the others. That was the point of everything: to protect them."

Lorand nodded gravely. Then, dropping a fraction of his composure, he gently rested a hand on her shoulder. "At times," he murmured, "I'm terrified watching how much you give of yourself to keep them safe."

A smile tugged at her lips. "It's not so different from how you throw yourself into every fight," she countered. "I watch you charge into a swarm of swords without a second thought."

That drew a half-chuckle from him, a faint relief shining in his eyes. He lifted his free hand, letting it settle over hers in her lap. The orchard's hush wrapped them in a bubble of warmth. Distantly, Elysia heard the baron's guards shift across the courtyard, rounding up saboteurs. The last traces of dust and smoke had begun to lift, letting the festival's music tentatively resume.

NINE

Silence stretched between them for several beats, just the hush of lantern-lit leaves overhead. Elysia found her breath slowing, back against the rough wood of the bench, Lorand's presence anchoring her in the swirl of post-adrenaline. Her gaze dropped to where he held her hand, his fingers curled around hers, the Valecrest signet ring glinting faintly. That ring once symbolized everything she resented about this forced union. Now, it felt strangely reassuring.

At length, she gathered her courage, turning to face him properly. "Thank you," she said, voice trembling with sincerity. "If you and Darius hadn't tackled those men, they might have pinned the blame entirely on my wards. Or worse. You stood by me in front of everyone. If you'd hesitated for even a heartbeat, Kester might have turned the crowd."

His gray eyes, steady and serious, found hers. "We said we stand or fall together—it's not just a line, Elysia." He swallowed. "I can't deny I once resented this betrothal more than anything. But after what we've endured, I'd choose it again if it meant keeping you by my side."

Her cheeks flushed. That direct statement battered at the last of her guarded composure. She parted her lips, but no easy reply came. Instead, she reached up slowly, letting her palm curl against his jaw. "Then you know I feel the same," she managed. "This isn't just to appease the monarchy anymore."

He breathed out slowly, a flicker of something raw brightening his eyes. In one fluid motion, he dipped his head and pressed his brow to hers. She could feel his heartbeat thrumming in the tension of the orchard's hush. The memory of their public kiss still burned on her lips, but this moment—private, quiet—felt just as significant. They had overcome sabotage, answered the monarchy, saved villagers. And they had done it side by side.

Elysia closed her eyes and soaked in the closeness, the calm after the storm. Gradually, her senses registered more normal details: the faint chirping of night insects in the orchard grass, the smell of apples and honey from a nearby stand, the distant hum of a hundred relieved voices. Each one reminded her that real life existed beyond sabotage and hidden conspirators. She exhaled.

A minute later, footsteps approached from behind the orchard's arch. She opened her eyes to see Darius, who wore a sheepish expression, as though he wished he could vanish and leave them in peace. He cleared his throat. "My lord, my lady," he said carefully, "the baron wants to speak with you one more time before he finalizes a statement.

Something about how you want Kester's men processed, and how to handle official charges with the monarchy's envoy."

Elysia withdrew her hand gently from Lorand's face, though she could see the regret in his eyes at the interruption. She nodded to Darius, tucking away the swirl of emotion behind a veneer of calm. "We'll come," she said, voice steadier now.

Darius gave a courteous bow and disappeared, leaving them alone again for only a breath. Lorand stood, offering his hand to help Elysia up from the bench. She accepted it, ignoring how her knees still felt a touch weak. Together, they stepped back toward the open courtyard. The orchard's glow faded behind them, replaced by the bustle of watchers, knights, and a few anxious townsfolk. The festival's center had begun to recover from the smoke and blasts: lanterns were being relit, and scuffed tables were tentatively righted by innkeepers determined to salvage the night.

In the middle of it all, the baron stood near Sir Remine, arms still crossed but with an air of less tension. He beckoned them over, an impatient swirl of his cloak. Elysia felt Lorand's subtle squeeze of her hand as they approached. The baron wasted no time. "We have Kester under guard," he said tersely. "A few of his men escaped, but we're searching the perimeter. Sir Remine is confident this ledger proves Kester financed the sabotage. We'll conduct a fuller interrogation first thing in the morning."

Elysia nodded, swallowing the dryness in her throat. "Good," she managed softly.

Sir Remine cleared his throat. "You realize," he intoned, "that calling the monarchy's inquisitor to question Kester is your next step. The baron's staff will handle the formalities of minor charges, but the sabotage attempt on your forced union is a matter for the king. Official depositions must be recorded."

Lorand's expression was grim. "We'll do whatever is needed. Kester can't be allowed to slip away from real consequences." His voice carried a protective edge that warmed Elysia's heart.

"Then see to it." The baron nodded. "I'll prepare the testimony from the men who seized that ledger. Also, the guard Kester tried to use as a scapegoat might speak on your behalf." He paused, letting the tension crackle. Then, with visible effort, he exhaled and offered an almost-smile. "Tonight's fiasco ended with a redeeming outcome. We should let the rest of Highdale see that their baron and the monarchy support your betrothal—a betrothal that seems all the more genuine."

A wry twitch crossed Elysia's lips. If only the baron knew how wholeheartedly they had just confirmed that bond in front of the entire courtyard. She inclined her head, meeting his gaze. "Thank you," she said softly, "for defending us publicly. Now we do the same for Highdale."

They spoke briefly of logistical details: how the knights would remain stationed until the festival ended, how Kester's men would be carted to the keep's holding cells. Then, with the air of a man who had survived too many battles in one day, the baron gestured for them to rejoin the festival as they saw fit. "Better to celebrate publicly," he muttered, "than to let fear linger."

That left Elysia and Lorand to roam the courtyard, reentering a swirl of festival-goers who looked both exhausted and relieved. Musicians tried to reignite a festive tone, playing a jaunty reel that previously would have drawn dancers. Now, only a few joined, though with uncertain energy. Elysia's heart twinged—these people had come expecting a night of camaraderie, not an explosive confrontation. Perhaps, though, they could still find some joy.

She glanced at Lorand. He lifted a brow, the corners of his mouth quirking. "Shall we?" he asked, voice low. "If not to dance, at least to show them we're still standing."

Her pulse fluttered at the idea of stepping into a dance after the raw intensity of the last hour. But she recognized a valuable truth: a demonstration of composure might reassure the barony that fear would not win. So, she gave a small nod, letting him guide her toward the flickers of music. The fiddles quickened, as if the players sensed the presence of the so-called betrothed heirs.

She braced her hand on Lorand's shoulder, the other twined with his, and they began moving in a slow circle, not exactly matching the sprightly steps of the reel but falling into their own gentle pattern. She felt the solidity of his body, the warmth of his breath, and the swirl of a gentle breeze that lifted the edges of her loose hair. A few watchers nodded in approval. No one jeered; no one hurled accusations of witchcraft. The hush from earlier had been replaced by a fragile sense of renewed celebration.

As they danced, Elysia let her eyes slip closed for a beat, inhaling the moment. They had done it. Kester's sabotage was unmasked for all to see. The monarchy's envoy, once so doubtful, stood convinced of their union's truth. And Lorand...Lorand danced with her in public as though it was the most natural thing in the world. In that swirl of lantern light and nerves, Elysia realized that her own reticence, the leftover desire to push him away, had evaporated in the wake of their shared battles.

The music ended, replaced by a wave of applause and relieved laughter from the crowd. Elysia opened her eyes, meeting Lorand's gaze through the gentle hush that followed. He lifted her hand and brushed it with his lips—softer than the urgent kiss from before, but no less charged. Her heart soared anew, and she fought not to let tears gather again.

A flood of well-wishers approached, praising them both. An older woman pressed a pastry into Elysia's hand, insisting she needed the strength after spending so much magic. A Valecrest knight clasped Lorand's shoulder in heartfelt thanks for driving off more saboteurs. Elysia found herself enveloped by a swirl of gratitude so intense she could only muster murmurs of acknowledgment. For so long, she had felt overshadowed by suspicion here in Highdale. Now, acceptance had blossomed, albeit in the aftermath of chaos.

Eventually, the press of people eased, and Elysia found herself at the courtyard's edge, shoulder to shoulder with

Lorand. Together, they looked upon the orchard, where festival lanterns still glowed, and across the cobblestones where children resumed small games. Sir Remine loitered near the dais, speaking with the baron—likely drafting the official statements. The sky overhead was a vast canopy of stars, so clear it felt like a promise of new beginnings.

She turned to Lorand, voice intimate. "This is all I ever wanted—for them to believe in us. I never dreamed it would come to this dramatic a showdown."

He let out a small, relieved laugh. "Dramatic is an understatement." Then he grew solemn. "But you proved yourself tonight. Or perhaps we proved ourselves. In front of the entire barony."

She nodded, leaning closer. "We'll see what tomorrow brings, once Kester's men are questioned. But at least now we face it together, not as stooges forced by an edict."

A gentle hush spilled over them. In that hush, she felt his hand find hers once more, fingers intertwining. The orchard leaves rustled softly, as if applauding a final time.

Eventually, they meandered away from the crowd that lingered near the dais. They found a quieter nook by a row of unlit torches, near the keep's side entrance. Elysia sank against the stone wall, letting the faint moonlight wash over her. Lorand braced an arm behind her, shielding her from any stray passersby. She could still feel her heart fluttering from the remnants of the night's excitement.

"This might be the first time in weeks we can truly breathe," she said, her voice a murmur. "Still, we can't ignore that tomorrow will see us drowning in official tasks."

He nodded. "We'll manage. We always do." His tone carried a soft confidence that warmed her from the inside. "And once it's all settled? Kester under formal trial, the monarchy's envoy satisfied—what then?"

She smiled, though it wobbled. "Then we start building the peace we've been promising. Valecrest knights, Kallendore wards, working together for the good of Highdale." After a pause, she added more softly, "And maybe... some time to figure out how to live as true partners—not because we have to, but because we choose to."

His gaze flicked down, and she sensed the swirl of emotion in him. "I want that." A small, self-deprecating laugh tinged his words, as if he marveled at how far they had come. "If you'd told me a month ago that I would not only tolerate Kallendore's 'witch powers' but welcome them, I might have strangled you for the suggestion." He lifted her hand and pressed it to his chest, letting her feel the steady thump of his heart. "But I can't imagine going back."

Neither could she. The air between them crackled with a charged hush. Finally, she pushed up onto her toes and pressed a gentle kiss to the corner of his mouth. "Then we go forward," she whispered, letting the orchard's sweet fragrance and the hum of distant fiddles envelop them.

He wrapped an arm around her waist, drawing her fully to him. The distant echoes of the festival's next tune swirled like a lullaby. Elysia closed her eyes, resting against his shoulder, fatigued but serene. Let tomorrow bring official statements and Kester's accusations. Let the monarchy's scribes comb through ledgers all day. Tonight, she had Lorand at her side and a quiet orchard as witness to the alliance they had forged in every possible sense.

In the background, the festival's spirit rekindled, music drifting gently, laughter following. Sabotage was undone, and Highdale's citizens had seen the truth. As the night swept onward, Elysia allowed a final wave of contentment to settle over her. After so many struggles—so many corners of doubt—here they stood, truly triumphant. And, for once, free to imagine a future no longer dictated by an edict, but by the bond of healing and steel they themselves had chosen.

TEN

A brittle hush clung to Highdale on the morning after Kester's arrest. Although the streets were bright with newly scrubbed cobblestones and the gentle warmth of early sunlight, an undercurrent of caution threaded through every conversation. Elysia Kallendore sensed it like a chill that no glow of magic could chase away. She stood at the edge of the bustling town square—where just last night the final festival events had descended into chaos—watching knots of villagers gather to read the royal notice newly posted on the wide central board.

A guard rapped the butt of his spear against the wooden planks, directing attention to the parchment. The crisp, curling edges of the notice showed the monarchy's seal in shining red wax. People jostled closer, reading: *LORD KESTER ACTED ALONE*, it proclaimed in neat calligraphy, and *ANY FURTHER ATTEMPT TO STOKE UNREST SHALL BE MET WITH ROYAL CONSEQUENCES.* Elysia's eyes skimmed the rest of the text. It reaffirmed not only Kester's guilt but also urged the barony to support the forced alliance between Houses Kallendore and Valecrest.

She inhaled slowly, battling a flutter of nerves. The monarchy was doing its part to quell lingering suspicions. Yet she saw the strain on the villagers' faces, especially those who had once whispered about "witch curses." Some stepped forward to read the notice with relief, while others hovered a few paces back, arms folded, distrustful frowns etched into their brows.

A sudden surge of footsteps rustled behind her. She turned to see the baron stepping onto a small stone dais, the same dais that had shaken beneath last night's sabotage. He had changed from the elaborate festival robes into a simpler dark cloak. His expression carried the weight of a man who had spent the night fending off rumor and panic.

"People of Highdale," he began, voice carrying despite his clear fatigue, "I stand before you to confirm what many of you have already heard: Lord Kester is under arrest. He sowed chaos to pit Kallendore and Valecrest against each other again, hoping to destroy their attempts at unification." The baron paused, letting that statement settle into the crowd. "Now, with the monarchy's newest notice, it's official. His sabotage is recognized at the highest level, and any of his remaining allies who try to stir up trouble will face royal justice."

A few uneasy murmurs followed. Elysia glanced around, disquiet pressing on her chest. The tension among the crowd was palpable. Just because the monarchy declared Kester a criminal didn't erase centuries of suspicion or hush those who still believed Kallendore's magic was the cause of every illness. She felt the weight of their stares, the half-lowered eyes that flicked toward her hair, her hands, as though she might conjure spells at any moment.

From off to the side, Lorand Valecrest stepped forward. His tall shape was unmistakable in a fitted crimson surcoat, a simpler version of ceremonial attire—no polished armor now, but still every inch a knight. He carried himself with unflinching composure, shoulders squared. The sunlight revealed faint shadows beneath his eyes, an echo of the near-sleepless night spent dealing with Kester's imprisoned associates, but he moved with unwavering confidence.

When he reached the dais, the baron gave Lorand an expectant nod. Elysia swallowed, resisting the urge to smooth her skirts. She followed Lorand, footsteps echoing on the stone. A hush rippled through the assembly of townsfolk as they realized the two betrothed heirs were about to address them.

Lorand's gaze found hers for a moment—just enough to exchange a silent vow of solidarity—before he turned to the crowd. "Yesterday was meant to celebrate the festival's final night," he said, his baritone resonant. "Instead, we faced blasts of sabotage and a brazen attempt by Lord Kester's men to sow panic. Many were injured, and Elysia Kallendore's wards helped protect those caught in the chaos."

She felt a faint, grateful warmth at his emphasis on her

magic. Even a week ago, he had bristled to speak of Kallendore "witchcraft" in a praising tone, but now he did so openly, with pride in his voice. That small shift of acceptance stirred something deep within her.

He continued, "I personally thank Lady Elysia for saving innocent bystanders last night—farmers, traveling merchants, and even some of my own knights." His words were clear and direct. Then, as if acknowledging the eyes of the crowd, he reached out and slid his hand around hers. Elysia's heart kicked in her chest. Immediately, she felt an unexpected hush over the townsfolk. Some parted their lips in faint surprise or wonder; others wore guarded expressions. She knew that for many of them, the sight of a Valecrest heir publicly aligning with a Kallendore mage —touching her hand as though it were the most natural gesture in the world—was startling.

Yet Lorand's grip was steady, and she managed to keep her chin high. She remembered the swirl of energy when she'd conjured wards last night, how she'd glimpsed him through the haze of smoke, sword drawn. The memory kindled her resolve to stand by him just as fiercely.

A murmur rose from the crowd—some whispers laced with relief; others tainted by skepticism. One woman with a basket of laundry clutched against her hip cried, "He's only saying that because the monarchy demands it!" And a younger man near the back gave a sharp retort that Kester's sabotage was proof enough that House Kallendore wasn't to blame. The baron hammered his staff against the dais, gaining enough quiet that Lorand could speak again.

"We can't force you to trust us overnight," Lorand said, voice low but carrying conviction. "But I've seen Elysia heal total strangers—people who once spat that she was a witch. She doesn't ask for gold or loyalty in return. Don't let Kester's lies keep you from seeing the good she can do... or the good both our houses can achieve together."

Emboldened by that, Elysia drew a breath. Her pulse drummed. "I ask only for a fair chance," she said, raising her voice. "What happened last night—what caused fear and injury—was not an act of magic, but an act of cruelty fueled by Kester's coin. If any of you need aid, if you're suffering from last night's blasts, come to me or the Kallendore watchers. We will not turn you away."

Her words settled, and in them, she tried to pour calm empathy. A cluster of watchers wearing Kallendore green nodded supportively. The baron, relieved that the speech wasn't devolving into arguments, announced that a healing tent had been set up by the orchard path for anyone still wounded. Then, quietly, he gestured for Elysia and Lorand to step back from the dais, signaling the end of the address.

As the crowd dispersed in uneasy clusters, Elysia caught sight of an older man shooting her a suspicious glance. There were pockets of unspoken hostility— probably supporters of Kester, or at least those who refused to abandon the idea that occult magic lurked behind everything. She ignored the sting of old wariness that rose inside her. The monarchy's decree had forced her and Lorand together... but no decree could force acceptance from hearts determined to cling to old grudges.

Lorand's hand was still in hers, the faint warmth of his palm a steady anchor. Only when they stepped away from the dais did he gently release her. She looked up at him, meeting his storm-gray gaze. "Thank you," she managed softly, sensing how his public defense of her might ruffle some Valecrest knights. "That speech... it couldn't have been easy to stand up and proclaim I saved your knights."

His lips curved, just a little. "I'm not sure I'd have managed it a month ago." A breath escaped him. "But after everything, I... it needs saying." With a sidelong glance, he added, "Your wards saved us all last night. Let them talk of curses if they wish. I know the truth."

She felt her throat tighten with quiet gratitude. The simple conviction in his voice was all she needed in this moment.

Nearby, the baron dismissed a handful of guards, instructing them to patrol for any rumor-mongers. Elysia let the swirl of crowd voices fade from her focus, turning to find Mira waiting for her by one of the orchard gates. Mira wore a pale green over-gown, her posture tense with concern and relief. When Elysia moved toward her, Lorand stepped aside with a final, steady look that promised he'd see her soon. The moment felt more intimate than a thousand elaborate court gestures.

She reached Mira, who gave an anxious smile. "I'm glad the baron made that announcement. Though from the looks of it, some of Kester's sympathizers remain unconvinced." Her gaze shifted to the orchard path, where a group of older men was already muttering under their breath.

Elysia nodded, shoulders sagging slightly. "It'll take time," she admitted. "But at least the monarchy's notice is posted." She paused, brushing a stray lock of hair from her cheek. "You look tired, Mira. Did you help at the healing tent last night?"

Mira exhaled. "Yes. So many small injuries from the blasts. And then a few panicked souls who just needed reassurance. I made them tea and listened to their fears. Spent half the night telling them Kallendore wards weren't behind the explosions." Her small, wry smile faded. "Of course, that doesn't stop the rumor that your spells can bend minds."

A weary laugh escaped Elysia. "I'd guess no rumor can be killed in a single day." She rubbed her temple, acutely aware of the lingering ache in her limbs from overextending her magic. "Today, I meant to help more. But the baron insisted we do this public address first. Now, I—" She broke off, feeling dizziness swirl in her. She hated the telltale sign of fatigue creeping up. "I may need a short rest before I can do more healing. Overextending last night took more out of me than I realized."

Sympathy softened Mira's features. "Your face is pale," she said kindly. "Why not let me brew you something in the keep's kitchens? A mild restorative infusion—herbs, a bit of honey. Then you can see who else needs help."

Elysia nodded, relieved at the suggestion. "Thank you. I'll meet you there soon." She gratefully watched Mira slip away toward the orchard's back gate, presumably heading inside the keep's side entrance. Elysia lingered, scanning the crowd in case someone called for her, but the townsfolk had scattered into smaller clusters. She caught a few stares—some curious, some grudging—and tried to give a gentle nod if they met her gaze directly. Yet no one approached her openly.

At length, she turned toward the keep's courtyard, weaving through a line of stalls that had once sold sweet pastries and spiced ciders. Many were shuttered; their owners too shaken to continue celebrating. Broken bits of festival ribbons lay strewn across the cobblestones, a reminder of how quickly sabotage had turned revelry to fear. The hush unsettled her, stirring memories of swirling smoke and frightened screams from last night.

She was so lost in thought that she nearly bumped into a wiry man who stepped into her path from behind a stall. She halted with a startled inward gasp, instincts tensing. He wore the rough-woven tunic of a local craftsman, but his expression looked pinched, torn between apology and hostility.

"Lady Kallendore?" the man asked in a low voice, confirming that indeed it was Elysia. A faint scowl tugged at the corners of his mouth. "I... I heard you'd be healing folks again."

Her pulse fluttered. She scanned him quickly for visible injuries—none that she could see aside from minor bruises on his arm. "Yes," she said gently. "If you're hurt, or if any of your family is—"

He cut her off with a grunt, half defensive. "I'm not here to cry about a bruise. I just..." He shifted on his feet, glancing aside. "Blast it, I'm no friend to your witchery, but my daughter—she got scratched up really bad in the panic. She's got a fever now, maybe from the dirt in her cuts. And the baron's men told me to ask you for help." His tone dared her to mock him, doubt bristling at every word.

Elysia softened. Tension and suspicion she could handle from grown men, but she refused to let it harm a child's wellbeing. "I'll come at once," she said. "Where is she?"

The man blinked. He seemed faintly surprised that she agreed so readily, no scorn in her voice. Clearing his throat, he gestured to the narrower lane leading behind the row of stalls. "I can take you. She's inside the cooper's shop. My sister's place." He hesitated. "Don't... don't try anything strange, all right?"

She bit back the retort that healing was "strange" by default to some. Instead, she offered a calm nod. "I promise, I only want to help her. Shall we go?" Gently, she angled her body in invitation for him to lead.

He stared a beat longer, then turned and walked, his shoulders hunched as though expecting glares from onlookers. Elysia fell into step behind him, ignoring the faint twinges of weakness in her calves. She had to be mindful of her magic reserves; last night she'd shielded so many and draining yourself twice in quick succession was dangerous. But how could she refuse a sick child?

They passed a clutter of overturned crates, the leftover debris from the frenzied crowd. The cooper's shop was set in a squat wooden building, the sign battered by last night's blasts. Inside, the air smelled of sawdust and stale smoke. A small girl lay on a makeshift cot near the back, whimpering softly. Two of her relatives stood at a distance, wringing their hands.

Elysia knelt, an ache tugging at her knees, and pressed gentle fingers to the child's brow. Warm, fevered. Multiple shallow cuts on her legs, one beginning to fester with a yellowish crust. Grimly, Elysia eased aside the girl's soiled bandage. "I'll clean it, all right?" she murmured in her gentlest voice. The girl's eyes fluttered open, big and frightened, but she didn't shrink away.

A quiet ring of watchers formed. The father hovered behind Elysia, tension rolling off him. She set aside her reservations and focused. First, a normal approach: herbs, a clean cloth, some boiled water if she could get it. She beckoned a cooper's apprentice. "Please bring some boiled water," she requested. He darted off. In the meantime, Elysia rummaged in her small pouch. The father twitched at the sight of small vials, as if expecting a cauldron of curses. She forced herself to remain calm and unhurried.

When the apprentice returned, Elysia used the water to wash the wound carefully. The girl let out a tiny whimper, so Elysia hummed a soft melody under her breath—an old tune from Kallendore halls. With sure, precise movements, she mixed a mild disinfecting salve from her pouch to rub onto the cuts, ignoring the father's watchful scowl.

Only when she'd applied the ointment did she settle her hand lightly over the most inflamed wound. She closed her eyes, inhaling a measured breath. She wouldn't conjure a full ward or risk deeper magic unless necessary;

for a minor infection, she could channel a small flow of healing energies. Her compassion rose, fueling the gentle light that glowed around her fingers—a faint golden shimmer that she guided into the child's torn skin.

Sweat gathered at Elysia's brow, and her pulse skittered. She reined in the healing flow to keep it from bleeding her strength too much. The brief flicker of magic was enough to coax the fever back from the brink and flush out the nascent infection. After a moment, she exhaled and removed her hand. The child's brow lost some of its heat. Her breathing calmed; cheeks no longer bright with fever. Elysia offered a small smile. "There," she murmured, smoothing the blanket. "Let the salve work. She should rest, but the fever won't worsen. Clean bandages each day—no more dust and dirt layering on top."

Around her, the watchers stood transfixed. Some stared with anxious awe at the faint ruminant glow that had scooped infection from the wound. The father stepped forward, kneeling by the girl. "Janine?" he whispered, as though half expecting her to vanish. She stirred, opened bleary eyes, and feebly reached for him. He swallowed hard, darting a sidelong glance at Elysia.

She rose to her feet carefully, ignoring the slight tremor in her legs. One of the father's relatives—an older woman with lines of worry across her face—mustered a nod of thanks. "I... we appreciate what you did." Then her voice tightened in suspicion. "You're sure you ain't left some curse behind?"

Elysia suppressed a sigh. "No. My wards don't cause curses, nor do they sow seeds of anything ill," she said softly. "I used a fraction of healing to encourage her body's own strength." Her gaze lingered on the father, who had turned to watch them. "She'll be fine, I promise."

An uneasy silence stretched, then the father gave a stiff nod. "You helped her," he said, his voice gruff. "Reckon I owe you." He shifted, looking away. "I... I'll pay if there's a fee. I'm no beggar."

Elysia's heart squeezed. House Kallendore had never required payment from those in the barony, not for essential healing—though the rumor that they demanded unholy tributes was common. "No fee," she said simply. "I ask only that you not spread false claims about me afterwards. That would be enough."

He blinked, as if uncertain how to respond. Finally, he let out a low grunt. "I'll... do my best to right rumors if I hear 'em." It was a reluctant vow, but a vow, nonetheless.

With a slight nod, Elysia turned and retreated, leaving them to fuss quietly over the child. The father's body no longer radiated such stark hostility. She stepped out into the lane, letting the midday glare wash over her face. The swirl of the orchard's breeze offered a welcome hush after the tension inside the cooper's shop.

Fatigue gnawed at her. That minor healing had taken more from her reserves than it should have—proof she was still recovering from the prior day's ordeal. She inhaled slowly, wishing for her bed in the Kallendore estate, or any restful corner far from suspicious eyes. But she had told Mira she'd find her for that infusion in the keep's kitchen. Summoning her last stores of composure, Elysia made her way toward the keep's side entrance. The dull ache in her temples throbbed with each step, a reminder that pushing her powers again tonight would be ill-advised.

Inside the keep, the corridor bustled with leftover festival staff tidying messes. The baron had apparently commanded a thorough scrubbing, to restore the estate's dignity after last night's chaos. Elysia nodded at a passing steward, who dipped a harried bow. She aimed for the small hallway off the main banquet area. Sure enough, Mira was there with a steaming cup.

"Here," Mira said gently, thrusting the cup into Elysia's hands. "Chamomile, honey, and a dash of ginger root. Drink up."

Grateful beyond words, Elysia cradled the cup, inhaling the soft herbal steam. Her shoulders unknotted fractionally at the first sip. The warmth slid through her, easing some tension. "Thank you," she whispered. Then she gave a rueful smile. "I just helped a child behind the cooper's shop. I was in time to prevent a deeper infection, but... I'm feeling it now."

Mira's brow creased. "Are you sure you shouldn't rest for a few hours? The baron can arrange other watchers to cover minor injuries."

Elysia shut her eyes briefly. She wanted to keep helping, especially while rumors plagued the town. But a wave of dizziness made her realize that continuing would be reckless. "I'll rest," she relented. "At least for a bit. But what about you? Any more visitors at the healing tent?"

"Not as many. A few folks wanting to confirm that you'd be there later." Mira set a hand on Elysia's elbow, guiding her toward a worn bench at the corridor's edge. "Sit, finish the tea. I'll gather more bandages in case more people arrive. Then maybe we can see about finding

Lorand or the baron for an update. They might have fresh concerns about Kester's supporters."

Nodding, Elysia sank onto the bench. Her thoughts drifted unbidden to Lorand. How earlier he'd unhesitatingly championed her in front of the townspeople. The memory brought a warmth to her cheeks, a sense of relief that she no longer stood alone under suspicious glares. She drank in silence, ignoring the swirl of servants in the corridor. A part of her longed to slip away somewhere quiet and reflect on how swiftly everything had changed since she and Lorand first embarked on their "goodwill tour." Then again, there was no time for private musings. Not yet.

She finished the tea. The gentle infusion did help, soothing some of her headache. Following Mira's advice, she retreated to a small side chamber near the keep's kitchens, a place typically used for storing linens. Mira snagged an extra cushion from a bench and insisted Elysia lie down. Reluctantly, Elysia complied. She draped her forearm over her eyes, letting the hush of stacked linens lull her. Now and then, footsteps thudded outside, a constant reminder that the keep's day-to-day chores marched on.

Sometime later—she wasn't sure if it was minutes or a full hour—discreet footsteps approached, stirring her half-awake senses. She lifted her arm from her eyes, blinking in the dim lamplight. The door cracked open. Lorand's voice, softly pitched: "Elysia?"

She rose on an elbow, heart fluttering. "Lorand," she murmured, surprise leaking through her tone. Her eyes adjusted to see him in the gloom, his profile backlit by the corridor's torchlight. He looked more exhausted than before, tension carved into the set of his jaw. Yet at the sight of her awake, his stance eased.

"Mira told me you were resting here," he said simply. He slipped inside, letting the door hush shut behind him. The small chamber's close air felt suddenly charged. "How are you feeling?"

She pushed upright. "Better," she said, though the word came out slightly breathless. "Just… drained, I suppose." She gestured at the folded linens around them. "Hardly the most dignified place for a rest, but it's quiet."

His lips quirked in a faint smile. "Quiet can be a welcome reprieve." He leaned back against a shelf, head tilting toward her. "The baron's posted more guards in the square and near the orchard. We've had a few scuffles—people cursing House Kallendore or claiming Valecrest manipulated everything to look heroic. But nothing as serious as last night's sabotage."

She rubbed her eyes, the mention of conflict renewing her fatigue. "So, the rumors keep swirling."

"Yes." He paused, crossing his arms. "But some vow that they saw you saving villagers, and if others contest it, they fight back. It's… complicated, but I'd say more are swayed in your favor than Kester's." After a beat, his gaze softened. "I know none of this erases the stares or the scornful whispers. But I hope it helps a little."

She gave a half nod. "It does." Sighing, she let her hand fall into her lap. "I sometimes feel foolish for letting it get to me. I've faced people's fear of Kallendore magic my whole life. But these past weeks, especially after we discovered Kester's sabotage... it's like every rumor about me roars even louder in my ears."

Lorand's posture shifted, and then—in a surprisingly gentle motion—he stepped closer and lowered himself to the bench beside her. The small space forced them into close proximity, his thigh near hers. She caught the faint scent of leather and a hint of musk from his surcoat. "I wish I could shield you from all that," he said quietly, setting an elbow on his knee. "I know I can't. But I'm here... if that counts for anything."

Something about that admission made her heart clench. She recalled how just a month or so earlier, standing near him felt like bristling hostility. Now, she wanted to lean toward him, to absorb the reassurance in his voice. "Thank you," she whispered. "It does count. More than you know."

He exhaled, and for a moment, they simply breathed in each other's presence, the hush thick with unsaid feelings. Outside, footsteps echoed, somebody calling the baron's name. But in this linen closet, the world felt still. Elysia's gaze fell to where Lorand had set his hand on the bench. She nearly placed her own atop it—an impulse that both thrilled and terrified her. Instead, she laced her fingers together in her lap.

Eventually, she broke the silence, voice hushed. "I should do more healing soon—there might be more villagers who need me."

He glanced at her, a flicker of worry in his eyes. "Not until you're certain you've recovered. You did enough,

Elysia. You saved my knights and countless others last night. Don't let the skepticism of a few push you to the brink of exhaustion."

She gave a small, grateful smile, touched by his protective concern. "I'll pace myself," she promised. Then, after a pause, she added softly, "But part of me wants to keep showing them, over and over, that I'm not the threat they think. Patience... is so difficult."

He reached out, in slow motion, and briefly—very briefly—settled his hand over hers. The contact was feather-light, yet a current of warmth flared through Elysia's veins. Even through the layer of cloth, she felt the raw sincerity in his gesture. "You'll prove it, in your own time," he said gruffly. "Just... keep some strength for yourself."

Then he squeezed her hand gently and withdrew, clearing his throat as though the moment was too charged. She felt a mingling of longing and relief. "Thank you," she repeated, quieter still.

Sudden footsteps sounded in the hallway. Elysia recognized Mira's voice speaking with Darius, mentioning the orchard. Lorand immediately straightened, maintaining a soldier's composure. Elysia swallowed, her pulse still unsteady. "We should probably go see if the baron needs us," she murmured.

"Yes," Lorand agreed, though his voice held a tinge of reluctance. "The baron wants to finalize statements to quell further unrest." He stood, offering Elysia a hand to help her up. She let him, ignoring the flicker of heat that raced through her at the contact.

Together, they left the storage chamber. The corridor's torchlight felt almost glaring after the dim hush. Mira and Darius stood near the archway, discussing guard rotations. At the sight of Lorand and Elysia, Mira's eyes flicked with faint amusement, but she schooled her expression. Darius inclined his head, greeting them with a respectful nod. "The baron's in the orchard," he said. "He asked me to fetch you. Something about publicly reaffirming that Kester stands alone—that no other houses are complicit."

Considering that possibility, Elysia nodded. She remembered how Kester had tried to incite strife by claiming Valecrest's knights attacked a Kallendore retainer. The baron likely wanted to assure the public that no other lesser lords had conspired with him. "All right," she said. "Let's go."

Mira gave Elysia's arm a gentle squeeze as they passed. "Feeling better?" she asked quietly.

"A bit," Elysia answered. "I'll manage."

They crossed the keep's courtyard, stepping through a side gate into the orchard behind the estate. A wide swath of apple trees formed a canopy of soft green above neatly lined pathways. Lanterns hung from low branches—a remnant of last night's festival décor. In broad daylight, their glow was feeble, but they still provided a whimsical note. The orchard's air smelled of fresh grass, faintly sweet from ripening fruit. It was there, near a wooden bench ringed by carefully tended flowerbeds, that the baron waited.

He was engaged in conversation with a handful of lesser nobles, presumably to confirm that no other families had aided Kester. Elysia recognized one older lady from a far-flung corner of Highdale, wearing a pin shaped like a bird. Another man wore a modest crest of a small estate. Their quiet voices drifted across the orchard, sounding half warmed by the midday light and half guarded from the night's fiasco.

When Elysia and Lorand approached, the baron spotted them and raised his hand. "Good," he said in relief, dismissing the lesser nobles with a polite word. They retreated, sparing Elysia brief glances—some friendlier than others. The baron motioned for Elysia, Lorand, Darius, and Mira to gather around him. "We've posted official statements that Kester's plot was orchestrated without any other local lord's involvement. That has calmed a portion of the rumor. But now there's talk that House Valecrest might have manipulated the outcome to make Kallendore appear heroic." His mouth tightened. "We can't let that nonsense take root."

Lorand's jaw clenched. "So, the rumor is flipping sides?"

"The rumor flips to any vantage that fosters distrust," the baron replied wearily. "Now a handful of Valecrest loyalists claim you staged the sabotage to cast Elysia in a saintly light. Utter hogwash, but hogwash often spreads faster than truth." His gaze flicked to Elysia. "I trust you're not pushing yourself? I'd call on your wards to highlight House Kallendore's genuine goodwill, but I don't want you fainting in front of half the orchard."

Elysia flushed. "I can do a simpler demonstration," she offered. "Though I shouldn't conjure large-scale wards—

I'd prefer to wait at least until evening to attempt anything that strenuous. But if needed, I can show a small ward or do a quick healing demonstration. Perhaps in front of the orchard workers? Something that proves we haven't faked caring for the barony's well-being."

The baron rubbed his chin, considering. "That might help. Let's arrange it for later, after you've recuperated more. The orchard staff have minor scrapes from last night's fiasco, so you can treat them in a calm, public manner." He shot her a pointed look. "No illusions, no dramatics—just practical help. Let people see you as a real person, not some mysterious figure."

Elysia's heart twisted with a mix of gratitude and frustration. At least the baron supported her. "I'll do it," she agreed.

Darius shifted; arms folded. "I can notify the orchard workers. They'll be dividing the last of the festival equipment today. We can gather them near the fountain so it's a bit more centralized."

"Good," the baron said. "Let's do that within the hour. Then hopefully by evening, the rumor that Valecrest orchestrated a Kallendore 'miracle' will wither."

Mira inclined her head. "I'll help Elysia if needed. But perhaps one or two Valecrest knights standing by would show collaboration. People would see that this isn't an act, but actual cooperation."

Lorand nodded, face solemn. "I'll arrange that detail."

The baron flicked his gaze between them, something like cautious optimism in his eyes. "We might yet salvage the spirit of unity after last night's fiasco. But let's remain vigilant—Kester may be locked up, but his old cronies might still sow doubt. One slip, and the monarchy's eyes will see a fractious barony, not a united one." He paused, giving Elysia and Lorand a tired smile. "Thank you both for standing firm. I'll handle the rest from here. Dismissed."

With that, the baron moved off, presumably to deal with more pressing tasks. Darius, too, took his leave, heading toward the orchard's far exit to find orchard workers. Elysia and Lorand lingered for a moment beneath the branches. A gentle breeze rustled overhead, drifting the faint scent of apples. Even with the hush, Elysia couldn't shake a swirl of conflict in her chest—frustration that no matter how many times she proved her healing, new rumors sprang up like weeds.

Mira touched her shoulder lightly. "I'll go gather a few Kallendore watchers to help with the supply of bandages. Meet us by the orchard fountain in a bit, yes?"

Elysia mustered a tight smile. "I will." Then she watched Mira slip away, leaving her alone with Lorand in the orchard's dappled sunlight. She found herself acutely aware of his presence, the memory of his hand on hers in that linen closet.

He cleared his throat, stepping closer so their conversation could remain private. "I hate that you keep having to prove yourself at every turn," he said quietly.

Her breath caught on a weak laugh. "I suppose that's the nature of bridging centuries of mistrust. One night's grand display won't fix everything. Or one arrest."

His gaze roamed her face, lingering for a moment on

the faint circles under her eyes. "I only wish—" He halted, words tangling. Then he grimaced, running a hand through his dark hair. "Kester caused all this, but even with him caged, suspicion persists. It makes me wonder how one man's manipulation could find such fertile ground. Maybe we Valecrests and Kallendores have clung to hatred so long that we'll seize any chance to see the other side as villains."

Her throat tightened. "We have both been taught from childhood that the other side is dangerous," she agreed, voice softer. "Though I never realized how foolish it was until these forced... travels." The corner of her lips quirked at the memory of that first ride in the carriage, the tension thick enough to choke. "It's not all undone overnight."

He studied her face for a heartbeat longer. "You should rest again before we do the orchard demonstration," he said at last. "I'll walk you back inside."

"Thank you," she said, ignoring the flutter in her belly. Let him fuss, if it meant they could savor these quiet moments. They left the orchard side by side, following a cobbled path that led toward the keep's western door. On the threshold, she paused, glancing sidelong at him. "We keep pressing forward. That's all we can do."

Lorand gave a firm nod. "Yes. And if any more Kester-worshipping fools spout nonsense, I'll handle them." A slight grin ghosted across his lips, dissolving the tension. Then he glanced behind her, as though ensuring no one was watching, and lowered his voice. "See you soon."

She realized how close they stood, inches apart in the corridor's hush. Her pulse hammered. The desire to tip her face up, to let their closeness become something more, nearly overwhelmed her. But the day's tasks beckoned. With a tiny nod of farewell, she slipped away, heart pounding at the swirl of longing and determination that anchored her next steps.

TWELVE

The sun hung high overhead when Elysia finally emerged into the orchard once more, guided by Mira and two watchers from House Kallendore who carried small caskets of healing supplies. Near the stone fountain—adorned with a carved griffin symbol—she found a handful of orchard workers nursing various minor scrapes. Overturned crates, upended barrels from last night's fiasco, still littered the edges. Darius stood to one side with two Valecrest knights, both wearing their house's colors, arms crossed in a stance of calm vigilance. Lorand wasn't present, though Elysia figured he might appear soon to lend authority to the demonstration.

Not many onlookers had gathered—only about a dozen, but each pair of eyes was significant. She recognized the father of the child she'd healed earlier, lingering at the orchard's perimeter. His expression was guarded but curious. Another figure stood in partial shade, wearing a hood lowered to hide half their face. Suspicion prickled at Elysia, but she focused on the orchard workers first.

She approached them with quiet confidence, setting down her supply chest. "Need any salve or bandages?" she asked, scanning the group. One older orchard hand had a shallow gash on his forearm from a falling wooden beam last night. Another complained of an ankle twist. Elysia listened patiently to their recounting of how the blasts had toppled crates, bruising them.

Then, calmly, she began to tend to each one. With Mira's help, she cleaned cuts, applied a mild ointment, and only once used a brief surge of magic to reduce swelling in the orchard hand's ankle. Onlookers watched, some leaning in to see if a swirl of evil energies might emerge, only to find that the faint shimmer of Elysia's magic brought relief instead of harm.

She offered explanations in a reassuring voice. "This salve is a mixture of thyme and comfrey to speed healing, and the small enchantment I used helps draw out inflammation. It won't burn or curse anything—it just helps your body mend quicker." The orchard hand tested his ankle, eyes widening when pain receded. Murmurs rippled among the watchers.

Darius took a measured step forward, projecting his Valecrest authority. "You see," he said, voice clear, "these orchard folks will be back at work by sundown, thanks to Lady Elysia's care. No illusions, no staged heroics—just genuine healing."

The orchard workers nodded politely, murmuring thanks. One even mustered a small, awkward bow. Elysia dipped her head in return, relief coursing through her. She sensed that every successful demonstration chipped away at the rumors.

Glancing around, she noticed the father from earlier. He was half turned, as though about to leave. Perhaps he could see her sincerity. Resisting an urge to run over and demand his acceptance, she instead offered him a slight nod. He caught her eye, then jerked his chin in a tentative, respectful gesture. It wasn't much, but it felt like a piece of the wall crumbling.

Then, near the orchard's entrance, footsteps announced a new arrival. She recognized Lorand's stride instantly. He emerged, scanning the scene. When he noted Elysia's calm, methodical healing routine, a flicker of satisfaction crossed his features. The orchard workers straightened slightly, mindful that a Valecrest heir had joined them. Lorand didn't interrupt; he simply stood by Darius; arms folded in a posture of approval.

A final orchard worker stepped up—an older woman who, upon removing her glove, revealed a deep splinter lodged in her palm. Wincing, Elysia coaxed out the splinter with a sterilized needle, handing Mira a pair of tweezers to help. The woman hissed in pain.

"Try to hold still," Elysia murmured, guiding a faint trickle of energy into the wound. "I'll numb the stinging." The orchard worker's face relaxed, surprise flickering in her eyes. Elysia glimpsed a droplet of blood welling up, but her magic eased the palm's tension so Mira could remove the splinter cleanly. Then Elysia pressed a small bandage patch on top. "There. Keep it clean, maybe rest it a day. You should be fine."

The older woman flexed her fingers, evidently astonished that it no longer hurt. Then she offered Elysia a shy, grateful smile. "I always thought your house's wards were just stories for the wealthy," she whispered. "Didn't realize they helped regular folks, too."

Elysia's throat was constricted. "We try," she managed softly, stepping back to let the orchard worker go. "That's all we want—to serve Highdale, not harm it." The woman nodded and ambled away, carefully cradling her bandaged hand. Elysia caught a surge of relief, as though each small acceptance was a candle lit against the darkness of suspicion.

She exhaled, pressing a hand to her chest. The orchard demonstration felt successful. Her powers were near their limit, but she had avoided pushing them too far. Beside her, Mira flashed an encouraging grin. Darius, glancing around at the watchers, gave a satisfied nod. Even the Valecrest knights looked less guarded, as though they recognized the sincerity in each healing act.

Elysia turned to Lorand, uncertain if he'd want to say something more, but he only gave her an approving look. She cleared her throat, addressing the small ring of onlookers, "If anyone needs further healing or consultation about last night's... events, I'll be here a little while, or you can find me in the keep." She hesitated, noticing the hooded figure on the far side of the orchard. They made no move to approach. Perhaps it was just an overanxious onlooker.

Gradually, the orchard crowd drifted back to their tasks. The father from before left, the orchard workers returned to clearing debris, and a few lingering watchers trickled out. Elysia sensed the tension in the orchard lighten, as though people finally believed the chaos was settling.

When the trickle of watchers ended, Elysia sank onto the edge of the fountain, letting the soft trickle of water behind her lend a soothing backdrop. Mira excused herself to store the supplies, Darius heading off with the knights to resume standard patrols. That left Elysia and Lorand alone, flanked by ripening apple trees and the sweet hush of midday. A shift of the breeze sent green leaves rustling overhead.

He approached, footsteps soft against the grass, then crouched so they were nearly at eye level. "You did well," he said gently.

Her cheeks warmed. "Thank you." She studied his face —saw the faint lines of strain near his eyes, the evidence of a man who had also borne too much stress in recent days. "How are you?" she asked quietly. "You look exhausted yourself."

He gave a noncommittal shrug. "I've been checking in with the Valecrest knights who were hurt last night. A few bruised ribs. Some singed hair from the blasts. Nothing dire." A pause, then his expression softened. "But I am tired of rifts that don't close. We put out one rumor, two more sprout. It's like whack-a-mole if I were to use a child's game as analogy."

A soft laugh escaped her, a genuine one. "I can't

picture you playing whack-a-mole," she teased, imagining a stoic, armor-clad Lorand hammering children's carnival contraptions. The mental image must have touched him too, because he cracked a rare grin.

"I suppose not," he admitted. Then his grin faded, replaced by a quiet intensity. "In any case, though I can't quell every rumor, I can stay by your side. I... want to stay by your side." The last words slipped out, carrying a warmth that made her heart flutter. He had not voiced such unguarded remarks often, and at the quiet vow in his tone, she felt a prickle of tears she stubbornly willed away.

She reached out, letting her fingertips graze the cuff of his sleeve. "That means more than I can say," she whispered. The orchard's hush wrapped around them, leaves murmuring overhead. For a long moment, neither spoke. They simply lingered, aware of how the day's demands would soon pull them elsewhere, but relishing this pocket of stillness.

Finally, she eased to her feet, ignoring the flush of longing that skittered up her spine. "It's nearly mid-afternoon," she observed, glancing skyward through the canopy. "I should gather my watchers, see if anyone else needs help. Then perhaps rest properly in the keep."

"Let me escort you," Lorand offered. "And then perhaps I'll speak with the baron about the next steps. We still need to finalize the official deposition against Kester, in case any even bolder rumors arise."

She nodded. "Agreed." They set off together, crossing the orchard path. This time, they walked side by side across the dappled light and shadow, a sense of easy camaraderie mingling with the tension that was never fully absent—tension that felt both political and deeply personal. Even the orchard's sweet air couldn't mask the swirl of half-formed longing inside her. Someday soon, she thought, they would need to speak openly about what truly lay between them. But for now, the tasks of Highdale took precedence.

BY LATE EVENING, the day's efforts at dispelling rumors had borne modest fruit. Word spread that Elysia administered to orchard hands who'd openly doubted her magic. A handful of minor lords signed statements supporting the arrest of Kester, swearing they had no part in his sabotage. The baron, in a fit of efficiency, posted a second notice near the keep's gates that any claim of "false sabotage" or "manufactured illusions" was patently untrue, punishable under Highdale law.

Still, the shadows of prejudice lingered. Elysia heard scattered accounts of people muttering in alleyways that House Kallendore's powers were unnatural or that Valecrest knights were covering for them. The baron's staff did what they could, encouraging local reeves to calm unrest, but Elysia knew an underlayer of suspicion would remain —like old scars that refused to fade.

Nightfall settled in, bringing a slight relief from the day's tensions. The keep's interior glowed with lanterns, and the staff lit torches in the courtyard. A quiet hush replaced the frantic bustle. Under the vaulted ceilings,

Elysia paused near a wide window, peering out at the star-freckled sky. She had planned to find Mira and slip away for a private chat, needing to confess her anxieties. Finally summoning the resolve, she moved deeper into the keep's corridors in search of her friend.

She found Mira in a lamplit side garden just off the eastern wing—a small haven of tilled earth, potted plants, and a stone bench. The moon now glimmered overhead, turning the leaves silver. Mira must have asked permission to use this peaceful spot for reflection. Elysia's heart eased at the sight of her friend humming quietly to herself while removing dead leaves from a potted herb. A single lantern hung from a wrought-iron hook, bathing them both in a gentle glow.

"Mira," Elysia said softly. The other woman turned, a sweet smile lighting her face.

"You found me." Mira motioned to the bench. "Come, sit. I was hoping we'd get a quiet moment."

Elysia gladly joined her, letting the hush envelope them. A trickle of water dripped from a small fountain at the garden's edge, echoing minimally in the mild night air. For a moment, neither spoke, simply savoring the calm after the day's strain.

Finally, Elysia inhaled. "It still hurts, you know," she confessed. "Hearing people call me a witch in hateful tones. I try to act strong about it, but..." She sighed, clasping her hands. "No matter how many people I help, there are always some who say I stage these rescues."

Mira's eyes softened. "I suspected as much." Gently,

she rested a hand over Elysia's clasped fingers. "Has Lorand said anything that eases it at all?"

A tremor of warmth sparked at the mention of his name. "He's been... unwavering," Elysia admitted. "Defending me publicly, telling me to rest. It's so surprising, I sometimes don't know how to respond. Part of me still recalls how we used to glare at each other, snapping about forced marriage. Now, though..." She trailed off, uncertain how to articulate the swirl in her chest.

Mira gave a sympathetic, almost teasing smile. "Now, you're hopelessly smitten?"

Elysia's cheeks heated. "Mira," she protested weakly. But a reluctant laugh escaped her. "All right, perhaps not hopeless. But I do feel—close to him. Safer when he's near. That's new for me."

Mira nodded in understanding. "It's natural that you'd form a bond after all you've endured together. No matter if the monarchy forced the betrothal, you two have made it real through your actions." She squeezed Elysia's hand. "If you trust him, if you want his presence to anchor you, I see nothing wrong in that. Especially if it helps ward off the negativity swirling around."

A lump rose in Elysia's throat. "But then I think about the rumors. If people see me leaning on a Valecrest knight, does it feed the notion that Kallendore is subordinate? Or if I stand too independent, do they claim I have something to hide?" She shook her head. "It's maddening."

Mira's expression turned earnest. "People will always twist a story if they want to see the worst. None of that changes the truth: you're saving lives, forging unity." She let out a soft sigh. "I know how heavy this is for you, but you don't have to shoulder it alone. House Kallendore stands with you, and Lorand—well, it's obvious he does, too. Let that be enough."

Elysia felt tears prick at the corners of her eyes. "You're right," she murmured, letting the hush of the garden soak into her bones. The gentle drip of water lulled her heart rate to a calmer beat. "And I can't let rumors shape how I live my life."

Mira's smile brightened. "Exactly. Or how you accept Lorand's affections." Her playful wink made Elysia huff a quiet laugh. But the next moment, Mira's expression sobered. "In all seriousness, Elysia, your gift has saved so many—even Lorand himself. Don't forget how he might not be standing if not for your healing that day you nearly drained yourself to save him. The best argument against the gossip is your repeated compassion."

Something inside Elysia eased, a knot of tension dissolving. She leaned her head back, gazing at the star-speckled sky through the greenhouse-like glass overhead. "Thank you," she said softly, tears receding, replaced by renewed resolve. "I needed this talk."

Mira nodded. "Anytime. And if new rumors arise tomorrow, we'll combat them the same way: with calm, unwavering demonstration of the truth. You're no malevolent witch. You're Elysia Kallendore, the mage who's fought and risked everything for Highdale."

A sudden swirl of gratitude for her friend welled up. Elysia nodded vigorously. "Together," she agreed. "We'll keep pressing forward." The hush of the garden embraced them. She sighed, letting the tension fade from her shoulders. "I should probably retire soon," she said after a moment. "There's sure to be more to handle in the morning... especially with the monarchy's envoy still lurking about, ready to pounce at any sign the alliance is fraudulent."

Mira stood, helping Elysia up. "Then rest well. I'll see you in the morning." She looped her arm briefly through Elysia's in a comforting gesture, and they made their way out of the little garden nook. The corridor beyond was quiet, lamps flickering along the stone walls.

They parted ways near the keep's main stair. Elysia felt lighter, if still weary. A part of her wished to see Lorand once more before bed, but she wasn't sure if she'd find him in the keep's halls or if he'd gone to finalize depositions with the baron. Hesitating, she stepped through the corridor toward her assigned chamber.

She had almost reached the door when she spotted a lone figure leaning against the wall, arms folded. Her heart jolted to see Lorand there, seemingly waiting. He looked up as her footsteps sounded, and a tiny, relieved twist softened his mouth.

"Elysia," he greeted, voice subdued.

She smiled. "You again." Quiet amusement colored her tone. "I was going to retire." A faint warmth spread across her skin, remembering how she'd told Mira that she sometimes yearned for his presence. Now, here he was, as though conjured by that wish.

He nodded. "Darius said you went to talk with Mira in the garden. I just wanted to confirm everything was all right. With the orchard demonstration done, the baron is finishing the depositions. I was free... well, free enough to check on you." He offered a half-shrug, as if abashed by his own concern.

Her heart flipped. "You've been pacing the corridor like a restless sentinel, then?" she teased gently. "Just waiting for a chance to have your wicked way with me?"

A grin touched his lips. "I always want to have my wicked way with you." Then, in a lower voice, "I wanted to make sure you weren't... overwhelmed by all that happened today."

She stepped closer, the corridor's lantern light reflecting in his storm-gray eyes. "I was," she murmured, "but Mira helped me see that I can't let these rumors break me. I feel... better now." She hesitated, pulse thrumming. "Thank you for caring enough to wait."

He caught her gaze, heat flaring in his expression. "Elysia." Her name lingered in the hush like its own promise. Then he inhaled. "I know we can't fix everything overnight, but—if you ever need my support...it's yours."

Emotion welled in her chest, an ache of gratitude and longing. She nodded, tears threatening again, though more from relief than sorrow. Without thinking, she curled her hand over his forearm, feeling the muscle beneath his surcoat. "I do. I will," she whispered.

He reached up, resting his other hand lightly against her cheek. They stood like that for a charged heartbeat, no grandeur of festival crowds, no baron or watchers. Just two people in a quiet corridor, hearts hammering with unspoken feelings. She leaned into his palm slightly, letting the warmth of that small contact soothe her.

For an instant, she thought he might close the distance, tilt her chin up for a kiss. A swirl of anticipation roared in her veins. But he seemed to rein himself in with visible effort, muscles tensing. After a weighted pause, he spoke, voice lower: "We should both rest. Tomorrow will bring new challenges."

She understood the subtext: not here, not now, not with a half-dozen potential eyes around every corner. Part of her wanted to protest. But another part recognized that pushing him or exposing themselves to gossip at this hour might only complicate matters further. With a soft nod, she let her hand slide free of his sleeve. "Yes," she breathed. "Tomorrow."

He exhaled, stepping back. The air between them thrummed with unanswered longing. Then his mouth lifted in a faint, reassuring smile. "Good night, Elysia."

"Good night," she echoed, voice unsteady. Her heart pounded as she turned the key in her chamber's lock, slipping inside. Only when the door closed behind her did she let out the breath she'd been holding. The hush of the room enveloped her, and she ventured to the small washbasin, rinsing her face from the day's dust.

By the time she settled into the bed, the fatigue she'd been fighting washed over her in waves. Tonight, would not be endless. She could rest... and tomorrow, she'd continue the long work of mending hearts, healing bruises, and dismantling rumor piece by determined piece. Lorand's vow echoed in her mind: If you ever need my support, it's yours.

And so, as she drifted off, the orchard's hushed breeze, Mira's reassurance, and Lorand's steady presence coalesced in her thoughts. Much remained uncertain, but she refused to bow to fear. Kester's influence had tried to tear them apart. Instead, it had shown Highdale just how fiercely Elysia and Lorand were willing to defend each other—and soon, she hoped, that reality would outshine any lingering rumor of "witchcraft" or staged alliances.

Her eyes fluttered shut. She let the stillness of the keep's night cradle her, the promise of a new dawn shaping her final thought: they had survived sabotage and scorn. They would endure the whispers, too—and find a way to leave the word witch behind, replaced by something far stronger: healer, partner, fierce defender of the realm, and perhaps—one day—beloved.

CHAPTER

THIRTEEN

Elysia's heart drummed with uneasy anticipation the moment sunlight crept through her chamber windows. Only two days separated her from the chaos of the festival sabotage, and yet here she stood—gaze flitting to the hazy sky, posture tight with lingering tension—summoned to a formal inquest by Sir Remine, the royal envoy who had quietly commanded so much scrutiny before. The monarchy wasted no time. They had dispatched him anew to Highdale, or perhaps he had never departed in full, staying just long enough to gather evidence. And if the rumors were correct, an official edict would once again hover like a blade over her and Lorand's tenuous union.

She closed her eyes and breathed in, bracing herself before she left her small, assigned chamber within the baron's keep. Her limbs still carried an echo of fatigue after the exhausting events of the festival. The courtyard blasts, the swirling accusations, and finally the arrest of

140

Lord Kester had drained her. Awareness of how each muscle still felt a touch leaden reminded her that peace was not always a simple exhale after a storm. Today might be as grueling as any battle, and just as precarious: a battle not of blades but of words, ledgers, and unspoken judgments.

A guard escorted her through the winding corridors: the keep's stony hush broken only by servants scurrying with polished trays or rolled documents. She offered them polite nods, though every step sharpened her nerves. The baron's reception hall—a place she once imagined might host only minor ceremonial gatherings—seemed to have become the epicenter of all Highdale's controversies.

When she arrived at the antechamber outside the reception hall, Mira stood waiting with a mixture of relief and anxiety in her kind eyes. "Elysia," she greeted softly. "Sir Remine arrived only moments ago. He traveled with two scribes—they're setting up in the hall."

Elysia tucked her arms tight around her middle. "Is Lorand already inside?"

Mira shook her head. "I saw him instructing Darius on something near the grand staircase—ensuring no disruptions while the inquest proceeds, I suspect. Valecrest knights are on edge. They..." She pressed her lips together. "They fear the monarchy might still question the authenticity of your alliance, no matter how thoroughly you two have proven yourselves."

A wave of quiet anger and exasperation coursed through Elysia. What more would it take? She and Lorand had fought side by side, braved sabotage, and publicly defended one another. Yet she understood the monarchy's perspective too: fear lingered whenever old feuds might erupt anew. She inhaled carefully, forcing calm. "Well, we'll face it," she said, voice steadier than she felt. "We can't linger in suspicion forever."

Mira nodded, giving her hand a quick, supportive squeeze. "I'll stay outside with the baron's staff. If you need me, just call."

Footsteps echoed behind them. Elysia turned. Lorand approached in his familiar, composed stride. The quiet ring of subtle armor—the breastplate across his crimson tunic—drew her attention. His hair, dark and neatly combed, accentuated the tension in his gray eyes. He carried himself with a soldier's discipline, but she recognized the slight clench of his jaw that revealed his worry. For an instant, their gazes locked in a silent exchange— she saw the memory of last night woven in his expression: how they'd parted in the corridor, arms brushing in reassurance but weighed by the knowledge of this morning's summons.

He halted beside her, inclining his head respectfully toward Mira before meeting Elysia's eyes. "Ready?" His voice was low, pitched only for her hearing.

"Ready enough," she managed, though her stomach still quivered with unease. "I hope you are as well."

He exhaled and offered a faint nod. "Remine's no fool. He wants to see if our bond is genuine or if we're... performing to avoid losing our titles. Let's show him the truth."

Elysia's cheeks warmed at the word performing—her

mind flicked back to that impulsive, desperate public kiss in the festival courtyard. She still felt the ghost of it on her lips whenever she recalled how, in the thick of chaos, Lorand's arms had felt like both shield and anchor. Clearing her throat, she tucked those thoughts away. "Then let's go," she whispered.

They entered the reception hall together. It was a grand space, with high-arched ceilings draped in banners of Highdale's crest—an interlaced design that symbolized the barony's fields and gentle hills. But Elysia sensed no gentle welcome. The air felt heavy as Sir Remine stood, clasping his hands behind his back in a posture of formal authority. Two palace scribes sat at a side table, quills poised above open ledgers, ready to record every word.

A hush fell as Elysia and Lorand approached. The baron was there as well, stationed near the far side of the chamber with arms folded. He looked wearier than ever— shadows under his eyes from nights spent overseeing Kester's arrest and the simmering tensions among the townsfolk. He gave them a small, tight nod, as if to say, "I'll do what I can, but this is between you and the monarchy now."

"Sir Remine," Lorand greeted, voice measured. "We answered your questions the day after the festival, but I understand you have more inquiries."

Remine inclined his head curtly. "Yes. The monarchy requires a thorough account. I have new instructions to finalize my assessment of your union's legitimacy. And, given the gravity of the sabotage, we must confirm that no shadow of deceit lingers. If your alliance were formed in convenience alone, that would be one matter. But if it is real... then, indeed, the crown will respect it."

Elysia's pulse fluttered. She forced composure. "We've complied with every request so far—we've handed over ledgers, statements from villagers. The watchers have testified to the sabotage. So, please, ask your questions, and we'll answer them the best we can."

He gestured for them to stand near a wide wooden table. The palace scribes, a man and a woman both in plain gray robes, glanced over with neutral expressions. "I have my doubts," Remine said plainly, "not about Kester's guilt—that is largely verified—but about whether your betrothal truly mended the feud. Suppose the monarchy allows you to keep your houses' noble status. Who's to say you won't unravel into animosity again?"

Lorand stepped forward, expression unwavering. "We have no intention of unraveling. We risked our lives to protect each other—and Highdale—against acts of sabotage meant to deepen the feud. My knights can attest to that. Elysia can confirm any further details."

The envoy turned a shrewd eye to Elysia. The weight of that gaze made her straighten. "Lady Elysia," Remine said, "speak plainly: how do you reconcile with the older generation in your house, the Kallendore relatives who despise Valecrest? Do you truly believe you can unify centuries of scorn?"

She inhaled and let the truth settle in her chest. "Despise is a strong word, sir. Yes, my family has harbored resentments. Some still do. But a forced betrothal compelled me to travel with Lorand—a man I once thought a proud swordsman with no respect for my magic. Over these weeks, I saw that he would defend my wards just as fiercely as he'd defend a Valecrest squire. My father and others witnessed me openly healing Valecrest knights, risking my strength for them. We've come too far to return to animosity." She paused, voice wavering only slightly. "This is not a charade."

Elysia's shot Lorand a look, their eyes locking in a heartbeat longer than necessary before they both turned away, their movements carefully choreographed. It was an art they had been forced to perfect—meeting each other's eyes just enough to satisfy the king's watchful scrutiny, their expressions neutral but tinged with the faintest trace of amicability.

The villagers nearby whispered among themselves, their attention divided between cups of spiced wine and the pair that symbolized the barony's fragile truce. Elysia let her lips curve into a small, unreadable smile, calculated to suggest neither disdain nor undue warmth.

Lorand's hand, resting on the edge of the table, twitched slightly before stilling. The layers of pretense between them weighed heavily, a silent contract neither could break. Any spark of genuine affection—a fleeting touch, a softened glance—would ignite the ire of their families, each side fiercely protective of their claim to power. But too much distance, too little civility, and the king's carefully laid plans would crumble, taking their respective houses down with them.

For a moment, as Lorand's hand brushed hers, the tension crackled in the air between them. Their eyes met again, and this time, there was an unspoken understanding beneath the façade. They were walking a knife's edge, balancing between the king's demands and their families' expectations, neither willing to fall—but unable to deny the danger of the tightrope they walked together.

Remine let out a slow exhale. "Your words sound genuine enough. But I must probe deeper." He glanced at the scribes. One scribble on the parchment already. "Tell me, what is the nature of your personal bond? Besides shared relief that you both avoided losing your noble titles, do you truly hold affection for one another?"

Elysia's cheeks heated more than she cared to admit. That question cut straight to the heart of everything. She chanced a look at Lorand, whose gaze flicked to her. In that silent beat—brief as a spark—she recalled a hundred moments: the scorch of adrenaline when she'd shielded him in a fight, the brush of his lips at the festival dais, the protective way he'd hovered when she was drained from overexerting her wards. She swallowed. "It goes beyond relief," she said softly. "If it had only been about titles, I doubt either of us would have risked our lives the way we did. There are... real feelings here."

Though her voice caught, Remine nodded once, then turned to Lorand. "And you, Lord Lorand Valecrest? Are you likewise prepared to claim genuine affection in front of the king's scribes?"

Lorand met Remine's gaze directly, jaw tight. "I am. I'd never have allowed Elysia to push herself so far in healing had I thought everything between us was false. I care for her well-being—as the mother of our future heirs who will inherit the barony." A flicker of wryness touched his mouth. "Neither of us wanted this union at first. Now, I see the...benefits of our union."

Elysia could feel her father's piercing gaze from across the hall, his dark eyes narrowing with every glance she exchanged with Lorand. At the same time, Lorand's mother, seated with the grace of a hawk poised to strike, scrutinized them with a sharp, practiced intensity that made Elysia's stomach twist. Their movements, their smiles, even the careful distance between their bodies—it was all under relentless observation. Elysia's fingers tightened around her goblet as she forced herself to laugh lightly at something Lorand had murmured, praying the sound carried the right mix of casual partnership without veering into warmth. Lorand, for his part, inclined his head toward her in a gesture so seamless it bordered on genuine affection, though she knew it was as calculated as her every breath. Their shared hope hung between them like a fragile thread: that this carefully curated performance would be enough to convince the two people most eager to spot a flaw in their charade.

Elysia felt the tension in the room shift: the baron's eyes flickered with faint surprise; the scribes paused mid-quill. Sir Remine's demeanor, however, remained firm. Instead of relaxing, he pressed further. "Feelings, however, sincerely stated, are intangible. The monarchy demands more than spoken devotion. We want to see that your households are cooperating fully."

Elysia's upthrust sense of hope wavered. "And if you decide we haven't met your definition of cooperation, you'll… revoke our noble standing anyway? Even after Kester's sabotage is exposed?"

Remine offered no comfort. "It's within the crown's prerogative."

Silence stretched. Elysia's chest tightened, fury blossoming at the notion they might be cast aside after everything. But she channeled it into composure. "Then let us know what specific proofs you seek. Our houses have begun coordinating watchers and knights. The baron can confirm."

The baron cleared his throat, stepping forward. "I've personally seen the forging of new guard rotations—Kallendore watchers assigned alongside Valecrest patrols. Elysia's wards aided the orchard workers. Lorand's men allocated resources to Kallendore retinues traveling outside the keep. Our local reeves have reported fewer rumors of renewed conflict." He cast a glance at Remine. "Surely that indicates progress."

Remine dipped his chin. "Provisional progress, perhaps. But we must be thorough." He motioned to the scribes. "I will require a final written statement from each house, pledging to maintain joint efforts for the next year —non-negotiable. I also request an itemized account of your combined enough-late-for-anyone defenses: how many Valecrest knights stand guard at Kallendore farmland, how many Kallendore watchers assist Valecrest training grounds, how resources are shared."

Elysia touched her pendant lightly, a reflex she performed when she needed grounding. "That's feasible. We can produce those details." She braced for some further blow, suspecting Remine might not stop at mere records.

Indeed, he continued, "Additionally, I will observe you more closely over the next few days—my scribes and I shall remain in Highdale. We'll evaluate your daily interactions: no more clandestine sabotage, no false courtesy. If it's real, we'll see it. If it's a pretense, you'll slip." His tone was cool. "Are we agreed?"

Lorand exhaled. "Agreed," he said firmly, though Elysia sensed the simmer in his posture. The monarchy's demands bordered on invasiveness. But neither of them could refuse if they hoped to preserve their houses' standing. And she saw no alternative but to yield, because if they did—for pride or frustration—Highdale would suffer the monarchy's wrath.

Remine gestured for the scribes to pause, then faced them with finality. "Thank you. We'll deliver your statements to the king as soon as you complete them. For now, you're dismissed—unless you have anything else to declare."

A momentary hush. Elysia shook her head. She wanted to rail against the monarchy's suspicion, but she held back. They had the rest of the day, perhaps more, to demonstrate the unity was no lie. Words alone wouldn't suffice.

The baron signaled for a steward to escort Remine to comfortable guest quarters, ensuring he and his scribes had all they needed for an extended stay. As they departed in measured steps, the tension seeped from Elysia's shoulders, only to be replaced by a different, subtler weight. The baron turned back to them.

"I'll begin drafting an official record of the watchers and knights you two reorganized," the baron said in a low voice. "That should help. But please—be careful. Remine is thorough, and even if he's personally convinced, he must answer to the monarchy's higher circles."

Lorand nodded, his expression grim. "We'll do everything in our power."

Elysia let out a slow breath, her eyes drifting closed for half a heartbeat. "Thank you, my lord baron. We'll comply."

The baron gave a curt nod. "We're all counting on you. If we lose noble status, Highdale will be thrown into even greater disarray. Kester might be in custody, but rabble-rousers remain. Let's not hand them another chance." With that, he strode out, muttering orders to a pair of advisors trailing behind him.

FOURTEEN

Elysia felt Lorand's presence beside her, silent, both of them likely reeling. Slowly, she shifted to face him. A swirl of myriad emotions flickered in his eyes—anger and weariness most of all. "We'll handle it," she murmured. The urge to reach for his hand filled her chest, and for once, she didn't resist it. Her fingers found his, lacing them together in a tight hold. "We've done so much already—he can observe if he wishes, but we have nothing to hide."

Lorand's palm was warm, the gentle squeeze he returned reminding her that strength could lie in such quiet gestures. "And if it's not enough?" His voice emerged in a husk of frustration. "Something about Remine's manner suggests he half-expects us to fail."

"We won't fail," she insisted softly. "He wants practical evidence... let's give him that. We can show him the orchard synergy, how watchers and knights coordinate. We'll answer questions about how we deal with villagers together. Everything. By the time he's returned to the capital, I want him to have no doubt."

Lorand's mouth curved into a faint, determined line. Then, unexpectedly, he lifted her joined hands and brushed a light kiss across her knuckles. The fleeting contact stirred her pulse in a slow, heated flutter. She glimpsed in his eyes a reflection of that same swirling mix of exasperation... and closeness. "All right," he said quietly. "We do it together."

She held his gaze a moment longer, feeling the shift from tension to a steadier sense of resolve, then stepped back. "Let's find the baron's clerk," she said. "We might as well begin drafting this statement of combined defenses. The sooner we produce the records, the better."

Lorand guided her out of the reception hall, their pace brisk. Ahead, the corridor branched left toward a smaller administrative wing, where the baron's clerk likely kept the necessary logs. Elysia felt an odd comfort trailing beside Lorand, as though the quiet click of their footsteps signified more than approaching a desk of official documents—it symbolized their shared path forward, reinforcing the alliance that once felt impossibly forced. She had to believe that no decree from the monarchy could break what they'd fought so hard to forge.

They found the baron's clerk—a lanky older man with spectacles perched on a narrow nose—amid stacks of parchment and leather-bound account books. He looked harried, and the disarray of his desk suggested he was juggling countless tasks. Nonetheless, he greeted them with a respectful bow. "My lord, my lady. I gather you need official rosters of watchers and knights?"

"Yes," Elysia confirmed gently, taking pity on his over-whelmed expression. "Could we gather the final rosters from each house? The monarchy's envoy wants an item-ized list of times, locations, assigned tasks. Anything that proves we're working together."

The clerk scrabbled through a shuffle of pages, pushing aside old festival receipts. "Certainly. The baron told me to make it a priority. House Valecrest's postings... I have them near the top... or so I thought." He rifled through a second stack, then finally located a small ledger. "Here we are—eight Valecrest knights rotating with four Kallendore watchers daily at the orchard, plus orchard staff who confirm each shift. I can expand these to note who's in command after nightfall, or if you'd like precise hours...?"

Lorand stepped closer, scanning the ledger with a soldier's efficiency. "Precisely that. Let's detail it thor-oughly. For Kallendore watchers, we should list Darius's involvement as a liaison, since he coordinates with them if a rumor or scuffle arises. And for Valecrest knights, mention Marcus or anyone else we used for orchard guard." He met Elysia's eye. "I recall you wanted watchers specifically assigned to farmland near the keep's perimeter too."

She nodded. "Yes, a few watchers who cycle every other day to examine if any minor sabotage is creeping back in. Should we also detail the ward spells we put in place?" She glanced uncertainly at the clerk. "Or is that superfluous?"

Lorand frowned thoughtfully. "Remine might see it as critical. You can disclaim that those wards are purely defensive, to ensure farmland health, not some clandestine Kallendore 'witchery.'"

She suppressed a wry smirk. If only Remine understood how many times she'd used such wards for the good of the entire barony. She turned to the clerk. "Yes—please note any farmland wards and how the watchers coordinate with Valecrest knights if external threats arise."

The clerk jotted frantic notes. "Certainly. I'll produce a polished draft by late afternoon. Then you or the baron can sign it, present it to the envoy?"

Elysia and Lorand traded looks, nodding in unison. "Yes," Elysia said. "We'll need it as soon as possible. Thank you."

They left the clerk to his work, stepping back into the corridor. The bustle of the keep felt subdued, as though everyone tiptoed around the presence of the monarchy's envoy. Elysia hummed under her breath, a subdued tune she recognized from her childhood—something her mother used to hum while sorting dried herbs. She hardly realized she was doing it until Lorand looked her way, brow slightly raised.

A faint laugh escaped her. "A habit," she murmured. "It helps me feel I'm doing something, even if small. My mind tends to race otherwise."

He smiled, a hint of warmth breaking through his

tension. "A good habit, I think. We'll need every bit of calm today." He paused, gaze skimming the corridor. "I wonder if Remine intends to watch our movements all day. Suppose we go speak to the orchard staff, see if any new problems surfaced overnight? That might fall under the monarchy's 'observing your daily interactions' clause. Better to let him see us in action."

Elysia considered the idea. "Yes. Let's do that. The orchard staff typically reconvene in the early afternoons, sorting any bruised fruit from last night's pick. We can help. Maybe fix some scrapes or check knights' bruises. That's cooperation in practice, right?" She realized how practical she sounded—like a list-checking function. But after everything, she suspected only tangible demonstration would sway Remine.

Lorand gave a resolute nod. "Then the orchard it is."

THEY LEFT the keep soon after, emerging into the midday sunlight that gilded the courtyard. Overhead, scattered clouds sailed across the bright sky. Elysia breathed in the outside air, grateful to escape the keep's stifling corridors. By now, the festival decorations had mostly been taken down: no more swirling ribbons or vibrant banners, replaced by the hush of a barony still recovering from sabotage. She glimpsed a few villagers passing near the gate, exchanging guarded smiles or civil nods. Some still carried wariness about Kallendore's "witchcraft." Others, she knew, had begun to accept her healing after the festival's dramatic unveiling of Kester's betrayal.

And in the corner near the stables, Elysia spotted Sir Remine himself, flanked by his scribes. They seemed to be quietly observing, making no attempt to hide the fact that they were paying attention to everything Elysia and Lorand did. The envoy's expression was inscrutable as they continued on foot, crossing the courtyard. She resisted the urge to bristle.

Lorand murmured in her ear, "He's watching. Let him."

She inhaled, relaxing her shoulders. "Absolutely. We have nothing to hide."

With that, they slipped out through the keep's rear gate, descending a gentle slope until the orchard spread out before them like a tapestry of green. Rows of apple and pear trees swayed under a mild breeze; overhead, faint birdsong threaded the air. This orchard had once been a place of uneasy gatherings—particularly during the festival fiasco. Now, it felt calmer, though Elysia still remembered the reek of sulfur from sabotage blasts near the orchard stalls. She prayed such horrors wouldn't repeat.

A group of orchard workers was already there, stacking wooden crates. Elysia recognized one older man who'd sustained a nasty splinter that she'd healed a few days prior. He glanced up, a flicker of wariness crossing his weathered features before he dipped his head politely. "My lord, my lady," he greeted.

Lorand nodded, stepping forward. "Any issues lately? Trouble with the orchard perimeter or leftover sabotage devices?"

One of the orchard maids, younger and wearing a worn apron, pushed a stray lock of hair aside. "None that we've seen. The watchers sometimes pass through at night, checking. They said we were safe from further tampering." She paused. "Is it... truly over, then? These blasts and potions that threatened us?"

Elysia felt the edges of old anger tighten her throat. She wanted to promise them absolute peace, but caution prevailed. "Kester's main conspirators are either captured or scattered. We're working with the baron to ensure no one tries anything so brazen again. But if you notice anything suspicious, let us or one of the watchers know."

Another orchard worker, a woman with a limp, set down her crate. "I had a question about the wards you put in place," she said hesitantly. "Some folks say you're weaving illusions to rope us into praising House Kallendore. Others disagree, saying your spells keep the orchard from catching blight." She fidgeted. "Could it be both? Or neither?"

Elysia's chest clenched with a familiar pang of frustration. "They're wards to repel pests and magical residue— nothing more," she explained, careful to keep her tone patient. "No illusions to trick you. If you doubt me, I'd be happy to demonstrate how it's done. You'll see it's not controlling your minds; it's basically a protective barrier that wards off harmful influences."

The orchard workers exchanged uncertain glances. Lorand cleared his throat. "I can vouch for Elysia's wards," he said firmly. "She's used them to help farmland beyond your orchard. My knights haven't seen a single sign of enthrallment or mind tricks. She's saved us from bandits —do you think she'd do that if she was out to manipulate you?"

One or two orchard hands nodded, calmer. The older man from earlier rubbed his bandaged palm from the day's splinter fiasco. "I appreciate what you did," he said gruffly to Elysia. "My hand's been fine since. Didn't even fester."

She allowed a small smile. "I'm glad." Then, with a flicker of an idea, she turned to the orchard maid. "If you have bruised fruit or minor injuries from picking overhead branches, let me see them. I can reapply salves or quick healing spells."

The orchard maid hesitated, glancing between Elysia and Lorand. "Well, I did twist my ankle stepping in a rabbit hole this morning. S'not too bad, but it's slowing me down."

In that moment, Elysia glimpsed Sir Remine's shadow near the orchard's entrance, lurking some distance away with a scribe. Observing. She inhaled and gestured for the orchard maid to step forward. "May I?"

The girl nodded. Carefully, Elysia knelt by the orchard worker's ankle and rolled back the edge of her sock. A mild swelling, nothing severe. She fished into her pouch for a small jar of thyme-and-comfrey ointment, then dabbed it gently. All around them, orchard leaves rustled, sunlight painting the grass pale gold. "This might sting a moment," Elysia murmured.

She whispered a short incantation, letting a gentle pulse of healing energy flow through her fingertips. It was a far cry from the large-scale wards or the desperate healing she'd once used to save Lorand's life. Just a mild, controlled channeling of warmth to ease the tendon. The orchard maid inhaled sharply, then tentatively shifted her weight onto that foot. "Oh," she breathed. "That's... a lot better."

Elysia smiled. "Just take care not to run on that foot for a bit. The ointment will help, but you should rest if you can." She rose, ignoring the wave of lightheadedness that often came from multiple small healings after so much magical strain in recent days.

Lorand, meanwhile, had turned to an orchard hand who needed help with hoisting a crate into the cart. He rolled up his sleeves and lifted it easily, reminding Elysia how his martial training and disciplined strength translated to quiet usefulness here. She watched as he placed the crate, exchanging a few calm words with the orchard worker. The man seemed thankful for the assistance. A memory flitted through her mind: in earlier days, she would have found it unthinkable to see a Valecrest heir stooping to help with manual orchard labor. But that was then. This was now.

Sir Remine's presence in the background weighed on her. She felt his scrutiny like a tangible force. But if the monarchy wanted to witness real cooperation, they had it right here: Kallendore wards, Valecrest muscle, orchard workers who now wore uncertain yet grateful expressions. She prayed it would suffice.

After a short lull, Lorand returned to Elysia's side, brushing dust from his forearms. "Shall we check the orchard's perimeter markers?" he suggested. "We might as well show them how watchers and knights coordinate on the outskirts."

She nodded. "Lead the way."

They made a short circuit around the orchard's boundary. At intervals, small stakes had been driven into the ground, each bearing a faint Kallendore sigil for protective wards, while a Valecrest insignia hung from small metal plates. Symbolic, but also practical: watchers from Kallendore recognized where to pulse the orchard wards, while Valecrest knights recognized that area as a patrol route. On their walk, Elysia crouched at one stake, murmuring a gentle incantation to refresh the faint glow of protective runes. Lorand lingered at her shoulder, watchful.

"Does it need frequent recharging?" he asked, curiosity in his tone.

"A little, yes," she explained. "Every few days. The orchard staff can do the rest of the day-to-day tasks. I just supply an extra push. If your knights see flickering wards, they know to inform me or another Kallendore mage."

He nodded, lips curving slightly in approval. "Seems efficient. And here I used to think wards were intangible nonsense."

She laughed. "You Valecrests rarely believed in anything intangible. But your doubt... well, it kept me on my toes."

Gaze warming, he extended a hand to help her rise. She took it, ignoring the pleasant spark that shot through her. "And your magic kept us alive more times than I can count," he murmured. "There's no going back to ignorance on that front."

FIFTEEN

As they moved onward, Elysia glimpsed the orchard staff watching with mild interest, and further behind them, Sir Remine's unobtrusive figure still followed at a distance. She wondered how closely the envoy listened to their conversation. Let him. She pushed away the flicker of discomfort. If it showed them as real and not contrived, so much the better.

Halfway around the orchard's edge, they encountered one of the watchers wearing Kallendore green. He bowed hastily. "My lady, my lord—I was just finishing a midday sweep. Nothing suspicious."

"Good," Lorand said. "We appreciate your vigilance." He gestured to the orchard markers. "Has the orchard staff voiced any new concerns about sabotage?"

The watcher shook his head. "No, my lord. I did overhear some of them worrying about potential orchard fires in the next festival. They mentioned scaremongers claiming Kallendore wards might spontaneously combust apple trees." He grimaced. "Absurd, obviously, but rumors have their own life."

Elysia pressed her lips together, exhaling. There was always some rumor. "We'll keep dispelling them as best we can," she said. "Thank you for letting us know."

The watcher saluted, stepping aside. Elysia stifled a weary sigh. Even after Kester's exposure, fear of "witchcraft" still thrived. But maybe with time, repeated cooperation would overshadow those old superstitions.

They finished the orchard circuit, verifying all the wards. The orchard staff, seeing no urgent tasks left undone, drifted back to their afternoon chores. Elysia and Lorand parted ways with them, turning back toward the keep's rear path. As they walked, she couldn't resist glancing over her shoulder to see if Sir Remine still trailed them. Sure enough, he and a scribe hovered near the orchard's entrance, scribbling notes. Her frustration rose, but she forced a neutral expression. She refused to give Remine any sign that might spark further suspicion.

Partway up the slope, Lorand cleared his throat. "We should check on the farmland watchers next, or would you prefer we speak with the knights first?"

She considered, scanning the bright midday sun overhead. "Let's speak with your knights. We can gather them near the keep's training yard and see if they have any new developments regarding raids or leftover sabotage. Then I can speak with farmland watchers before evening."

He agreed easily. "If Darius or Marcus have found anything, they'll share it. Let's go."

Their footsteps sounded on the gravel, the orchard

behind them now. Elysia's mind buzzed with the juggling of tasks: appease Remine, show real cooperation, quell rumors in every quarter. And, she realized with a soft pang, she needed to find a moment alone to gather her strength. Using small healings all day added up. Still, she walked onward, determined.

BACK AT THE KEEP, they entered the wide courtyard used primarily for drilling knights. A lively ring of Valecrest men, some in partial armor, sparred with wooden swords. Overseeing them stood Darius, a large figure in scuffed armor, whose friendly grin broke into a broader smile when he noticed Elysia and Lorand approach. He motioned for the knights to pause.

"Lady Elysia, Lord Lorand," he greeted, saluting lightly. "We were just running a few drills. After the fiasco at the festival, the men insisted on being thoroughly prepared in case of more sabotage. Care to watch?"

Lorand nodded. "Certainly. Also, if any of the knights have injuries or concerns, Elysia can attend to them. We're keeping things coordinated."

At that, Darius turned to the ring of knights. "Anyone still nursing bruises from that orchard scuffle or festival blasts? Step forward, get them checked. We can't have you compromising your sword arms in a real fight."

A couple knights hesitated, exchanging glances. One eventually stepped out: a broad-shouldered Valecrest guard with a faint limp. Another followed, complaining of a muscle strain in his sword arm. Elysia moved toward them, scanning each with a practiced eye. The first had a bruised calf that hadn't healed properly, the second carried a mild sprain near the elbow.

She applied a gentle salve to the bruised calf—just enough to accelerate normal healing—and gave a slight magical nudge to the sprain. Each time, she felt the prickle of dizziness that warned her magic reserves were not limitless. She couldn't help but recall that desperate day in the forest pass, when she'd poured so much of her life force into Lorand. This was mild by comparison, yet the cumulative effect wore her down. Still, she forced a reassuring smile for the knights.

They murmured thanks in low voices, still somewhat uneasy about receiving "witch healing." She recognized that tension in their stances, but the relief on their faces as the pain ebbed was genuine enough. And from the corner of her eye, she saw Lorand standing at her shoulder, exuding quiet reassurance. The knights trusted him— thus, by extension, they trusted her. A precarious trust, but progress, nonetheless.

Darius watched the healing with approving calm. "You know," he said quietly, "these men used to say a Kallendore witch's kiss was lethal. Now they're grateful for your 'witchly' touch." He gave a wry grin. "How quickly times change."

Elysia's lips skewed into a rueful smile. "I suspect we still have a way to go. But if even a handful see the difference between illusions and real healing, that's a start.

Darius nodded. "I'll keep encouraging them to rely on you when needed, as you do with them."

Lorand raked a hand through his hair, glancing around at the ring of practicing knights. "Good. We want to show the monarchy that Valecrest men trust Kallendore wards, and Kallendore watchers stand guard alongside Valecrest. This demonstration will help when Remine asks for more proof. And I stand testament that a witch's kiss isn't lethal," Lorand said with a bow and smile.

At that, Darius's expression brightened slightly. "Remine has an uncanny knack for sniffing out the slightest sign of façade. I hope he sees the real cooperation here."

Elysia pressed a hand over the pocket where her small store of herbs lay. "We're doing what we can—a public demonstration, the orchard perimeter, these knights' treatments. I'll speak with farmland watchers later. If that doesn't satisfy him, I don't know what else will." A quaver of bitterness entered her voice, unbidden. She pressed her lips together. She hadn't meant to let frustration slip through but these silly misconceptions about witches were providing hard to overcome.

Darius offered a grimly sympathetic look. "I'll make sure the men confirm your help to Remine if he inquires. We all saw how you shielded some of them from blasts during the sabotage. If that's not genuine unity, I don't know what is."

Warm gratitude uncurled in Elysia's chest. "Thank you," she said softly. She knew how much prejudice lingered among Valecrest ranks, so Darius's unwavering support felt like a boon.

Lorand turned to watch the two younger knights resume sparring. "We'll remain for a bit, observe the drills. Let the monarchy see we're not hiding." He cast a glance at Elysia, voice dropping lower. "Will you be all right standing? You look a bit pale."

She gave a tiny nod, touched by his concern. "I'm fine," she whispered, though she felt the edge of fatigue. "Just a little tired from all the minor healings. I can manage."

He studied her face, then nodded. "We won't linger too long."

They stepped aside to the courtyard's edge, letting the knights continue their drills. Elysia folded her arms, watching wooden swords clash in a steady, rhythmic pattern. Darius barked occasional corrections or encouragement. Meanwhile, she felt Lorand close beside her, his posture that of a guard ensuring she didn't overstrain. A small current of warmth tugged at her heart—this man, once so hostile to her magic, now watched vigilantly for her comfort, not out of grudging duty but out of something deeper.

She was so absorbed in the subtle comfort of his nearness that she nearly jumped at the sound of footsteps behind them. Spinning, she found Sir Remine again—in fact, the envoy had approached within a dozen paces, scribes in tow, as though testing just how often they might be caught unaware.

"Busy day," Remine commented, surveying the training yard. His gaze flicked from Lorand to Elysia, then to Darius. The scribes hovered with quills poised. "I see you have Valecrest knights drilling, and Lady Elysia personally tending their injuries. Interesting."

Lorand's expression tightened. "Is that not precisely what a unified barony would do—train together, heal together?"

Remine inclined his head, not quite a nod of agreement but not refuting it either. "Indeed. One might even suspect you knew I'd be watching. You orchestrated this demonstration for my benefit, yes?"

Elysia's temper flared. She tempered it with a deep breath. "We can't keep the knights idle simply to avoid looking staged, sir. And I genuinely prefer healing them. If a few days from now you ask around, they'll confirm it was no act."

The envoy studied her, an unreadable gleam in his eyes. Then he turned to a couple of knights finishing a drill. "You there," he said, voice carrying. "Are you comfortable receiving magical healing from a Kallendore mage? Or do you resent it?"

The knight, flushed from exertion, glanced anxiously at Lorand, then stiffened. "M-my lord envoy, I was uncertain at first, but her remedies fixed my arm after the sabotage. I'd be a fool to refuse such help. So, yes, comfortable enough." He looked away, clearing his throat.

Remine's scribe jotted a note. A hush lingered. Elysia let relief well within her, though she worried the knight's forced honesty might sound suspicious, as if he'd only said it out of fear. But at least it was positive.

Next, Remine swung his attention to Elysia. "And how

do you feel, Lady Kallendore, assisting knights who once belittled your so-called witch powers?"

She bristled at how easily he tossed the phrase around. "I do what I must to keep the barony safe," she said evenly. "Hearts won't change in a single day, but if healing them can gradually undo old grudges... I'll keep doing it."

Remine studied her another moment, then gave an almost imperceptible nod. "A pragmatic approach. Very well. I'll continue observing. Carry on." He turned away without further courtesy, the scribes scuttling behind him.

Elysia let out a shaky breath, tension loosening from her spine. That exchange could have gone far worse. Lorand placed a comforting hand against the small of her back—so fleeting and light she wasn't sure if it was conscious. But the warmth of his touch lingered.

"That was well-handled," he murmured. "He's definitely testing us."

Her shoulders sagged. "Testing us is an understatement. But we'll not give him reason to doubt." She straightened, looking up at Lorand. "Thank you for standing by me."

He offered a half-smile tinged with both frustration and quiet gratitude. "We stand or fall together, remember?"

And for all the tension swirling around them, that statement flooded Elysia with renewed confidence. "Yes," she whispered, "together."

They lingered only a short while longer to finalize a few details with Darius, ensuring Remine could see them coordinate an actual day's plan: farmland watchers, orchard staff check, and potential border patrol lists. Elysia documented the times she or other Kallendore watchers would inspect wards. Lorand arranged the knights' shift schedules. Through it all, Remine and his scribes hovered on the periphery, listening. Elysia decided it was best not to let their presence rattle her further. Let them witness the genuine synergy—maybe then they'd accept what she and Lorand already knew: that House Valecrest and House Kallendore were no longer adversaries.

SIXTEEN

By late afternoon, Elysia's legs ached from walking and standing, her mind buzzing with a low-grade exhaustion from repeated small healings. She and Lorand returned to the keep, found a quiet nook just off the main hall—an alcove with a single bench near a tapestry. It was hardly private, but at least it was out of the main flow of traffic. She sank onto the bench, pressing her palm to her forehead.

"Let me get you something," Lorand offered, voice hushed. "Water? Or if you'd prefer, we can go to the keep's kitchens. A honeyed infusion helps, yes?"

Warmth for him rose in her chest at his attentiveness. "That'd be nice," she admitted. "If we have a break before the next wave of scrutiny."

He nodded. "Stay here. I'll be quick."

She watched him stride away, shoulders set, purposeful but worried. The sense of closeness thrummed in her chest. Rarely had she seen Lorand so openly concerned for her well-being—not as forced courtesy but from genuine care. She recalled the countless times they'd glared at each other in the earlier days, riling each other's temper just by breathing the same air. Now, that memory felt distant, almost surreal.

Left alone for a moment, Elysia breathed slowly, letting her shoulders slump. Exhaustion pulsed behind her eyes. She hadn't done anything grandiose today, but the repeated small healings added up, layered over the stress of the monarchy's watchful envoy. The bench's wooden surface pressed into her back, but she welcomed the mild discomfort as an anchor.

A soft shuffle of footsteps made her look up. Sir Remine stood just a yard away, the scribe absent for once. Elysia tensed, expecting more questions. But the envoy only inclined his head. "You appear tired," he observed.

She mustered a polite half-smile. "Yes. Healing can do that."

Remine watched her carefully. "And yet you persist in offering it even to those who once doubted you. That's remarkable, Lady Kallendore. Not every forced union fosters such... perseverance."

Her heart pounded. She studied him, searching for sarcasm, but saw none in his austere features. "We've traveled together for weeks, faced sabotage," she said. "It taught me that trust isn't built by waiting. We have to actively create it."

"Indeed." He paused, glancing briefly at the tapestry on the wall—a woven design featuring Highdale's farmland. "I wondered, initially, if you and Lord Lorand were just performing for me. But you truly do care for the barony, don't you?"

A flicker of hope ignited in her chest. "Yes," she insisted softly. "I know you've seen centuries of feuds. But times can change. Valecrest knights and Kallendore watchers are working together better than I imagined possible. We're not feigning it for your sake."

Remine's scrutiny bore down once more—though a fraction gentler. Slowly, he nodded. "I needed to see some tangible sign that hearts had changed, not only logistical rosters. Perhaps I have." Another measured pause. "Continue as you are. I'll compile a final report soon enough."

Without waiting for her reply, he pivoted and strode off, boots echoing in the hallway. Elysia stared after him, chest tight. It wasn't a promise, but for once, she sensed no scorn in his words. A subtle shift in his tone... maybe the monarchy wasn't wholly immovable.

Moments later, Lorand returned, carrying a wooden mug. "One of the kitchen servants prepared a mild tea with honey—no time for a full infusion, but this should help," he said. "You all right?"

Elysia accepted the mug and sipped, warmth flooding her mouth. "I am now," she said softly, thinking of Remine's cryptic words. "Remine spoke to me while you were gone. He seemed... less hostile, though not exactly friendly."

Lorand's gaze sharpened with interest. "That's progress, I suppose. Maybe we're wearing down his suspicion."

She shrugged, drinking more tea. "I hope so." The

sweet tang coated her throat, soothing some of the dryness. She realized how much she needed a reprieve. "Thanks for the tea. Shall we rest a moment? Then we must finalize the rosters with the baron's clerk and deliver them to Remine."

Lorand nodded, sitting beside her on the bench. The corridor was quiet save for the occasional distant footsteps. They sat in companionable silence, close enough that their shoulders brushed. Elysia felt the tension in her body slowly abate. She took another sip, savoring the honey flavor.

She let her eyes slip closed, leaning fractionally against him, trusting no one would wander by or misunderstand this fleeting moment of respite. After a beat, he slid an arm lightly around her shoulders, gentle, steady. She felt his chest rise and fall, each breath resonating through the space between them.

They spent the remainder of the afternoon with the baron's clerk, meticulously itemizing every detail: which watchers patrolled farmland, which knights handled orchard security, how many hours each shift ran, and what protocols they used for reporting suspicious activity. Elysia outlined the minimal wards along the orchard boundary, explaining how watchers would check them. Lorand listed the times knights would escort supply wagons or cross patrolled roads. The clerk wrote swiftly, producing multiple sheets of parchment.

By early evening, the final drafts glimmered with official thoroughness. The baron popped in only briefly to add his seal, acknowledging that these rosters reflected the barony's official stance. Then they carried the documents to the reception hall, where Sir Remine awaited. The two scribes sat at a large table, which was already laden with various statements from orchard staff, peasants who had witnessed sabotage, even guards verifying Kester's ledger. Elysia placed their rosters on top, her heart pounding at the precariousness of it all.

Carefully, Remine examined the rosters, flipping through each page. The scribes hovered, copying details. At last, he peeled his gaze from the writing. "These are… quite thorough," he said, voice subdued. "I see joint operations in orchard defense and farmland patrol. You've documented watchers and knights cross-reporting. And the baron's seal legitimizes it."

"Yes," Lorand said. "We'll continue adjusting and refining if new threats arise. But as you can see, our houses are cooperating in day-to-day tasks, not just staging a show for you."

Elysia felt a faint tremor in her hands, but she kept her tone level. "We want the monarchy to recognize our sincerity."

Remine set the rosters aside, leaning back in his seat. "I will. My scribes and I will compile our findings. You'll have our official verdict soon, likely within two days—depending on how quickly we can cross-check every-thing." He eyed them for a heartbeat. "If what we've seen holds up under quiet inquiry—unplanned observations, random statements from villagers—then I suspect you'll find no trouble with your noble status."

A hush washed over them. Relief, cautious but potent,

pulsed in Elysia's veins. Lorand exhaled softly. "Thank you, Sir Remine," he said.

The envoy's features remained composed, but Elysia caught a subtle softening. "Don't thank me just yet, Lord Lorand. My mission isn't to be your friend—it's to ensure the monarchy's edict is upheld. If you truly have forged unity, my job is done. If not..." He trailed off. No need to finish.

She swallowed. "Understood."

Remine nodded. "Now—go and rest. You both seem to have worked tirelessly. Unless you're off to do more orchard rounds?" His mouth quirked in something faintly resembling humor.

Elysia blinked, slow to parse that he might be jesting. Then she summoned a small, tired smile. "We've done enough for one day."

He gestured dismissal. With that, Elysia and Lorand turned, leaving the reception hall. The tension still churned—two days or more of secret observation remained. But for the moment, at least, no further demands weighed on them.

They walked in silence down the corridor, the flickering torches marking their path. Outside a tall window, the sky had deepened into dusk. Elysia realized her entire day had been consumed with proving sincerity. Not in grand, heroic battles, but in everyday tasks: orchard bruises, farmland wards, knights' bruised arms. Strange how it all felt as draining as rallying for a pitched confrontation.

When they finally reached a quieter side passage,

Lorand turned to her, voice subdued. "How do you feel now?"

She forced a small grin. "We survived day one of Remine's inquest. And from what I see, he's not unconvinced. That's progress, right?"

His eyes glinted in the torchlight. "More than progress. I half expected he'd tear our rosters apart or dismiss them as an empty performance. But he didn't. He saw us in the orchard, the training yard… saw you healing people who once mocked you. That's genuine."

"And he recognized it," Elysia finished, catching a note of wonder in her own voice. She rubbed her arms, chasing away a chill that wasn't from the ambient temperature but from the daily tension. "I want it to be over. I'm beyond ready to coordinate peacefully without a monarchy official peering over my shoulder."

Lorand's fingertips grazed Elysia's shoulder before sliding down to the curve of her arm, leaving a trail of heat in their wake. The gentle yet deliberate touch sent a shiver skittering through her, igniting every nerve despite her exhaustion. His presence, so near, seemed to envelop her, the faint scent of leather and something earthy, undeniably him, weaving through her senses.

"Soon," he promised, his voice low and rough, the sound of it curling through her like a spark catching kindling. "Once he leaves, we can continue this under our terms—not because of a decree, but because we choose it."

Her breath caught as she turned to him, their faces mere inches apart. His gaze locked onto hers, dark and smoldering, his raw sincerity cutting through her defenses. That same determination—the fire that had burned in his eyes when he'd risked himself for her and her wards—was there, but now it was paired with something deeper. Hunger. Need.

Her pulse thundered as her hand rose instinctively, sliding up his chest. Beneath the fabric of his tunic, she felt the steady, insistent beat of his heart. Her fingers trembled as she splayed them there, his heat seeping into her palm.

Lorand's breath hitched, and she caught the faint clench of his jaw as he stepped closer, closing the last sliver of distance between them. His hand skimmed along her waist, his touch branding her even through the layers of her gown. She leaned into him, her body betraying her will with the aching way it pressed toward his, as though drawn by a force she couldn't resist.

When his lips met hers, the world melted away. It wasn't a hesitant brush but a claiming, deep and thorough. His mouth moved over hers with a precision that stole her breath, each kiss fanning the flames of desire coursing through her. She tilted her head, her free hand curling into the fabric of his tunic, pulling him closer as her body melted against his.

Her skin burned where his other hand skimmed her side, his fingers flexing as if he fought to hold himself back. But she didn't want restraint; she wanted the storm, the chaos of their shared hunger. Her body thrummed with the raw energy of it, the electric pull between them undeniable, unstoppable.

Lorand broke the kiss just enough to speak, his lips brushing against hers as he murmured, "If we keep this up, I won't be able to stop."

Elysia's chest heaved, her forehead pressing against his as she fought to catch her breath. "Then don't." Her voice was barely a whisper, and yet it carried the weight of her longing, her lips brushing his once more, drawing him back to her.

His groan was low, guttural, a sound that sent a fresh wave of heat spiraling through her. His hands moved more boldly now, sliding down to grip her hips, anchoring her against him as though to steady himself against the force of his desire. Her heart raced as his body responded to hers, the tension between them an intoxicating blend of restraint and want.

When they finally pulled apart, both breathless, Elysia's cheeks were flushed, her lips tingling from the fervor of their kiss. Lorand's eyes burned with unspoken promises, his chest rising and falling as though he'd been running. For a moment, neither spoke, their shared silence heavy with the weight of everything they couldn't say but had just shown.

"We're supposed to be behaving," she said softly, her voice trembling with a mix of laughter and lingering desire.

Lorand's lips curved into a crooked smile, his thumb brushing her cheek as he stared at her like she was the only thing in the world. "If anyone saw us, they'd certainly believe this wasn't a sham." His smirk faded, replaced by something more tender. "But for now, let's keep this between us."

Elysia nodded, her heart still hammering as she stepped back, his touch lingering on her skin long after it was gone. "Agreed," she whispered, though her body screamed for more.

He chuckled softly, the sound low and intimate, before taking her hand and pressing a kiss to her knuckles. "Then let's get you to your chamber before I lose what little control I have left."

Her smile trembled as she allowed him to lead her away, her body still buzzing from their stolen moment, her mind already yearning for the next.

Together they navigated the corridors, passing only a few patrolling guards. The hush of early evening lay thick around them, a hush that promised the keep's residents some reprieve after a day of unrelenting scrutiny. At her chamber door, Lorand paused, dropping a soft kiss on her brow.

Elysia's heart twisted at the sweetness of it, so distant from the forced betrothal they'd both despised. "Goodnight," she murmured, stepping inside.

The wooden door shut between them. For a moment, she leaned against it, heart still fluttering. Outside, she heard his footsteps fade, presumably heading to meet Darius. She exhaled a slow, shaky breath. In the hush of her chamber, her thoughts whirled with the day's trials—Remine's watchful eye, orchard demonstrations, the rosters, knights' bruises. And that kiss.

Exhaustion soon took hold, overshadowing every flutter. She traversed the small space, setting her herb pouch on the table. The bed beckoned. She shrugged off her overgown, leaving only the simplest shift. With measured movements, she lit a single lamp, rummaged for a mild salve to rub across her temples—anything to keep her from collapsing under stress-laden sleep.

As she unbraided her hair, her gaze flicked toward the softly flickering lamp. The monarchy's final say remained uncertain. Yes, they had impressed Remine somewhat, but would it be enough? She recalled how easily an entire barony's fate could shift on royal whim. Tucking away that worry, she reminded herself: we've done everything we can. And we have each other, truly. That knowledge had to count for something.

Dimness settled in, the lamp's glow dancing on the walls. She crawled into bed, nestling her head against a pillow that smelled faintly of lavender from a sachet Mira had left. Her limbs felt heavy, her mind drifting. Moments of the day flitted behind her eyelids: orchard sunlight, the swirl of wards at each marker, Lorand's presence always there, quiet smiles from knights who once glared at her. Then that final corridor hush, warm lips meeting hers in a gentle promise that overcame all sense of contrivance.

Her last conscious thought was a whispered vow: let Remine observe, let him test them further—she and Lorand would show that no sabotage, no monarchy edict, could overshadow the love they had for each other.

SEVENTEEN

Elysia felt an all-too-familiar tension coiling in her gut as she stood among the gathered nobles in the baron's conference hall. Shadows from the tall hearth flickered across the chamber's stone walls, creating shifting patches of light that made the assembly seem even more volatile. Kallendore greens and Valecrest crimsons mingled in a blur of sharp glares and rigid postures. Though the chilly, late-afternoon sunlight filtered in from a narrow window near the far end of the room, the heat of argument pressed down like a palpable weight.

Her father, Lord Daryon Kallendore, paced on one side of the circular oak table that dominated the space. His dark green robes swished around his ankles, and his lined face was drawn taut with indignation. Opposite him stood Sir Balin, the older knight who had all but raised Lorand after his father's passing. Sir Balin's scarred temple gleamed in the dancing light of the fireplace; the old knight was not loud, but every terse word landed like a blade on marble.

Elysia picked up the clipped edges of their debate: father accusing Valecrest knights of drawing steel too eagerly, Sir Balin retorting that Kallendore's "secrecy and wards" had sown discord for decades. Beneath the surface, the conversation spiraled toward old grudges that no arrest or monarchy edict had entirely erased.

Standing just behind Sir Balin was Lady Devia Valecrest, Lorand's mother. Her erect stance and well-tailored crimson gown gave her an imposing presence even before she spoke. She gripped the top rail of a carved wooden chair, her knuckles whitening each time Sir Balin spat out an especially stinging barb. Now and again, Devia cast her son a look: a mixture of concern, steely frustration, and a cautious flicker of hope—like she wanted Lorand to intervene, to calm the storm. But so many times in the past, Valecrest pride had demanded they never seem weak.

The conversation pitched when a Valecrest retainer in the corner said something about Kallendore wards "breeding superstition," prompting Elysia's father to hiss back that at least wards could heal farmland, rather than "sticking swords at peasants." Elysia's cheeks flared hot. How many times would they circle the same horrors of the feud? Didn't they see how deeply she and Lorand had grown past this?

She swept her gaze over the rest of the room. The baron stood at the far side; his broad shoulders set in tired resignation. A handful of watchers from both families— lesser uncles, loyal cousins—murmured among themselves, eyes occasionally darting to Elysia. To Elysia's left, Mira hovered with an anxious expression, fiddling with the hem of her gown. And a few paces away, Darius—broad-shouldered and clad in Valecrest colors—exchanged uneasy looks with her friend. She felt the tension in the air like a brewing thundercloud.

But it was Lorand's presence that rooted her. He stood near Elysia, one step behind Sir Balin and Lady Devia, his posture clenched as though containing a wellspring of frustration. She didn't need to see the set of his jaw to sense his anger thrumming. She felt it in the quiet, shallow breath he drew. This entire debate, after all they had survived, threatened to unravel the precarious unity they'd fought so hard to claim.

Her father—waving a hand in exasperation—spoke again: "House Valecrest fosters cruelty in its knights. How else do you explain the manhandling of Kallendore watchers at the southern orchard last summer? If they truly sought peace, they wouldn't resort to intimidation!"

Sir Balin bristled, lines deepening at the edge of his scar. "And House Kallendore's clandestine spells in the farmland near our fortress? We had wards flaring at all hours, stirred by your watchers' incantations. I recall a milling family nearly run off their land, suspecting your magic tampered with their well."

Elysia had heard enough; she parted her lips to intervene, but Lady Devia abruptly spoke for the first time. "Balin," she said sharply, "we must consider that not all wards are malicious. Elysia's magic has proven beneficial many times these recent weeks." Her gaze flicked to Elysia, lips pressed thin, as though disclaiming the grudging compliment. Then Devia's attention pivoted to Daryon. "But that doesn't excuse House Kallendore from ignoring how our knights might be... threatened or misled by illusions. We never had full cooperation in defensive strategies. Perhaps if your watchers had been more forthright—"

Lord Daryon scoffed. "Forthright? It's Valecrest that sought to corner us from the start. You can hardly expect Kallendore to share every layer of magical knowledge when you call it witchcraft at every turn."

And so, it went. Elysia felt her teeth set. She glanced again at Lorand; his brow furrowed; mouth twisted in a barely contained snarl. She remembered how he had once believed those same rumors about her magic—and how far they had come. That memory brightened in her chest, reminding her there was a more hopeful path than this ugly bickering. She slowly drew herself upright.

"Father," she said, voice carefully even. "Must we dredge up orchard tales from last year? We know how easily rumor can overshadow fact. Our watchers—"

But Daryon talked right over her. "Elysia, you haven't seen half the scorn we endured for letting Valecrest knights prowl our farmland even after the sabotage fiasco. Folks accused us of inviting brutes into our orchard. The Kallendore name was tarnished because we were forced to yield under the monarchy's glare!"

Elysia's frustration stirred with a jolt. The monarchy's glare, yes. But all that compulsion was meant to unify them, not chain them to pettiness. She clenched her fists.

"We tried unity at the festival. House Valecrest faced sabotage orchestrated by Kester," she said, voice beginning to tighten. "You cannot lay blame for intimidation at Lorand's feet when we've seen him risking his own life to defend Kallendore watchers. He nearly died in that forest pass—"

Sir Balin cut in: "Only because he was chasing bandits financed by Kallendore's old grievances. Some lesser allies of your house might have set the stage. We heard rumors that certain Kallendore outliers wanted to sabotage the wedding."

"Stop," Lorand muttered, his voice dangerously low. The single syllable reverberated across the hall. His posture was so rigid Elysia thought he might snap. Slowly, he stepped forward, ignoring Lady Devia's small gesture of caution. His eyes, storm-gray, swept over the older men. "You're all describing ghosts," he said harshly. "Specters of grudges that belong in the past. Kester orchestrated sabotage—both Kallendore and Valecrest nearly fell apart over it. We found proof. The monarchy recognized it. And yet you stand here, flailing your old resentments."

Sir Balin's lips pressed together in a grim line. "Lorand, you're letting your sentiments blind you to—"

"To what?" Lorand exclaimed, voice rising. "To the fact that without Elysia's wards, more knights would have died? That without her healing, we'd have lost half the orchard workers. Stop painting Kallendore caretakers as potential saboteurs."

Elysia's pulse hammered, relief warring with new tension. Even Lady Devia blinked, uncertain how to react to Lorand's vehement outburst. In that moment, he seemed to embody all the frustration she herself felt that they were re-litigating every scrap of old animosity rather than acknowledging the present truth. The truth that Elysia and Lorand had discovered a different way forward.

Her father's cheeks flushed. "And we are to forget that Valecrest knights once belittled her magic, that they still gossip about witches in the orchard? You think the older generation just forgives that?"

A spike of fury shot through Elysia. She moved beside Lorand, voice trembling with pent-up frustration. "What good does endless blame do? We've proven that our union —yes, forced or not—saved this barony from a worse crisis. You all saw the sabotage. You saw how we responded together."

The hush that fell was peppered with muttering. Both Kallendore and Valecrest supporters looked poised to argue again. At Elysia's side, Lorand inhaled sharply, and for an instant, the entire swirl of voices blurred into the background of Elysia's hearing. She felt the tension radiating from him—knew her own stance mirrored that heat.

She stepped forward. "Your bitterness, your fragile pride... it helps no one. If you keep clinging to these grudges, it's as though you want Kester's sabotage to succeed even now."

A few hearts might have twinged at that. Elysia spotted the baron near the wall, half-lifting a hand to intervene, but Sir Balin's voice cut in again, flooded with old bitterness. "You speak as though we can dismiss centuries of Valecrest scorn. We bled on the battlefield protecting farmland Kallendore refused to share, we—"

Elysia's father roared, "You speak of battles? My father—"

"Enough!"

Lorand's voice tore through the chaos. Elysia's heart pounded at the raw edge in his tone. He advanced, ignoring Lady Devia's attempt to hold him back. "Enough," he repeated, more quietly. "I will not let you degrade what Elysia and I have accomplished for this barony. I nearly bled out in a forest pass. She poured her life force into saving me. If that doesn't prove the sincerity of House Kallendore, what will?"

Elysia's breath caught. She felt eyes pivoting to her, some hostile, some uncertain. A new wave of murmuring erupted. This time, Elysia's father looked momentarily wrong-footed, brow pinching. She sensed him trying to reconcile his protective instincts with his resentment. Meanwhile, a flicker of sympathy crossed Lady Devia's face, though she kept her spine rigid.

"Lorand," Sir Balin said softly, "I raised you to be proud of Valecrest. Not to forget how we—"

Lorand turned on him. "Have you not seen how prejudice blinds you? I once felt it, too—fearing Kallendore magic because I was taught to. But I've learned, with Elysia at my side, that we can do far more working together. If you can't accept that, you're the one tarnishing Valecrest pride, not me."

Those words seemed to slam Sir Balin back a step. For a heartbeat, no one spoke.

Elysia's father tried to regain footing, his voice a hiss of frustration. "So, you'd have us simply yield? Bow to Kallendore wards? Let your knights stand idle while a swirl of incantations flood the orchard?"

At that, Elysia's restraint dissolved. "Father, you're the one ignoring that we've integrated watchers into Valecrest patrols. We've done so for weeks—house synergy is real, not lip service. You're the one clinging to some misguided notion that letting Valecrest knights near our farmland soils Kallendore traditions!"

"Elysia," her father warned, eyes narrowing. "You speak as if—"

She cut him off, voice trembling with anger. "I speak as if I'm done letting old slights overshadow the present. Don't you see that we almost lost everything—our title, the barony's safety, any hope of genuine acceptance of magic? Did you think that while cowering behind your arrogance, we'd hold the monarchy at bay forever?"

Beside her, Lorand exhaled a ragged breath. "We risk losing more than titles if we tear each other apart," he said. "We risk shredding whatever fragile trust has grown among the people. Are you so determined to prove the marriage worthless that you'd condemn all Highdale to more suspicion and fear?"

Silence fell, thick as stagnant water. Elysia's gaze darted along the ring of watchers. Some Valecrests folded their arms, scowling under pinned brows; some Kallendores stared at Elysia, unsettled. She realized she was trembling, chest tight with a swirl of heartbreak and fury. She didn't want these old men—fathers, uncles, mentors

—bellowing half truths about a feud that was, in her mind, finally beginning to mend.

As if sensing her agitation, Lorand's hand lifted, almost imperceptibly, toward her back. He did not fully touch her, but the gesture anchored her. Something in the air crackled. She glanced at him, eyes meeting with his in a flash of mutual exasperation, frustration, and—beneath it all—solidarity.

Her father opened his mouth again, presumably to fling more blame, but Elysia's voice beat him to it. "If you truly think these grudges are worth more than the lives we've saved, you're living in a ghost world," she said, not caring that her own father might take offense. She stepped closer to Lorand, chest rising and falling in short, heated breaths. "And I won't stand for it."

In the hush that followed, a small wave of heat coursed through Elysia's body. The intensity of her own emotions—anger, fear, and a sudden upswell of longing— tumbled together. Lorand turned, and their gazes locked. She saw in him that same swirl: the frustration at being misunderstood, the fierce loyalty, the memory of how she had saved his life, how he had defended her in turn. It all coalesced into a single charged instant; tension wound so tightly that it tipped over the edge into something else.

CHAPTER

EIGHTEEN

He reached for her.

She didn't care that the entire chamber was watching. She let out a noise—half gasp, half exhale—and met him in an abrupt, searing kiss. It felt as though a dam had burst, unleashing the pent-up swirl of terror, relief, anger, and desire they'd carried all this time. The world constricted to the space between them, the press of chest against chest, the warm shock of his mouth covering hers, the heady sensation of his arm sliding firmly around her waist. She heard an outcry of gasps and low curses from onlookers, but it all receded into the background roar of her heart.

Her lips parted against his, and for once, Elysia allowed herself no reservations, no caution. This was the truth beyond monarchy edicts, beyond forced ceremonies. The taste of his breath, the tension in his body, the trembling in her knees—everything ignited a molten warmth that banished the conference hall's cold shadows. She clung to him, inhaling the faint scent of leather and the echo of orchard breezes. The intensity of it, the raw melding of frustration and deep longing, made her dizzy.

Somewhere, someone shouted her name. Possibly her father. Possibly Sir Balin was calling Lorand. She could have sworn she heard Lady Devia's voice rise in protest or alarm. None of it mattered in that suspended moment. The kiss was more than a meeting of lips; it was a fierce statement that the old feud had no hold on them anymore.

After a breathless eternity—likely only a few seconds—Lorand pulled back. His face hovered inches from hers. Elysia's pulse pounded as the hush in the room snapped back into focus. She saw shock etched into half the watchers' faces, some older Valecrests slack-jawed, a few Kallendore mages exchanging wide-eyed stares. A swirl of confusion reeled through her. Did she regret it? No—her heart thrummed with a sudden, incandescent clarity. She wanted them all to know they were serious about forging a new path.

She felt the nervous tremor in Lorand's body, saw the unmasked yearning in his eyes. He tore his gaze away from her just enough to speak, voice hoarse. "We refuse to be caged by your grudges," he managed, breath hitching. "Elysia and I stand together, as truly as any two heirs ever have. If you want to cling to the past, do it away from us."

Her father tried to speak, looking furious and astonished all at once. Before he could, Elysia found her own voice, shaky but resolute. "The feud must die," she announced, turning to glare at both Valecrest and Kallendore faces. "We gave too much, risked too much. We won't let your bitterness tear the barony apart again."

Some older family members bristled, sputtering in shock. Sir Balin's mouth hung open, disbelief warring with paternal concern for Lorand. Lady Devia's eyes glowed with a potent mix of confusion, pride, and shame. A half-dozen murmurs flared at once: half condemnation, half unsettled acceptance.

In the midst of that confusion, Darius stepped forward from the side, forging a path with his broad frame. "You heard them," he said, voice calm but firm. "Whether forced or not, they've proven the marriage stands on more than reluctance. Let's not forget the sabotage fiasco, the orchard fiasco, the forest fiasco—one after another, and these two overcame it all side by side."

Mira stepped up from the other side. Her color was high, but her voice trembled with determination. "Truer words... you can't deny what Elysia and Lorand have accomplished. If you truly care for Highdale, you'll help them shape unity, not dredge past blame."

Darius turned to the gathered crowd, his broad shoulders squared and his voice ringing with unexpected fervor. "My lady speaks of unity, of loyalty to Highdale and to what we've built here," he began, his eyes scanning the room, daring anyone to interrupt. "But I'll tell you what true loyalty is. It's standing by someone when the odds are against them, when others doubt, and when it would be easier to walk away. I've seen that kind of loyalty first-hand, not in grand speeches or alliances, but in Mira of House Kallendore."

Elysia's heart twisted as Darius's gaze finally landed on Mira, her cousin's face pale but her eyes wide, shimmering with unspoken emotion. The crowd shifted uncomfortably, whispers threading through the hall, but Darius ignored them all. His voice dropped, rich and steady. "She's been the voice of reason when tempers flared, the steady hand when others faltered. Mira is the kind of person who doesn't just dream of better—she fights for it. And I love her for it. I love her with every part of me."

The room fell silent, the weight of his declaration settling over them all. Elysia could hardly breathe as Darius took a step toward Mira, his expression softening as though the rest of the world had vanished, leaving only the two of them.

"Mira," he said, his tone quiet but still carrying, "I've held back for too long, thinking it wasn't the right time, that I had no right to hope for more. But I can't do that anymore. I love you. And if you'll have me, I will stand by you for the rest of my life."

Elysia watched as Mira's hand fluttered to her chest, her color high, her breath visibly unsteady. Her cousin, so often calm and composed, looked utterly undone as she stared at Darius. For a moment, Elysia feared Mira wouldn't respond, but then she stepped forward, closing the distance between them.

"I never thought you'd say those words," Mira whispered, her voice trembling yet clear enough for all to hear. "I thought I was alone in this. But I love you too, Darius. I always have."

Elysia's throat tightened as the two came together, their kiss unhurried but powerful, a promise forged in the presence of every doubting eye. Around the room, expressions softened—some skeptical, some begrudgingly admiring—but none could deny what they'd just witnessed. For the first time in what felt like forever, Elysia allowed herself a small smile. Amid the tension and endless schemes, love had staked its claim in the unlikeliest of places.

NINETEEN

The baron cleared his throat from across the hall, a depth of relief on his weary face. "Yes," he said, letting his authority ring out. "We are done indulging old grudges. This is not a negotiation. The monarchy's edict forced them together, but we see clearly: they stand strong now by choice. Let us move beyond this endless rehash of slights or watch Highdale unravel. Enough."

A series of grumbles followed—nobody wanted to be the first to yield. But Elysia sensed the moment slipping from the old generation's control. She felt Lorand's hand on her back again, a reassuring warmth that stoked the embers still burning inside her. She turned, meeting his gaze. The fervent flush on his cheeks mirrored what she felt in her own.

"Let's get out of here for a moment," she whispered shakily, aware that if she stayed in the ring of onlookers, her anger might flare again—or she'd do something even more impulsive. He nodded; tension still etched around his eyes. Without waiting for any formal dismissal, they slipped between the parted ranks of watchers. Darius and Mira smoothly blocked any attempt at pursuit, stammering some excuse about letting them gather their composure. Lord Daryon's voice rose in disjointed protest, but Elysia ignored it. She didn't want to give him or anyone else another second to corner them.

They stepped out into the corridor. It was cooler here, the only light coming from widely spaced torches that made elongated shadows across the stone floor. Elysia realized her hands were trembling—she wasn't sure if from fury or from the aftershock of that kiss. Her mind reeled: had she really done that, seized him like that in front of everyone?

Lorand's breath was as ragged as her own. "Elysia," he managed softly. "Are you all right?"

Leaning a hand against the cold stone wall, she nodded, though her heart pounded in her throat. "Yes," she said. "Yes, I... I'm only shaky." Slowly, she straightened. "That was... quite a scene."

His lips twitched, shaping a rueful half-smile. "I suppose it was," he murmured, stepping closer. The corridor was deserted; behind them, muffled voices continued to surge in the conference hall. "I lost my temper, but I don't regret it."

"Nor do I," she whispered. Her gaze flicked to his mouth, memory of that explosive contact coursing through her. Heat coiled low in her abdomen. Another wave of longing threatened to surge. "We had to show them we're not simply fulfilling a monarchy script."

"Indeed." He was silent for a moment, expression shifting to raw vulnerability. Then his voice dropped to a hush. "But that kiss—Elysia, was that just...demonstration?"

She swallowed hard. "I don't know," she admitted. "Perhaps it was at first, but also something else. I can't deny that I—" Her words tangled. She had known she cared for him, that their bond had grown, but the ferocity of that kiss, the utter disregard for an entire chamber of watchers, suggested a deeper tide.

He nodded, gaze dipping. A single step, and he was in front of her, towering in the dim corridor. She felt the warmth of him, the tension coiled beneath the stiff lines of his posture. "I feel it too," he said gently. "This pull that's been building... I fear it's more than a fleeting spark. Elysia, can we... talk somewhere private?" His tone carried more than a request for conversation; a subtle tremor of longing made her pulse leap.

"Yes," she breathed. She remembered the cluster of lesser-known Valecrest guards posted just outside the main hall and knew the baron's staff scurried in the adjacent corridors. That left the adjoining tower steps or a vacant side room deeper in the keep. Another wave of heat flickered in her cheeks. She jerked her chin toward a smaller corridor that branched off this main one. "This way."

They moved quickly, half hoping not to be intercepted by a meddling relative. Elysia's feet carried her down a narrower hallway, unadorned by tapestries or official crests. Partway down, a plain wooden door marked a storage or some lesser-used chamber. She tested the latch, found it unlocked, and slipped inside, Lorand right behind her.

A rush of stale air greeted them: a room with shelves stacked haphazardly, half-laden with linen. Old festival decorations—wilted ribbons and folded cloth—occupied one corner. At least there was enough space to stand without stepping on crates. By the sparse lantern light from the hallway, she caught Lorand's face—palms braced on the closed door, chest rising in a shallow, unsteady rhythm.

She pressed her back against a nearby shelf, heart pounding. The door latched with a light click. They were alone. The hush felt doubly loud after the clamor of the conference hall. He moved closer, eyes lingering on her parted lips, as though asking permission. She urged him on with a faint tilt of her chin, blood roaring in her ears.

Slowly, almost reverently, he lifted a hand to brush the backs of his fingers against her cheek. That gentle contact, after the heated swirl in the hall, sparked a delicious shiver down her spine. "I hate how they make you defend yourself," he said, voice low. "I've seen all you've done. I despise hearing them question it."

Her throat ached with unshed tears—equal parts fury and relief. "I hate that they question you too," she managed. "Like you're a brute who wields a sword without conscience." She exhaled shakily. "We've shown them our intentions, over and over. Why can't they let it rest?"

His hand grazed her jaw, thumb stroking lightly. "Old

grudges die slowly," he said, bitterness shading his tone. "But ours... ours is no longer forced. You and I, we—" He broke off, gaze flicking downward. "It's real, Elysia. Whatever the monarchy demanded, I'm here because I want to be."

Fresh warmth flooded her chest. It was one thing for him to defend her publicly, quite another to reveal this quiet confession. Without speaking, she slid her palm over his chest, feeling the steady hammer of his heart through his tunic. That closeness made her breath catch again, and the tension crackling between them flared brightly. The argument in the hall, the forced betrothal, the swirl of rumors—they all seemed to fade into the corners of this musty storeroom. Only Lorand's voice, his nearness, and the heat in her veins felt real.

She tipped her head up, parted her lips—and in that instant, their mouths met again. This time, the kiss was less a clash of anger than a slow merging of want, a tentative confirmation that yes, they absolutely could choose each other. Despite the tight ache in her chest, Elysia inhaled him, savoring the way he steadied her by sliding an arm around her waist. Her hands found the broad lines of his shoulders, his tunic bunching beneath her fingers. She sensed the faint taste of leftover tension, but it mingled with desire until it was simply them, no watchers, no condemnation.

He broke the kiss to draw a ragged breath, dipping his forehead against hers. "We can't stay in here forever," he said, voice still hushed with restrained passion.

She freed a trembling laugh, pressing a hand to her

heated cheek. "No... but I'm not ready to face them, not yet." Her voice cracked. "Father. Sir Balin. Lady Devia. All those watchers with their eyes. They'll have a storm of questions. I—" She swallowed. "I don't want to let go of this moment."

He nodded. "Nor do I." His hand slid to cradle the back of her neck. She felt the warmth of his calloused palm, and her eyes fluttered shut. The last few months reeled through her mind: the forced ceremonies, the orchard sabotage, the tense carriage rides, the near-fatal forest pass, the healing that nearly drained her lifeblood to save him. She realized she wanted this closeness not simply as defiance, but as a promise. A promise that they would be stronger together.

She rose on her toes, brushing another soft kiss to his lips. He responded with a gentle hunger that made her blood sing. Heart drumming, she let herself melt into him, ignoring the dusty linen smell of the storeroom, ignoring the swirl of panic just outside these walls. For a few heartbeats, they explored this new intimacy with unhurried tenderness, each brush of lips or slide of hands unveiling a deeper longing that had simmered beneath their friction.

Lorand hesitated, breath caught. "Elysia," he murmured into her hair. "I— I can't hide how much I want you. But I also don't want to presume."

She exhaled, feeling a throbbing current of warmth, part embarrassment, part desire. "You're not presuming. I —" She rested her forehead against his chest, inhaling the faint aroma of leather and his underlying musk. "I feel the same," she whispered. Emboldened by the swirl in her limbs, she lifted her gaze. "There's a small cloakroom, I think, further down the corridor. It locks. Perhaps—"

His eyes darkened, not in anger but in a wave of intense longing that made her stomach flip. "Show me," he said quietly.

She managed a shaky nod. They slipped back into the corridor, checking for watchers. It was empty. Her ears pounded with the blood rush of what they were about to do, the knowledge that everything had changed in that hall. She led him down a few steps to a narrower branching corridor used by servants. At the end, a short door led to a cloakroom or storage for old festival costumes—she wasn't entirely sure. But she knew it was rarely used. Her heart hammered as she opened that door and stepped inside, lighting a small lantern perched on a dusty shelf.

The place was hardly romantic: old racks for outer garments, a few rotted crates, and a single rickety bench. Motes of dust drifted in the lantern's glow. She shut the door behind them, then threw the latch. Privacy.

She turned to face Lorand. The moment their eyes met, the tension ignited anew, a hush of anticipation that coiled tight in her belly. Gently, he reached for her again. "Only if you're certain," he murmured, voice tremulous.

Her blood roared. She stepped into his arms, sliding her hands up around his shoulders. "I am," she whispered. She rose on tiptoe, and his lips descended on hers, slow at first, then deeper, more wanting.

He kissed like a man starved: each press of his mouth urgent, fervent, yet overlaid with a careful gentleness that revealed just how much he cherished her. Elysia answered in kind, matching his intensity, letting her fingers thread through his close-cropped hair. She'd never felt so simultaneously shaky and secure. The months of forced proximity, suspicion, near-death rescues—every piece had built up to this raw expression of mutual acceptance.

As they stumbled backward, Lorand eased her onto the small bench, never breaking the warm press of lips. The shift made her heart hammer faster, and she let out a faint noise high in her throat. They parted for a single breath. "You're sure?" he repeated, his voice low, laced with longing. She slid her hands down to his waist, hooking her fingers in the sash.

She nodded, heart thudding. "Yes. Let me have this." Her cheeks flushed with vulnerability. "Let me have you. Even if everything outside that door is chaos, let me have this moment of—of closeness. Please."

A shudder went through him. Then he leaned in, his breath ghosting her ear. "I want nothing more," he confessed. "You, Elysia. I want you."

She framed his face in her hands and lost herself in another kiss, this one slow and exploring, their tongues meeting in a languid dance. The tang of salt and the faint taste of honey lingered on his breath. She felt the shift of his strong arms as he braced them on either side of her, enveloping her in that protective warmth she'd come to trust. Her entire being buzzed with awareness—the glide of his palm down her back, the way her own breathing hitched as she let him in.

As their kisses deepened, a swirl of heady anticipation and tender caution guided them. Elysia's heart soared, her mind dizzy with the realization that all that forced formality had led, ironically, to a genuine bond she no longer wanted to deny. His hands trembled slightly as they slid along the curve of her waist, carefully exploring. She moaned softly, focusing only on the heated friction of his tunic against her bodice, the way his thigh brushed hers, sending sparks shooting through her nerves.

At some point, they both stopped speaking entirely, lost in the hush of breath and the rustle of clothing. Elysia could hear the faint pounding of her pulse in her ears, each beat thrumming with longing. She let Lorand ease her cloak off her shoulders, lowering it onto the bench behind her. Her heart threatened to burst with how right it felt—and how terrifying it was to be so vulnerable.

In that dusty cloakroom, they indulged in this closeness, uncertain how much time passed. Distantly, Elysia knew the families might still be in uproar. But here, behind a locked door, she and Lorand found a hush that no decree or argument could shatter. They sank into each other with gentle touches and murmured reassurances, pushing aside the swirl of tension from outside.

Elysia's entire body hummed, a flush staining her cheeks. She realized tears shimmered at the corners of her eyes—tears of release, gratitude, something akin to relief.

Lorand's voice was husky. "I... I never imagined it could feel like this. With you."

She swallowed. "Neither did I," she whispered. A shaky laugh escaped her. "I used to resent you so fiercely.

But now, it's like all that pent-up feeling became... something else."

His mouth quirked in a tender half-smile. "A far better use of our energy," he said wryly, brushing a thumb over her month. She gave a tremulous laugh, heart still pounding. She curled her arms around his neck, inhaling the comforting spice of him. For a moment, they were content merely to hold each other, letting the hush cradle them. Elysia closed her eyes, letting the warmth of his arms anchor her in the midst of everything.

After a while, he shifted, pressing a soft kiss to her temple. "I'd keep you here forever, but they might tear down the door," he murmured. "And I suspect the baron wants to finalize something about the families' terms of peace. We might have to return eventually."

She sighed, reluctant. "They'll want some dramatic explanation, I'm sure, for that scene. For... well, this." She sat up, smoothing her gown. A slight creak of the bench reminded her how precarious it was to linger in a dusty cloakroom. "But... I need a moment longer. Just one more moment alone. Then we'll face them. Together. Right?"

"Together," he echoed firmly. He laced his fingers with hers, lifting her knuckles to his lips in a tender gesture. "We're not cowering from them. We're forging forward, letting them see we will not yield to their tired grudges."

His vow warmed her. She took several breaths, letting the tension in her shoulders ease. Slowly, she stood, smoothing her skirt and retucking a stray lock of hair that had come loose during their embrace. Lorand hurriedly ran a hand through his hair, trying to restore some semblance of composure—though the flush in his cheeks betrayed how deeply he'd been affected.

A small, shy grin tugged at Elysia's lips. "We look quite undone," she said softly.

Lorand let out a quiet chuckle, leaning in to press a last, fleeting kiss to the corner of her mouth. "Better undone than living in false dignity," he teased gently. Then, more somberly, "Are you ready?"

She swallowed, steeling herself. Thinking of her father's flustered scorn, Sir Balin's disapproval, Lady Devia's uncertain acceptance. The entire swirl of watchers, some of whom still saw them as forced participants in a show. Let them watch. The memory of that searing kiss in front of everyone filled her with fresh fortitude. "Yes," she said. "We've ended that pointless argument, or at least... we've made our stance clear."

He nodded. "Then let's face them." With a final squeeze of her hand, he unlatched the door. Together, they stepped into the corridor.

TWENTY

The hallway beyond was still empty, albeit with more distant echoes of voices. Elysia suspected that Darius, Mira, and possibly the baron's staff had managed to keep prying eyes away from this route. She and Lorand walked side by side, hearts still racing, each footstep echoing in the hush of the keep.

As they neared the main corridor leading back to the conference hall, they saw Mira lurking near a tall candelabra. Her eyes widened with relief when she spotted them. She hurried over, whispering, "They're all in a stir. The baron's trying to calm them. Your father is furious, Elysia. Sir Balin looks pale as a ghost. But I think Darius and the baron might have hammered out a line: something about letting you both speak for yourselves."

Elysia took a steady breath. "Thank you, Mira," she said softly. Gods, she was grateful that her friend had her back.

Mira's gaze flicked between Elysia and Lorand, noting

their slightly disheveled appearances, the bright flush in their cheeks. A wry smile curved her lips. "I see the two of you… found a moment to reflect," she teased gently. Elysia's ears burned, but she summoned a small smile.

Lorand cleared his throat, posture stiffening in mild embarrassment. "We did," he said. "We're ready now."

Mira nodded. "I think your father wants a formal apology or explanation, Elysia. But the baron insists on a structured discourse. If you two stand firm, you might end the entire meeting on your own terms." Her glance at Elysia brimmed with reassurance.

Elysia firmed her jaw. "All right." She slid her hand unconsciously into Lorand's. He squeezed it, conveying silent solidarity. With Mira in tow, they followed the corridor back to the conference hall.

The moment they reentered, a hush fell. The baron, still stationed near the far wall, looked mightily relieved. Lord Daryon, who was in mid-rant with another Kallendore relative, whirled to face them. Sir Balin's posture was rigid, arms folded, expression guarded. Lady Devia stood near him, a faint furrow in her brow. Across the table lay a swirl of lesser cousins, retinues, and watchers, all wearing stunned or wary expressions as they took in Elysia and Lorand's linked hands.

Elysia breathed deeply. Her father recovered from his shock first, turning his fury-lashed glare upon them. "Elysia," he snapped, "that public display was outlandish and—"

She raised her chin. "And truthful," she interrupted. Her father blinked. She cast her gaze around the entire chamber, taking in Valecrest stares as well. "We stand by it. You might find it scandalous, but we would rather show our genuine unity than feign polite courtesy while you tear each other to shreds."

A few watchers murmured in dismay. But the baron stepped forward, voice weary but firm. "I, for one, welcome a genuine expression of union," he said. "If your families are wise, you'll put aside the meltdown we witnessed. Let them speak without interruption. Then we can all move on."

Lorand's grip on Elysia's hand tightened imperceptibly. He nodded to the baron. "Thank you, my lord. We've proven we fight for Highdale's well-being. Our... demonstration in the orchard sabotage, our public vow to stand by each other, the synergy we forged in punishing Kester's scheming—it's real. If any of you doubt it, we can prove it again. But we refuse to cower while you hurl old accusations."

Silence stretched. An inner swirl of tension thrummed through Elysia. She caught glimpses: some Kallendores looked guilty, recalling how Elysia had saved them from suspicion, then from sabotage. A few Valecrest knights stared at Lorand with shock or grudging respect. Lady Devia's expression softened by a hairsbreadth, as if acknowledging that her son had chosen his path. And somewhere near the back, she noticed Sir Balin bowing his head slightly, as though trying to gather composure.

Finally, Lord Daryon let out a long breath. "If your hearts are truly aligned," he murmured, voice strangely subdued, "then who am I to stand in your way? I simply... I worry, Elysia. The monarchy forced this union. I feared you'd be overshadowed, or your magic exploited."

Elysia's heart squeezed. She recognized the paternal fear behind his bluster. "Father," she said quietly, "I appreciate your concern. But I'm not overshadowed. If anything, Lorand has given me more space to heal and help than any forced edict could. He defends me when others question my wards. I do the same when folks call him a brutish knight. We made it work."

A dip of her father's head signaled reluctant acceptance. Elysia felt Lorand exhale softly at her side. That single breath was a balm. Then, shots of discussion began again among the watchers, the older relatives still complaining or muttering. But this time, there was a new undercurrent—one of grudging recognition that times really were changing, that Elysia and Lorand were no longer enemies playing a role.

The baron cleared his throat. "Anyone else wish to speak?" He cast a pointed look around the table. "No more endless feuding. We focus on the next steps. House Kallendore and Valecrest remain allied. If your pride can't stomach that, you can remove yourself from these proceedings."

A hush. Some watchers shifted uncomfortably but said nothing. Elysia let herself hope that perhaps the worst was done—that the families, though still simmering with complicated feelings, might not lunge back into another full-blown argument.

Sir Balin finally broke the silence, voice gruff. "Lorand," he said, "I... see your conviction. Perhaps I forget that you're a man grown, forging your own path. I only hope Kallendore proves as steadfast as you claim. My loyalty was to your father, and I'd do anything to keep the Valecrest name proud."

Lorand inclined his head, tension easing in his stance. "House Valecrest remains proud if we stand with Kallendore for what's right," he said. "You'll see it's not an idle fancy."

The old knight gave a curt nod. Elysia sensed that was as close to acceptance as Sir Balin would offer right now. Still, it was something.

Lady Devia's gaze flickered from Lorand to Elysia, a curious mixture of caution and empathy. "We have no choice but to move forward, do we?" she said softly. "I'll trust my son's judgment."

Elysia and Lorand both exhaled. In small pockets, conversation resumed, calmer now, while the baron signaled for a steward to bring a formal list of potential agreements—assigning watchers to farmland, knights to orchard patrol, and other items. Elysia suspected the rest of the meeting would revolve around hammering out some cohesive structure. But one thing was clear: there would be no more hurling of centuries-old blame, not tonight. That kiss had shattered the old lines.

As the baron stepped forward to read the documents, Lorand guided Elysia aside. He murmured in her ear, "They'll handle official business. Should we stay, or slip out again?"

Her lips twitched into a faint smile. The swirl of relief and lingering warmth from their stolen moment in the cloakroom still coursed through her. "We'll stay a bit," she whispered. "Watch them formalize something that might, at long last, outlive these grudges." Her eyes met his, a slight flush reigniting. "The next time I slip away with you; I want fewer prying eyes. We've had enough scandal for one day."

His answering looks gleamed with mischief and something deeper. "Agreed," he murmured.

They found a spot near the baron—close enough to observe the calm drafting of unity terms. Mira sidled up to Elysia's other side, giving her a subtle grin of approval. Meanwhile, Darius and a handful of Valecrest knights engaged in subdued conversation about orchard shifts and farmland rotation. Sir Balin loitered behind them, arms crossed, no longer spitting accusations but merely watching with hooded eyes.

Soon, the hush gave way to practical talk. The baron read out the new schedule ensuring watchers and knights patrolled together. Elysia's father offered occasional nods of agreement, though he kept a wary set to his jaw. Lady Devia contributed refinements, ensuring the farmland wards were updated. Each refinement felt like a small step away from centuries of enmity.

Elysia felt Lorand's hand brush hers again in an unspoken gesture of solidarity. Her entire soul felt lighter. They had faced the storm—and though the families weren't entirely at peace, the worst of it had been forced into submission by a single, undeniable truth: Elysia and Lorand wanted this alliance for themselves, not just because of a royal threat.

Finally, the baron concluded, "We'll codify these points in writing tomorrow. For now, let us adjourn. I believe we've had quite enough tension for one day." A bittersweet smile tugged his lips. "And Elysia, Lorand—I trust you'll continue demonstrating real cooperation. Do keep at it, for Highdale's sake."

Elysia dipped her head. "We will, my lord." Lorand echoed the sentiment, voice steady.

The assembly broke into clusters. Lord Daryon hovered, looking like he wanted to speak privately to Elysia, but Mira stepped in with a quick question about some farm detail, diverting him tactfully. Elysia silently thanked her friend's well-timed intervention. She wasn't ready for a deep father-daughter conversation. Not yet.

Lorand gestured for Elysia to walk with him. They drifted to a quieter corner of the hall. A swirl of half-lowered voices surrounded them as the rest filed out or gathered parchments. Elysia caught glimpses of Valecrest knights sipping from tankards, Kallendore watchers quietly conferring with the baron's steward. But she and Lorand stood apart from the bustle, a small bubble of calm.

He slid a hand over hers. The lingering flush in his face, the softness in his expression, made her chest tighten with tenderness. "We officially survived," he murmured, a wry note in his voice. "Though I suspect we'll have more battles to fight, they've come face to face with our unwavering stance."

Elysia nodded, pressing her free hand to the front of his tunic where she could feel his steady heartbeat. "Yes.

We have more to do. Many remaining pockets of bitterness, and we need to show them all it's possible to mend. But at least we're not alone anymore."

He threaded his fingers through hers. "Indeed. Let them see we're not just forging unity out of necessity. We're... forging something real."

She felt tears threaten. "There's strength in that," she said softly, remembering the swirl of desire in the cloakroom. "Strength I no longer want to hide."

A half-smile curved his lips. "Nor I." He dipped his head, planting a whisper of a kiss on her forehead. It was a far cry from the searing, desperate kiss that brought the entire hall to shocked silence, but it carried a gentler, no less significant vow. Her pulse skittered in response. She pressed closer, letting the rest of the room fade from her awareness. She had no illusions that this was the end of all tensions, but for now, it was enough to claim a measure of victory.

Around them, the last of the watchers drifted away, presumably to discuss the final details. Elysia heard her father's voice somewhere behind her, calmer now, possibly speaking with Lady Devia. Sir Balin still lingered, but he kept his distance, perhaps seeing Lorand in a new light.

Elysia let out a slow breath. "Shall we find Mira, or Darius? We might help finalize tomorrow's schedule with the baron," she offered.

"We shall," Lorand agreed, though he squeezed her hand once more, eyes shining with unspoken warmth. "But let's do so together—and let's not linger too long.

We'll want some time to rest ourselves, after this… dramatic day."

She laughed quietly at that understatement. "Agreed. A quiet corner suits me just fine," she said, recalling how the cloakroom had provided a fleeting sanctuary. And maybe, once the keep fell silent tonight, they'd find a better sanctuary for themselves—no interruptions, just a chance to speak openly about what they had discovered in their hearts.

They left the corner and made their way across the hall. Darius caught sight of them and beckoned them over to a side table, where the baron was discussing orchard expansions with a few lesser nobles. Elysia and Lorand joined amicably. Though Elysia's face still felt warm, she lifted her chin high, letting the sense of shared purpose gird her. The stares from a handful of onlookers held curiosity, perhaps mild scandal. But no one dared belittle them now. They had upended the old grudges with a single, powerful demonstration of devotion.

Yes, there would be more confrontation ahead—she knew that centuries of animosity didn't vanish in a single day. But in that hush of the baron's conference hall, Elysia felt the surety of Lorand's presence, the ember of promise that had sparked into genuine fire. As she fielded questions about farmland wards and orchard rosters, a small, secret smile curved her lips. Let them watch. She and Lorand were done hiding or apologizing. The feud was dying, and in its place, a new beginning bloomed—carried on the breath of their shared courage and the warmth of an undeniable, fervent bond.

Later, long after the baron's session ended, Elysia and Lorand found themselves pausing at a corridor junction, the castle's torches fluttering with night's chill. They were alone again—the keep's bustle winding down. He reached for her hand. She gazed up at him, her chest blooming with quiet affection.

"There's a small lounge by the southwestern tower," he murmured, a glint in his eye. "Might be more comfortable than a dusty cloakroom if you... wanted more time together before we retire."

A swirl of warmth fluttered in her belly. She recalled the cloakroom's hush, that near-tangible sense of shared breath and racing hearts. A flush spread across her cheeks anew. "Yes," she whispered. "Let's go."

TWENTY-ONE

Elysia Kallendore stood in a small alcove outside the baron's main hall, pressing one palm to her thrumming heart. She drew in a careful breath, letting her gaze roam over the corridor's high stone walls, the banners in Highdale's colors draped overhead. Murmuring voices drifted from the hall beyond—lesser nobles talking in close clusters, the scrape of boots on tile, the shifting of chairs. She sensed tension crackling like static in the air, though it was more subdued than the violent confrontations of the past weeks. Today was a day for formality and declarations, not sabotage and open hostility.

At her side, Mira hovered with an encouraging look. "You're ready," her friend whispered, straightening the hem of Elysia's deep green gown. "We both know you can handle anything they hurl at you."

Elysia attempted a small, wry smile. "I've healed arrows and magical blasts. Surely a mass of skeptical nobles is nothing to fear." Yet a flutter of nerves coiled in her belly. She had faced battles, yes, but there remained something uniquely daunting about an official gathering —entrenched tradition and watchful eyes overshadowing any single confrontation. Everything hinged upon the demonstration she and Lorand were about to give.

Lorand's gaze shifted to hers across the short distance, and he gave her a subtle nod—silent reassurance. She inclined her head in answer, exhaling to steady herself. The monarchy's envoy, Sir Remine, was in attendance, quill-inclined scribes likely at his side, ready to record every detail. And the baron had invited a throng of lesser lords, each hoping or dreading that Kallendore and Valecrest might at last step beyond centuries of mutual contempt.

"Lady Elysia," Mira murmured, leaning closer, "just remember the orchard—how you and Lorand worked together to calm the staff. This is only a grander stage, that's all."

Elysia curved her lips in thanks, recalling that orchard synergy and the relief on the workers' faces when Valecrest knights and Kallendore watchers patrolled in harmony. If they could do it there, they could do it here. She let out a final breath and moved forward, feeling Lorand step in pace with her as they reached the double doors that led into the baron's main hall.

A guard in the baron's livery opened them. Elysia blinked as she entered beneath the archway into a broad chamber of polished stone and tall pillars, illuminated by torches bracketed around the walls. Banners bearing Highdale's crest hung from overhead rafters, and a wide circle of seats surrounded a central dais. On the dais stood the baron himself, broad-shouldered, posture slightly stooped from age and frustration. Sir Remine stood to one side, watchful, his scribe perched at a small table with parchment at the ready.

All around, Elysia recognized familiar faces: lesser nobles from both sides, each faction wearing crest pins or color-coded attire—greens, crimsons, occasionally neutral browns from minor families who'd tried to stay out of the feud. In the front row, Elysia spotted her father, Lord Daryon, wearing his customary dark green robes. His face, lined with worry and a measure of pride, flicked to hers as she approached. On the opposite side, Lady Devia was seated with an erect spine, her attire formal and composed. Neither parent offered more than the faintest nod, but that was more than they might have done weeks ago, Elysia thought. Once, they couldn't have been in the same room without trading barbed words.

Gently, Lorand touched Elysia's elbow, guiding her toward the dais' steps. She reached the base of it, aware that every eye followed them. The baron raised his hand. "My lords and ladies," he intoned, his baritone carrying in the hush. "We gather today for a formal proclamation of cooperation between House Kallendore and House Valecrest. Given the sabotage we've all endured, and the monarchy's scrutiny, we must be certain no question remains about the sincerity of this alliance."

Elysia swallowed. A tense stir rippled through the seated onlookers—some Valecrest knights shifting in their chairs, some Kallendore watchers exchanging skeptical glances, a handful of neighbors she barely recognized leaning forward with curiosity. She didn't miss the faint flicker of disapproval in a few gazes. Even after Kester's downfall and the public revelations of sabotage, prejudice still lurked in corners.

Sir Remine took a step forward, slim figure framed by the torchlight. "Yes," he said, voice cool. "As the king's envoy, I have come again to observe how House Kallendore and House Valecrest implement the baron's directives. Too many times have we seen forced alliances unravel. This time, the monarchy demands a final, binding demonstration—one that leaves no doubt." He paused, letting that sink in. The hall stayed quiet.

Lorand stepped up beside Elysia, posture straight. "We're prepared," he said, loud enough for all to hear. "Let us show you how Kallendore healing and Valecrest discipline can merge for the good of Highdale."

A flicker of warmth registered in Elysia's chest in his certainty. She cleared her throat. "Yes," she added, and her voice carried surprisingly well. "If anyone still fears that Kallendore wards are illusions meant to trick or harm Valecrest knights, let them watch how we put our skills to use." She glanced at the baron.

The baron nodded, stepping aside. "I believe you requested that we bring forth the retainer injured this morning?" He turned, beckoning a squire waiting near the back of the dais. The squire disappeared behind the row of lesser nobles, then returned, guiding a Valecrest retainer —a young man named Gared, if Elysia recalled correctly.

He walked with a struggle, his right arm in a makeshift sling. Telltale lines of pain etched his features.

A hush fell again, punctuated by the retainer's labored breathing. Elysia's pulse sped. Even though she had performed healing a thousand times, never before had she done it under such an openly evaluative crowd, with Sir Remine's scribe ready to note every subtlety. The monarchy wanted proof, and they'd get it, but pronouncing healing spells in front of so many was still daunting.

"Come," Lorand said softly, motioning Gared closer. The retainer obeyed stiffly, face flushed—whether from pain or apprehension Elysia couldn't be sure. Lorand gestured for him to stand near Elysia. "Lady Elysia will see to that wound."

She forced a calm smile to reassure Gared. "You took a deep gash in sword practice, I understand?"

Gared managed a nod. "Aye, my lady. Cut across the bicep. The physician tried stitching it, but it tore again." His voice wavered with embarrassment.

From the corner of her vision, Elysia glimpsed her father seated with crossed arms, evaluating. She also noticed Lady Devia's unblinking stare. Let them watch, Elysia thought. Taking a steadying breath, she laid a gentle hand on Gared's shoulder. "I'll need to see it properly. With your permission?"

He swallowed and nodded. Carefully, she slipped the sling aside. Gared inhaled sharply as the slightest jostle sent fresh pain lancing through him. The cloth fell away, revealing a long slash bound haphazardly with bandages already soaked through. Elysia pressed her lips together—no wonder he'd been in agony. This needed thorough cleansing under normal conditions, but the monarchy insisted on drama, so here they were, midpoint in a grand hall. She shot Lorand a brief look of exasperation, but he only met her gaze with silent empathy, then gave Gared a steadying pat on the other arm.

"Easy," Lorand murmured to his retainer, quietly demonstrating the protective side Elysia had come to rely on. There was no scorn for her magic in his tone, only encouragement for Gared to accept healing from Kallendore's so-called "witch powers." A small, potent wave of gratitude coursed through Elysia. She steeled herself and focused.

"Hold still," she told Gared. In a fluid motion, she tugged open the bandage, revealing a raw slash along the upper muscle. The wound looked red and inflamed—likely from overextension during practice. She pressed her palm near the slash, ignoring the faint cringe from Gared as her fingers hovered an inch from raw flesh. Then she let her mind turn inward, summoning the gentle invocation she'd used so many times. She pictured the swirl of energies she labeled her "healing aura," an extension of the Kallendore gift. Magic tingled behind her eyes. Slowly, she exhaled, sending a warm pulse through her hand into Gared's torn muscle.

A hush fell across the hall so complete that Elysia heard her own heartbeat. Gared let out a strangled gasp—shock, not pain, for the warmth radiating through the wound would feel strange at first, like stepping into soothing bathwater after a day in cold armor. She concentrated, feeling how the magic threaded over torn fibers. She used another breath to direct that energy deeper, coaxing the muscle tissue to knit. Her chest squeezed with a mild ache. She'd done bigger healings, but it still cost her —especially with so many watchful eyes.

Gradually, Gared's breathing stabilized. The tension across his face ebbed, though he trembled under her hands. Elysia took another calming breath, letting the final wave of healing settle the surrounding tissue. Then she eased her hand away.

"It's done," she said softly, stepping back. She offered a cloth to Gared so he could wipe away the last traces of blood. As he gingerly tested his arm, the crowd leaned forward—some in awe, some with suspicion that any moment trickery might manifest. But Gared flexed his bicep with a look of mingled wonder and relief.

He stared at his forearm. "It... it doesn't hurt," he mumbled. A faint sheen of sweat dotted his brow, but the pain lines had vanished. He hesitated, then carefully rolled the shoulder, eyes going wide at the unimpeded movement. "Gods, that's incredible. It's like I never got cut at all—"

"Don't overstrain it immediately," Elysia advised, coaxing a half-smile. "Give it time to settle. But you won't need stitches anymore."

Gared swung toward Lorand, saluting with genuine gratitude. "My lord, I— My thanks. And to you, Lady Elysia." He bowed his head, voice hoarse with emotion.

At that, Elysia noticed the hush in the chamber had

shifted—from stiff suspicion to a rippling undercurrent of astonishment. A small dart of triumph blossomed in her chest. She could practically hear some watchful cynics reevaluating their doubts. Even so, she was painfully aware that a single demonstration might not fully conquer generational fear. Some watchers might call it a glamorous parlor trick. But many onlookers had to see that Gared's wound genuinely vanished under her gift, and he displayed no sign of mindless enthrallment—only gratitude.

She turned, meeting Lorand's eyes. The quiet warmth there steadied her more than any applause could have. In that look, she recalled how, in a far more dire moment, she had done something similar for him—risking her own life force to save him from a mortal wound. That day had changed them both. She swallowed, forcing her attention back to the crowd.

Sir Remine cleared his throat with audible skepticism. He stepped forward, scribes in tow. "That was... impressive. And quite thorough, from all appearances. The retainer can attest if the injury truly is gone?"

Gared braced his newly healed arm across his chest and gave it a full rotation. "Completely gone, sir," he declared, voice filled with relief. "No pain, no weakness."

The envoy made a small, thoughtful noise. "So, it seems." The scribes scribbled notes. Some lesser nobles muttered in the background, but Elysia caught glimpses of changing expressions. The man Gared had faced in the training yard that morning—another Valecrest soldier—

now stared as though everything he'd once believed about Kallendore magic had cracked.

Mira, still standing near the dais, offered Elysia a subtle grin of encouragement. Even the baron's features softened with something akin to pride. Elysia let out a low breath, more relieved than she cared to admit. One step done. She only hoped it would seal the argument that had circled for so long: that Kallendore "witchcraft" might be malevolent. Enough injuries had been alleviated by her hand to prove otherwise, yet the final wedge of doubt always lingered.

Before the hush devolved, Lorand stepped forward. "If that does not prove trust, I don't know what does," he said, letting his baritone carry. "Lady Elysia has no reason to sabotage our people. She stands ready to heal any Valecrest retainer as she would a Kallendore ally. That's the unity we're determined to uphold."

The retainer, Gared, nodded gratefully and bowed himself away, retreating to the seats. Elysia exhaled once more, focusing on calm as Lorand spoke again, addressing the assembled crowd. "Now, with the baron's approval, we'd like to formalize an arrangement that merges Kallendore watchers with Valecrest knights. A single vigilant guard—trained in martial discipline yet guided by Kallendore wards. No more separate patrols glaring at each other across the farmland. If we truly stand as one barony, we must demonstrate it day by day."

A few people stirred in their seats. Elysia watched how the lesser nobles assessed Lorand's words. She spotted one Kallendore uncle whispering something to his neighbor, but it didn't look outright hostile. And across the aisle, a Valecrest man in battered leathers scratched his chin, as if uncertain what to do with this concept but not outright condemning it either.

Lorand pressed on. "My knights will share watch rotations with watchers from Kallendore. We'll unify the chain of command so no sabotage can slip between the cracks. If Kester or any hidden conspirators remain lurking, we won't let them flourish in the gap between our houses."

Elysia felt her chest tighten at the memory of Kester's sabotage: the explosions in the festival courtyard, the staged illusions that tried to incite a riot against her supposed "witch powers." The monarchy's edict had forced her and Lorand together, but Kester had tried to tear them apart. Only by unmasking him had they proved a true alliance was possible. She prayed no new threat lingered in the shadows. At least not now, with Sir Remine scrutinizing every step.

Lord Daryon Kallendore cleared his throat. "And how, precisely, does this new guard handle farmland wards?" he asked, voice resonant, though not as confrontational as it might have been weeks ago. "Will Kallendore watchers still maintain magical protections?"

Lorand inclined his head respectfully in Lord Daryon's direction. "Yes, my lord. Elysia and her watchers will keep the wards that repel minor threats—rot, pests, or residual sabotage. Valecrest knights stand guard, ensuring the farmland's physically protected from bandits or infiltration." He paused. "We will share intelligence, so if watchers suspect foul play, the knight in command knows and can intervene. And if a knight spots suspicious magical residue, he calls on watchers to examine it."

A stir of hushed conversation spread across the hall, not all of it negative. Some watchers nodded, seeing sense in a system that leveraged both abilities. Elysia dared a surprised flicker of hope. It seemed that each time Lorand spoke, he chipped away at old grudges by simply acknowledging her house's specialized strengths. The baron took advantage of the lull, calling for an attendant to bring a ledger to a small side table. The baron's clerk hustled over; arms loaded with parchment.

TWENTY-TWO

"We have documentation here," the baron announced, "of the proposed schedules, roles, and responsibilities. I plan to sign an official record on behalf of Highdale. We'll present this plan to the monarchy. The new watch will begin immediate operation, with you, Lady Elysia, and you, Lord Lorand, overseeing its smooth implementation."

Elysia stepped forward, meeting the baron's gaze. "We're ready," she said. She didn't let herself think about how complicated it might be to coordinate so many watchers and knights. They would find a way. Because the alternative—letting fear and sabotage fester—had nearly destroyed Highdale before. She had no desire to repeat it.

A low murmur of acceptance rippled through the crowd, mingled with a few harder stares from older individuals. Elysia caught glimpses of doubt on some faces—like Sir Balin's scarred temple creasing with subdued wariness. Even so, no one voiced outright opposition. If a challenge lurked, it remained silent.

"Then let us do it," the baron said, and beckoned the clerk to set up a small table near the dais. Ink and quills were laid out. Elysia sensed a charged anticipation rolling through the hall, as though they hovered on the cusp of sealing an unprecedented pact.

Sir Remine approached, his scribe in tow. "Should you sign this record publicly, we of the monarchy's delegation will append an additional note verifying that Kallendore and Valecrest have acted in unison to bring stability. If all stands consistent, that note will depart for the capital in the next courier run, which may well finalize the monarchy's acceptance." He paused, scanning them. "You realize the king can still revoke the alliance if you backslide?"

A flicker of tension clipped Elysia's spine. She nodded, forcing composure. "We do."

Lorand's voice carried quiet steel. "We won't backslide."

The envoy didn't respond with a smile—merely a curt nod. "Very well." Then he stepped aside to allow the baron to seat himself at the small table. A hush fell like a drawn breath.

The baron gripped a quill, eyes flicking between Elysia and Lorand. "Before I sign, does anyone wish to speak for or against this measure?" he asked, glancing around the gathered assembly.

The hush stretched. Elysia's heartbeat drummed in her ears. Finally, one lesser noble from Valecrest's periphery coughed awkwardly. "We... we have concerns about trusting watchers with farmland wards," he began, posture stiff. "But after seeing repeated sabotage and how quickly Kallendore wards contained orchard blight, perhaps it's time we overcame that fear."

This earned a subdued chorus of agreement or at least wavering acceptance. From the Kallendore side, an older cousin of Elysia got to her feet, jaw set in a mixture of resignation and faint hope. "We also fear Valecrest men might strong-arm watchers on the roads. But if we do not try an integrated approach now, I suspect we never will. House Kallendore stands behind Elysia's decision."

The baron's gaze flicked to each side, satisfied. "Any further objections?" Silence. "Then let us proceed." He dipped the quill into ink. Elysia felt her breath catch as the baron's pen scrawled across the official record. Then, carefully, he set down his signature. Next, he offered the quill to Sir Remine, who took it and appended the monarchy's own notation of observation. Finally, the baron extended the quill to Elysia and Lorand in turn.

Lorand motioned for her to go first, his gray eyes offering encouragement. Heart pounding, Elysia approached. She bent over the parchment. The words might have looked dry or bureaucratic—guard rotations, farmland wards, orchard watch duties—but to her, they embodied everything she and Lorand had fought for. She signed her name, Elysia Kallendore, letting the ink settle as she lifted the quill. Then she stepped aside and watched Lorand produce his own signature under hers, a flourish that sealed House Valecrest's commitment. When he finished, a hush of finality pierced the air.

There it was. The official record of their cooperative watch, recognized by the monarchy's envoy. Elysia's pulse seized with a swirl of relief and a quiet, sharp longing for this to be truly real—for no lingering prejudice to sabotage them from within. She sensed the same tension in Lorand's stance as he straightened, signet ring glinting.

The baron picked up the parchment, holding it before him as if to show the watchers. "Then it is done. Let all present bear witness to this measure and abide by it." His voice resonated, and a wave of subdued applause rose around the hall. Not resounding or jubilant, perhaps, but applause, nonetheless. Elysia swallowed, her eyes prickling at the corners. This was more acceptance than she'd believed possible even a month ago.

In that moment, Lorand turned to her, eyes shining with unguarded warmth. She felt the hush ripple again, watchers and knights shifting, uncertain how to respond. Summoning quiet courage, Lorand lifted a hand to brush the backs of his fingers against her cheek.

Her breath caught at the tender contact. The baron had hammered out the official procedure, but Lorand's expression said something else—that he recognized the personal meaning behind all of this: the healing she had just demonstrated, the synergy of merging watchers with knights, the willingness they both had found to trust. Not from forced duty but from genuine choice.

He leaned in, cupping her cheek with gentle reverence. Elysia was dimly conscious of gasps from the nearest onlookers. She might have blushed, but she found herself stepping closer. The entire hall seemed to fade around them. Then his mouth met hers in a gentle, unhurried kiss. It wasn't a dramatic or desperate clash. Instead, it radiated a quiet, certain tenderness that stilled her heart and lit every nerve with a warmth that had very little to do with healing magic.

She could sense the surprise in the crowd—someone let out a startled exclamation, but no condemnation followed. The hush was laced with stunned fascination, perhaps even a reluctant acceptance that Elysia Kallendore and Lorand Valecrest truly meant to stand together. Her father, her Kallendore kin, the Valecrest knights, all bearing silent witness to a moment that hammered in so many final nails on the coffin of the old feud.

When Lorand pulled back, Elysia exhaled unsteadily, leaning into him just a fraction, eyes half-lidded with a rush of emotion. Electricity hummed in her every pore, not the raw, tangled fury that once sparked between them, but an abiding warmth that promised they truly had turned a page. A scattering of applause rose again, more emboldened this time, and she realized that from the dais, the baron wore a faint grin and fiddled with the newly signed document. Even Sir Remine looked grudgingly pleased, though he swiftly tried to school his expression into neutrality.

Finally, Elysia and Lorand stepped apart, just enough to address the assembly. The quiet swirl of acceptance was almost as staggering as any cheers. Elysia's lips tingled from that brief contact, her cheeks ablaze. She squared her shoulders, forcing her voice not to quiver. "Thank you," she managed. "We are... deeply grateful for the chance to bring order and hope to Highdale."

Lorand, looking likewise stirred but composed, inclined his head toward the baron. "As of now, House Kallendore and House Valecrest stand together." He let his gaze travel around the hall—pausing on stunned Valecrest knights, then on Kallendore watchers who had once threatened his men. "We shall see that this unified guard works effectively, and we encourage every retainer, every lesser noble, to support it."

A murmur of agreement rippled through the crowd. Elysia caught sight of her father's set jaw, but no outright scowl tinted his features. Perhaps even Lord Daryon realized it was futile to cling to the last shreds of an old feud when so much had changed. Across the aisle, Lady Devia Valecrest watched with a hint of resigned acceptance, her chin lifted. The baron cleared his throat, capturing their attention: "That concludes this formal proclamation. However, I'd welcome any final remarks from Kallendore or Valecrest."

For a moment, no one stirred. Then one Valecrest knight stood, a broad-chested older man with silver threading his hair. Elysia recognized him from prior guard rotations in the orchard. He rapped his fist on his chest in a sign of respect. "My lord Valecrest," he said to Lorand, his tone steady but touched by residual caution. "I was among those who doubted you, who feared Kallendore wards might lure us into dependence. But now, I see a difference. Let it be known that I, Sir Rellen, place my sword at your side and relinquish the old distrust."

The sincerity in his vow stirred something in Elysia's chest. She recalled that orchard shift when he'd refused her offer to mend his bruised ribs. Now, he stood publicly acknowledging her house's help. Perhaps old grudges could be undone, thread by thread.

"Thank you, Sir Rellen," Lorand said, voice tight with emotion. He put a hand over his chest in a rare display of heartfelt gratitude. Elysia had never seen him quite so close to letting raw relief break the shield of his composure.

A Kallendore mage—an older woman who'd once accompanied Elysia to farmland wards—rose, lifting her chin. "We, too, will do our part. I... regret the years we spent mistrusting any Valecrest presence on our grounds." She dipped her head in Elysia's direction. "If House Kallendore's heir sees fit to join with Lord Lorand, then we will heed her leadership as well."

Elysia felt a tremor run through her at so many turns of acceptance, albeit grudging or slow. The monarchy's forced betrothal had forced them onto this path, but only their own efforts—shared sacrifice, mutual healing, a willingness to stand against conspirators—had brought them to this day. She felt Lorand's hand brush hers, just for a heartbeat, under the watchful stares. Even that small contact grounded her.

The baron waited until the voices softened, then straightened in his seat. "Very good," he said, relief audible in his words. "We have the formal record. We have Sir Remine's witness. We have your signed agreement. Let any who doubt see how a single training yard and farmland ward system can strengthen Highdale, rather than tear it further apart."

Sir Remine, flipping through a small ledger, nodded once. "I shall return to the capital soon. My scribes and I will finalize a positive recommendation to the monarchy, verifying that, in my observation, your bond appears genuine." He glanced meaningfully at Elysia and Lorand. "But remember, I can only present the truth. If trouble arises after I depart, the crown still has the power to revoke your noble status—betrothal or not."

A flicker of defiance stirred in Elysia. She met Lorand's gaze, finding the same iron resolution there. "We understand," she said aloud. She doubted trouble would arise from either house now that they'd come so far. Unless, of course, a new fiend like Kester crawled out of the woodwork. But that was a fear for another day.

With that final warning, Sir Remine stepped back. The baron turned to the assembly and lifted his arms in a gesture of dismissal. "This session is concluded. You may remain to speak among yourselves or depart if you wish. Let it be known that official records of this new watch shall be circulated by tomorrow. My staff will be on hand to answer questions."

A wave of movement swept the hall as chairs scraped and people rose, some drifting forward to offer shy words to Elysia or Lorand, others grouping into quiet pockets. Elysia massaged the tension from her neck, half-shocked at how anticlimactic the release felt. Yet in a sense, it was a triumph. They had done it, publicly and legally. For weeks, she had dreaded the monarchy's final verdict—now, it stood within reach that they'd be free from further suspicion.

A swirl of lesser nobles approached a few politely bowing to Elysia. To her relief, most offered small acknowledgments of respect, or nods of agreement that farmland wards might prove helpful. Lorand, likewise, exchanged formal greetings with individuals from both sides. Elysia felt a new confidence in how the day had unfolded, even if a few suspicious glances lingered.

Mira appeared at her elbow, eyes shining. "Well done," she whispered. "That was more subdued than I expected. No shouting matches at all. Perhaps that final kiss hushed them better than any speech."

Elysia flushed. She wanted to protest that the kiss hadn't been intended purely to quell rumor—it was real. But she only let out a wry laugh, glancing around to ensure no one overheard. A moment later, her father approached. She braced inwardly, uncertain if he came to scold or congratulate.

Lord Daryon paused, arms folded in his robes, expression unreadable. For several heartbeats, he surveyed her face, then flicked his gaze to Lorand—who was occupied with a Valecrest cousin nearby. "That was... skillful healing," Lord Daryon said, voice carefully measured. "I sense you've refined your powers further since the orchard fiasco."

Elysia took a breath. "I've practiced as needed. My father, do you... object to this arrangement?"

A muscle in his jaw worked. "I object to our house being forced by monarchy decree. But I see you've found a measure of true partnership, even so." He let out a quiet sigh. "I only fear what the future holds. Our family has endured generations of mistrust, and it doesn't vanish with a single signature."

She studied his face. The flicker of paternal concern overshadowed the pride that usually dominated his features. "It won't vanish in a single day," she conceded softly. "But we can create something better if we keep pushing. Valecrest knights need not be my adversaries. They never did, strictly speaking. The feud persisted because... everyone was too proud to let it die."

"If you truly believe so, Elysia, then I'll stand aside. But watch yourself well." He paused, something akin to regret in his gaze. "I suppose I should also thank you for representing House Kallendore honorably. We remain in possession of our noble rights, in large part because you risked your gifts. Just... be cautious."

It wasn't exactly a paternal embrace, but it was as close to an olive branch as Elysia had ever seen in him on this matter. She dipped her head, feeling a pang. "I understand. Thank you, Father." Then he turned and drifted away, merging with a pool of Kallendore kin. Elysia released her breath. Their relationship would always be tinged with complexities, but perhaps a corner had turned.

On the dais, the baron spent a few minutes conferring with staff, then motioned for Elysia and Lorand. They approached, weaving through the thinning crowd. The baron wore a look of exhausted relief. "You both did well," he said in a low tone. "Today's demonstration will echo throughout Highdale. Now, finalize your guard plan. I'll dispatch official messengers to farmland outposts by dawn."

Lorand nodded. "We'll meet with watchers and knights tonight or first thing tomorrow. Darius can help coordinate. Elysia can begin adjusting orchard wards and farmland markers so watchers can find them more easily."

Elysia nodded, mind thrumming with a swirl of tasks: rosters, ward updates, farmland oversight. It might take weeks to fully train everyone. But she was oddly eager to begin. She realized she wanted to see Valecrest knights fully accept the wards, just as she wanted watchers to trust Valecrest steel at their backs. She'd grown tired of cautioning watchers to "mind the Valecrest scorn." Enough was enough.

The baron gave them a half-smile, relief pulling at the corners of his eyes. Then he stepped away to speak with Sir Remine's scribe. Elysia turned, finding Lorand at her side, gaze flicking over the receding crowd until it landed on her.

He offered a small, rueful half-grin. "So," he murmured. "All that remains is sustaining this unity in practice, day by day, so the monarchy never has cause to question it again."

She reached for his hand, ignoring the faint stares from passersby. "Yes. We'll show them. I have no desire to see a single orchard sabotaged again or a single farmland burned on account of old grudges." She hesitated, voice gentling. "And... thank you for that reassurance earlier, that moment we shared. It helped me more than I can say."

A slight flush warmed his cheeks. "You mean the kiss?" His tone carried an undercurrent of playful guilt, as though uncertain if he'd overstepped. "I couldn't help myself. The moment felt... right, I suppose. We've come so far."

She let her fingers squeeze his. "It was right," she affirmed quietly. Her heart still fluttered at the memory. The unspoken tension that had simmered from the start—initially expressed in anger—had transformed into something deeper and sweeter. Now, instead of fueling a feud, that energy fueled a budding union that neither had anticipated.

With a soft laugh, Lorand shifted to face her properly, ignoring the remains of the crowd. "You told me once that I was the proudest swordsman in Highdale. Perhaps that was true at the time. But I've realized that letting go of pride is not weakness. It's necessary if we want this to flourish."

Heart twisting, Elysia brushed her free hand lightly over his forearm. "And you once said you'd never rely on a Kallendore ward to save your life," she teased, remembering his older scorn. "Yet you've accepted my magic multiple times now, including a moment that nearly cost me everything." Her voice fell quieter, recalling the forest pass where she'd poured her life force into him to keep him alive.

He lowered his head in acknowledgment. "I'll never forget that. Not as a debt, but as a bond." He paused, searching her eyes. "Shall we step outside for a breath of air? The hall's grown stifling."

She peered around. Indeed, the throng was dispersing. She glimpsed Mira near the far corner, busily moving chairs aside with a few other staff, and Darius conferring with a Valecrest squire about rosters. The official portion was clearly over, leaving them in a swirl of logistical tasks. "Yes," she agreed. "Just a moment, please. Let me gather my wits."

They slipped past the baron's dais, greeting a straggling lesser noble who offered clipped but polite congratulations, then moved into the corridor. The stone hallway was quieter, lined with muted torch sconces that cast long shadows. Outside, through an open arch, the courtyard beckoned with early afternoon sunlight that slanted across the cobblestones.

Elysia inhaled the fresh air as they stepped into the courtyard. Only a few footmen bustled about, tidying up or carting supplies to the baron's storehouse. Overhead, a faint breeze rustled the banners. She felt the tension in her shoulders gradually unwind, replaced by moody relief. They had done it. The monarchy's final step—a thorough stamp of approval—seemed well within reach.

TWENTY-THREE

Lorand led her to a spot near the old stone fountain at the courtyard's center. Water trickled softly, mischievous droplets catching the sun. Elysia brushed her hand along the fountain's edge—cool, smooth stone. He turned to face her, expression thoughtful.

"We've signed so many documents these past weeks," he mused, "but this one truly changes Highdale. We finally have a formal plan to merge watchers and knights. No more living in fear that Kallendore magic undermines Valecrest steel, or that Valecrest swordsmen might harass watchers."

Elysia nodded, remembering the orchard staff's relief each time watchers and knights showed they could cooperate. "If the monarchy endorses it—and I trust Sir Remine's thoroughness—then we can build a lasting peace. Perhaps no lesser noble will attempt sabotage again." A wry twist shaped her mouth. "Though it seems there will always be some pockets of doubt."

He tilted his head, acknowledging the hard truth. "Yes. But doubt fades over time, given enough proof." He paused, glancing around, ensuring no eavesdroppers stood near. Then, more softly, "And we, you and I... how are you feeling about all this? The monarchy's scrutiny, the endless ceremony?" His tone carried more personal concern, not the official posture she saw him use with the baron or knights.

Her heart squeezed. "I'm... relieved, mostly. Exhausted. But—" She stilled, letting her free hand rise to lightly graze the front of his crimson tunic, feeling the steady beat of his heart underneath. "I'm also grateful. That enforced betrothal once felt like a prison. Now it feels like we've carved our own path out of it. We can love or not love at our own discretion, monarchy be damned. And I do choose... well, this. Us."

He exhaled, tension flickering across his features. She realized how rarely they directly named the shift in their relationship. For so long, it had been drowned by sabotage, conspiracies, and forced formalities. But now, they had a chance to breathe in the aftermath.

His hand settled around her waist, gentle but sure. "I choose it, too," he said, voice low. "I never planned to find real closeness in a forced union. But I can't imagine life without you now."

The honesty there hit her heart with quiet force. Elysia let her forehead rest against his chest momentarily, listening to his breath. "And we still have a thousand tasks," she said wryly, muffled in the folds of his tunic. "Merging watchers with knights, meeting farmland reeves, ensuring orchard wards stay stable. But yes... I want it all—this new future we're shaping." She pulled back, meeting his gaze. "Shall we get started?"

He brushed his thumb along her jaw, an affectionate gesture that made her breath hitch. "Yes," he whispered. "But first, allow me another small indulgence, if you're willing."

She tilted her face up, pulse fluttering. He leaned in, pressing his mouth to hers in a kiss more private than the one in the hall, but no less tender. She let herself melt into it, letting the hush of the courtyard embrace them. The fountain's burble, the gentle breeze, the distant rustle of banners overhead—everything seemed to cradle that moment of closeness. When at last they drew apart, Elysia's pulse thrummed, her lips tingling.

She smiled softly. "I suspect we can find many such moments, once all the watchers and knights are sorted out."

A slow grin curved his mouth. "We shall. Let them see we're not just performing for a monarchy scribe. This is ours to keep."

Stepping hand in hand away from the fountain, they headed back toward the keep's interior where Darius, Mira, and the baron's clerk were already sorting rosters. The remainder of the day stretched ahead, brimming with details for guard posts and farmland tours. Yet Elysia felt no dread at the prospect. If she and Lorand had emerged from sabotage, feuding relatives, and monarchy inquests with their bond still intact, then a day of administrative tasks was hardly foreboding.

Indeed, as they moved down the corridor, staff parted with respectful nods, and Elysia glimpsed the seeds of something new in their expressions. Fewer wary stares, more genuine acceptance. Not universal but growing. She recalled how, only weeks before, she'd walked these halls under suspicion, bristling at Valecrest knights who flung the word "witch" around like a curse. Now some of those same knights were prepared to sign up for the merged guard.

They found Darius in a small side chamber, hunched over a wide table cluttered with parchment. He straightened as Elysia and Lorand entered, saluting. "My lord, my lady," he said, voice wry. "I gather the official signing is done. Congratulations."

Lorand nodded. "Yes. Are you gathering the names of volunteers for the first integrated shift?"

Darius tapped the page. "I have eight watchers from Kallendore, some of them suggested by Lady Elysia's father. And from Valecrest, six knights who are open-minded enough to step in right away." He paused. "We can start them at the orchard and farmland closest to the keep, then expand as we see success."

Elysia peered at the list. She recognized a few watchers who had once been extremely wary of Valecrest. Surprising to see them volunteer so quickly. Perhaps the daily chaos had taught them that hostility gained nothing. She traced her finger down the names, nodding. "That's a good start." She glanced at Lorand. "Should we plan a brief orientation session with them tomorrow morning? Teach them how wards and watch rotations will overlap?"

Darius interjected, "Yes. I'd also suggest a second group for the night shift. We must not leave farmland unguarded once the sun sets—there's always a risk of bandits or leftover saboteurs."

Lorand grimaced. "True. Let's schedule it." He penciled a note next to Darius's list. "We'll talk to them, walk them through orchard perimeter markers, show them the wards so they understand it's not... some mind-control or anything ridiculous like that."

Elysia suppressed a chuckle, recalling how many times the orchard staff had questioned the wards. "I'll keep the incantations transparent," she said. "If they see me place a fresh ward, they'll know exactly what it does."

Darius nodded. "That will help. The more open you are, the quicker fear will fade."

They spent the next half hour refining schedules, marking times for watchers and knights to swap shifts, discussing how best to handle an emergency. Elysia felt an odd sense of satisfaction in the mundane practicality of it —a far cry from dramatic sabotage at festivals or near-fatal ambushes in a forest pass. Yet it all contributed to a sustainable peace. Mira joined them at some point, offering her own suggestions for farmland watchers who specialized in anti-blight wards. The subdued tension lifted each time Lorand or Elysia made an effort to incorporate feedback from both sides. By the time they concluded, a workable plan had taken shape.

As they folded up the final parchments, Elysia realized the sun had begun slanting lower. She glimpsed golden light streaming through a tall window, the corridor beyond tinted with late-afternoon warmth. The baron had likely retreated to handle an administrative dinner or greet lesser nobles before they departed. Sir Remine was probably reviewing notes to send to the monarchy. Elysia felt a twinge of tiredness behind her eyes—it had been a long day.

Mira, noticing her fatigue, set aside a quill. "You need rest, Elysia," she said gently. "You've performed a healing in front of half the aristocracy, fielded questions, and hammered out rosters. If you push yourself too hard, you'll risk magical burnout." There was a subtle worry in her tone, recalling how Elysia had once nearly overtaxed her life force.

Lorand's expression filled with concern. "Mira's right. You look pale, my lady," he said quietly, using that formal address in a tone that was anything but formal. "Why not retire for an hour or so? I can finalize a few more details with Darius."

Elysia suppressed a pang of guilt. She knew from experience that small spells, even a moderately sized cut healing, could accumulate in their toll. But she also knew her own limits better these days. "Perhaps half an hour," she allowed. "I can rest in the keep's smaller lounge, away from the bustle. Then we can reconvene at dinner to finalize anything urgent."

Lorand's eyes glinted with relief. "I'll escort you," he offered, then turned to Darius. "Stay here and ensure the second shift watches are confirmed. I'll be back shortly."

Darius saluted with a lopsided grin. "Understood. And

Lady Elysia—no pushing yourself further than you should."

Elysia mustered a grateful smile. "I promise." Then she and Lorand set off, navigating the corridor's mild bustle. They passed a handful of watchers and knights—some nodded politely, others peered curiously but no longer with suspicion. Down one flight of stairs, they reached a lesser-used hallway that led to a small lounge, usually reserved for visiting dignitaries who wanted brief privacy. A single guard stood posted near the door.

Lorand spoke quietly to the guard, who dipped his head and moved aside. Elysia entered the lounge, a comfortable space with a modest fireplace, two cushioned chairs, and a window overlooking the orchard in partial silhouette. The sun was dipping, painting the sky in soft oranges and pinks. She felt her tired muscles relax. The door clicked shut, leaving just the two of them in the hush.

She sank into one of the chairs, letting a slight groan escape. Her body ached from the tension of the day; plus, the magic she'd channeled into Gared's wound. Lorand set aside his sword belt—he never truly parted from his blade but resting it against the chair's side was enough to ease the weight from his hip. Then he lowered himself to the other chair, close enough that she could catch the warm spice of his presence.

"Rest," he reminded her softly. "Close your eyes if you must. I'll stay until you're ready to continue."

She leaned her head back against the cushion, letting her eyes slip shut for a moment. "Thank you," she whispered. "Not just for this, but for... everything today. You handled their questions about watchers and knights so gracefully." She pictured how confident he had looked, speaking of wards without a hint of condescension. She recalled how he'd kissed her in front of a hundred awestruck onlookers, sealing the new unity with a gentle vow. The memory sent a ripple of warmth down her spine.

"You're the one who courageously healed a retainer before the entire hall," Lorand said, voice resonating with understated pride. "I think you swayed half of them simply by letting them witness that." He paused. "I can't believe we've reached this point. If someone had told me a month ago that I'd publicly defend Kallendore wards and sign them into integrated guard duty, I'd have laughed them out of the training yard."

She opened her eyes, glancing at him. Moonlight would soon replace the sunset glow, but for now the traces of golden light edged his features, highlighting the flickers of humor in his gray eyes. "I would have firmly told them they were mad as well. Yet here we are."

They shared a smile. Elysia found herself wanting to savor the hush, the comforting knowledge that outside these walls, Highdale was taking its first genuine steps toward unity in generations. She could almost taste the relief of a barony that might finally put old grudges to rest.

"I'll only stay a few minutes," she said, "then we can find dinner. Or if you prefer, we could slip into the orchard before nightfall. Release some tension walking among the trees. We might see illusions if leftover sabotage lingers— though I suspect all those bursts have fizzled out."

Lorand nodded slowly. "A walk in the orchard might

do us good." His gaze shifted toward her mouth; a subtle flicker of longing that made her chest tighten. Ever since that moment in the hallway after the last inquest, she'd noticed how easily they gravitated toward each other in quiet corners—like magnets drawn by a force that neither fully controlled.

She let out a soft breath. "Perhaps after a walk, we can rejoin Darius, finalize the rosters, and be done for the day. We can let everyone see that we're truly functioning as one."

He leaned forward, gently curling his fingers around hers. "Yes. We'll do just that." A pause. "Elysia," he said softly, "I'm proud of us—truly. I never thought I'd say that out loud. But you've shown me how healing and might can coexist. I only wish the monarchy had realized it sooner, without forcing this betrothal upon us. Though —" he hesitated, "I also can't regret that it led me here, to you."

Her throat constricted. "Nor can I." She lifted his hand to her lips, pressing a delicate kiss to his knuckles. The gesture felt natural; a mirror of the comfort he so often offered her. As she lowered his hand, she caught the glimmer of emotion on his face. She marveled how, once, she had believed him cold and arrogant. Now, she recognized quiet depth and a fierce protectiveness that matched her own devotion to healing. The vow they had made, written on official parchment, was only an echo of the vow written in their hearts.

They stayed like that for another minute, exchanging hushed confidences until Elysia felt her mind clear of exhaustion. Then, steeling herself, she rose. "Come," she murmured. "Let's go see if the orchard is as peaceful in the twilight as it ever was. We can take that short walk and remind ourselves why we're doing this."

Lorand rose at once, collecting his sword belt and buckling it around his waist again, the metal discreetly clinking. He extended an arm. "Lead on, my lady."

Together, they left the lounge. The corridor was quieter than before, most staff presumably at mealtime. The single guard at the door saluted them briefly as they walked past, stepped out into the keep's courtyard, and then continued out a side gate that opened onto a gently sloping path. The orchard spread out in front of them, rows of leafy trees swaying in the mild breeze. Though the sun had nearly dipped below the horizon, the sky retained a faint shimmer of pink and gold streaks. Lanterns along the orchard path cast soft, flickering halos on the ground.

Elysia breathed in the smell of grass and ripening fruit. This orchard had witnessed so many tense moments and small triumphs—where sabotage blasts had once echoed, where watchers and knights had patrolled side by side. Now it felt calm, brimming with potential. She reached out to run her fingertips along a pear tree's bark, ensuring the wards were stable. A mild hum of protective magic vibrated under her touch. Good. No sign of meddling.

Lorand walked at her side, gaze scanning the horizon as though by habit. After a short distance, he let out a satisfied breath. "No sign of anything amiss. The orchard staff appear to have gone in for the evening. Are you finishing the day's ward checks?"

She nodded. "Just a quick pass. Then I'll be content to call it done." She paused under a curved branch, muttering a brief incantation to refresh a minor ward that helped repel pests. A faint glow shimmered around her fingertips, then diffused into the bark. She felt Lorand's presence close behind, warm and steady.

"You never tire of ensuring everyone's safety," he noted quietly.

She smiled, smoothing a hand over the newly pulsing rune. "I'm a healer. I thrive on ensuring well-being. Even if the injured party is farmland." She turned to face him. "And you, you never tire of scanning for threats."

His lips twitched. "I'm a swordsman. Protecting every vantage point is as natural for me as breathing. It's what I do."

She raised an eyebrow. "Then we truly are a fitting pair, aren't we?"

He let a soft chuckle escape, stepping closer so their arms brushed. "Yes, we are." Then, gently, he reached to tuck a stray strand of her hair behind her ear, letting his fingertips linger near her jaw. Her heart gave a sudden flutter. The orchard's hush slipped around them like a soft blanket, a moment of pure closeness, no baron's announcements or monarchy scribes. This place, at twilight, belonged to them and their fledgling union.

She pressed one hand lightly against his breastplate. "You're so warm," she murmured. A distant memory of that day in the forest pass flickered over her mind, him nearly dying in her arms, her magic draining dangerously to save him. And then the unfolding days, each new moment of trust bridging the yawning gap once carved by feuding families. They had come far indeed.

He freed a gentle sigh. "That's you," he said simply, covering her hand with his. "All your healing, your compassion. You warm everything you touch." His expression softened. "I love you, Elysia."

Her heart surged. She found she wanted to say the words back, wanted to tether them to the orchard hush. "I love you, Lorand." The confession spilled from her lips with a calm certainty that overshadowed all the forced formalities of the monarchy's betrothal. This was real. She stood on her own terms, choosing this path not because of a decree but because of the bond forged in bravery, synergy, and abiding care.

He dipped his head, brushing another kiss across her lips—soft, unhurried, tasting of orchard air and promise. She reciprocated, letting her fingers curl around the back of his neck, her pulse thrumming. The orchard's last bird-calls piped in the distance, but otherwise the world felt remote from them, as if time had briefly halted so they could rest in each other's arms.

When at length they parted, the orchard dimmed further, night's gentle cloak beginning to settle. Elysia inhaled deeply, steadying her breath. "Should we head back and find dinner, coordinate with Darius and Mira?"

He nodded, though reluctance flickered in his eyes. "Yes, we should. Before night is fully upon us. People will wonder where we've gone."

She laced her fingers with his, leading the way back along the orchard path. "Let them wonder. If it fosters a rumor that we're truly together, so be it." She still recalled how, weeks ago, every rumor had been that their betrothal was a sham. Now, ironically, the monarchy seemed convinced of their sincerity. She felt half-tempted to laugh at fate's twists.

Lorand snorted softly. "I don't think we'll have to worry about that rumor not spreading. Half the keep saw that kiss."

She grinned, letting the orchard's gentle quiet guide them toward the keep's gate. "Serves them right. We've done enough to prove ourselves. Maybe for once, rumor will become a force for good."

They strolled back through the orchard in companionable silence, stepping around the last patches of tall grass. Before long, they emerged at the keep's outer courtyard, where a few lanterns glimmered. Elysia spotted the main doors, warm light spilling out from within, hinting at supper in the works. As they ascended the steps, Elysia's stomach gave a little rumble, prompting a shared smile.

"Rest, dinner, then finishing up guard rosters," she recapped. "And after that, maybe we can find a moment to ourselves again, away from official eyes. I'll need more than one final walk in the orchard to recover from all this."

Lorand's expression brightened. "Agreed. We'll take it one day at a time," he said. "Tomorrow, we'll see watchers and knights form ranks side by side. I can't wait to see how that changes the mood among them."

She squeezed his hand. "It might be awkward at first, but we'll push through. If we've learned anything, it's that patience and steady devotion wear down old grudges."

They entered the keep's main door, the hallway glowing with torchlight. Voices echoed from the direction of the dining hall, presumably lesser nobles lingering for the baron's hospitality. Elysia suppressed a small laugh, imagining the swirl of conversation about the new "proclamation of harmony." She and Lorand were about to become the talk of Highdale once more, but this time for a reason that offered hope rather than fueling a feud.

She turned to Lorand, ignoring a flicker of startled glances from passing staff. "Let's face this dinner as though it's yet another orchard round—another chore that helps unify Highdale. Together."

He lifted her hand, pressing a soft kiss to her knuckles. The small, intimate gesture felt like a secret promise. Then he tucked her hand in the crook of his arm and guided her toward the dining hall. "Together," he said. "Always."

TWENTY-FOUR

Beneath the broad summer sky, Elysia Kallendore stood at the threshold of Highdale Keep's courtyard with jagged anticipation fluttering in her chest. A gentle breeze stirred loose locks of her dark hair, carrying the hum of a gathered crowd: farmers who'd abandoned their fields early, curious townsfolk eager for a glimpse of spectacle, even watchful noble cousins who had once scoffed at the notion of Kallendore and Valecrest forging anything that resembled real unity.

Yet here she was—on the cusp of making a vow that was no longer forced by parchment or monarchy but offered freely.

She took a slow inhale, savoring the mingled scents of wildflowers and the faint waft of roasting onions from a vendor near the outer wall. Above, bright pennants in swirling green and crimson rippled from tall poles: Kallendore's colors, Valecrest's colors, twined together. Within the courtyard's center, an arched trellis stood draped in ribbons—some vibrant green, some deep crimson. The baron's staff had spent the early morning weaving fresh sprays of small white blossoms through them, giving the arch a living grace.

Elysia's pulse gave a nervous thump. Moments from now, she would walk beneath that arch and speak vows that once seemed impossible to utter honestly. She swallowed, recalling a time when the very mention of Lorand Valecrest had provoked her frustration and pride. Now, her heart beat with a conflicting sense of thrill and gravity, as though the entire barony were poised at this same threshold with her.

Mira stood by her side, fussing with the final folds of Elysia's gown. The gentle friend tucked a loose strand of hair behind Elysia's ear. "You look radiant," she said quietly. Her voice trembled with genuine emotion. "Better than you did at the... the first ceremony."

A small smile tugged at Elysia's lips. That first forced betrothal, overshadowed by resentment and tension, felt like a lifetime ago. She could still picture the stiff posture of her father, Lord Daryon, in the crowd—how disappointed and furious he'd looked. She could recall the hush that fell when she and Lorand had exchanged the barest brush of a kiss, both of them bristling at the monarchy's imposition. Even so, the king's edict had been uncompromising, penned on thick parchment, and sealed in wax that threatened to strip both houses of their noble titles.

But the world had shifted, again and again, each shift forging a new link between her and Lorand. The memory sparked a flicker of warmth deep in Elysia's chest. She stepped forward, letting her fingertips graze the smooth, pale stone that formed the courtyard's outer staging area. People milled about; voices muted with anticipation. On a small dais near the arch, the baron waited with the town's clergyman. Off to one side, Elysia glimpsed a handful of Valecrest knights in meticulous formation, and beyond them, the swirl of Kallendore watchers.

She exhaled, and with a slight effort of will, calmed down the faint tingle of magical energy that coursed through her. She wanted to remain steady during the vow, not trembling as though she might unleash a healing spell by accident.

"Ready?" Mira murmured.

Elysia dipped her head. They moved into the open courtyard, crossing beneath fluttering pennants. The quiet that fell was nearly absolute. She spied Lorand at once. He stood beside the baron's dais, shoulders squared, clad in subtle Valecrest finery: a fitted tunic of crimson with gold piping, embroidered lightly across the chest. He wore no armor, but there was, as always, a disciplined poise to him. Elysia took in his short dark hair, the faint angles of tension in his broad shoulders—and, most of all, the quiet intensity in his gray eyes as he watched her approach.

Their gazes caught. Something inside her chest quivered, both bold and tender. He gave a slight inclination of his head, an unmistakable gentleness blossoming in the midst of all this ceremonial formality. She answered with a small smile she hoped would convey how deeply she shared that sense of reverent relief—that they'd survived to see this day.

Her father, Lord Daryon, stepped forward from somewhere near the dais to offer his arm. The lines of concern on his face, etched deeper by the months of tension, were softened by paternal pride. He gave her a grave nod, and though he did not speak, Elysia detected the flicker of acceptance in his eyes. Slowly, she placed her hand on his arm, allowing him to escort her the final steps toward the waiting arch.

Lorand's mother, Lady Devia Valecrest, also stood near the dais. She wore Valecrest's red in an elegantly cut gown that complemented her proud bearing. Elysia's father paused a step away from Lady Devia, and Elysia felt a swift pang of memory: once, these two had hardly been able to share a single corridor without spitting old grievances. Today, though tension still lurked in their gazes, there was an uneasy, grudging acknowledgment that their children had outgrown centuries of hate—and perhaps that was enough to earn a fragile truce between them as well.

The baron gave a somber nod, gesturing Elysia forward. She released her father's arm and ascended the dais next to Lorand. A hush rose among the crowd—a hush tinted with expectant warmth. The baron wore his official mantle, and beside him stood the clergyman in simple vestments. A slender stand of polished wood held the newly drafted parchment that bore the "final wedding" officialities. Elysia spared it only a brief glance. More important by far was the man at her side.

Lorand turned to her. She noted the faint swirl of color high on his cheeks, the slight shift in his posture. Once, she might have called him aloof, or haughty, or simply an unyielding soldier. But now she saw something else: an earnest vulnerability that spoke volumes. Elysia's heart fluttered, recalling the times she had seen him risk his life —for her, for the farmland, for the villagers who once jeered at Kallendore magic. She thought of the nights he'd stood by her while she gathered the energy to heal the wounded, how he'd pressed water into her shaking hands afterward, murmuring a soldier's reassurance in a voice gone unexpectedly gentle.

Gazing around, Elysia sensed the silence. The entire crowd, from the orchard workers to the traveling cloth merchants, nobles to baronial guards, seemed suspended in a single breath. Off to one side, Sir Remine, the king's envoy, observed with a critical yet tempered eye, scribes at the ready. Elysia felt a faint jolt of memory: that same envoy had expressed so much suspicion once, searching for any sign that this union was a fraud. Now, she caught the faint curve of satisfaction in his expression, as though even he couldn't deny that the closeness between her and Lorand had become palpable and real.

The baron stepped forward, raising both hands for silence. "We gather here today," he began in a firm, resonant voice, "to witness the true, final vows of House Kallendore and House Valecrest. As you all know, a royal decree once demanded this union. Yet in recent weeks, it has been proven by heart and deed that these two heirs stand willing to seal their bond not out of fear, but out of choice."

He paused, letting the breeze tug at the edges of his

cloak. "We have satisfied the Crown's requirements," he went on, nodding toward Sir Remine, "and we have the monarchy's recognition of Highdale's new peace. But" he said, turning to Elysia and Lorand, "today's vows are yours alone. No edict compels you to speak them. We gather to honor the pledge you give each other of your own free will."

A rustle spread through the onlookers, but no one spoke. Elysia breathed in, her heart pounding a slow, heavy rhythm. The baron met her gaze, then Lorand's. "When you're ready," he murmured.

Lorand offered Elysia a hand. She placed her palm against his, and a jolt of warmth ran through her, as if her magic had flared in gentle recognition of his presence. He pulled her a half step closer, each motion deliberate under the crowd's scrutiny. Then he turned to face her fully, expression open, storm-gray eyes reflecting a swirl of emotions she'd once thought impossible for him.

She licked her lips, drawing courage from the swirling green and crimson ribbons overhead. "My lord Lorand," she began softly, employing the formal address despite the closeness between them. Her voice echoed in the hush, carrying across the courtyard. "I stand before you not because of an edict, but because, through trials and storms, we've found something beyond grudges. In your steadfast presence, I learned that a Valecrest sword can defend more than a border—it can defend a life. My life." Her voice trembled. "You've saved me and accepted my magic when it mattered most. You've proven your loyalty to all of Highdale, and to me."

She paused, feeling tears prickle at the back of her eyes. Around them, the crowd lingered in breathless quiet. She swallowed and continued, "I promise to honor your courage, your discipline, and the oath that binds us not in resentment, but in hope. I vow to stand beside you, to heal and to protect as I can; to trust that together we mend what centuries of hatred tore apart. My father's house taught me healing is more than a spell— it's an act of faith. Today, it is an act of faith I give to you."

She finished, breath quivering, her gaze locked on Lorand's. Her cheeks grew hot, but she held that eye contact. The weight of the moment felt immense. The baron had told them to speak from the heart, and she had. No illusions, no forced stiff recitation. Only truth.

Lorand's hand tightened around hers. She felt the tension in his grip, the same mixture of awe and determination likely shining on her own face. He exhaled, shoulders lifting in a subtle gesture. Then, in a voice hushed but steady, he answered, "Lady Elysia, I once feared your magic, as Valecrest tradition taught me. I once believed the sword alone embodied honor. But you showed me there is honor in saving, not just in fighting. You risked your own life to heal mine,"—his voice caught— "and in that moment, I realized I would give anything to keep you safe. Not because the monarchy said so, but because my heart demands it."

A low undercurrent of murmurs swept through some watchers at those words. Elysia's throat tightened, recalling the day she'd poured her lifeblood into healing him, driven by more than duty—a moment that had changed everything between them.

Lorand swallowed, gazing unwavering at her. "I vow to protect you, not only from the threats we know, but from any future danger that lurks in Highdale. I vow to respect your power, to never again brand it 'witchery' or treat it with suspicion. I vow to build with you what our houses never imagined possible: a bond stronger than stone walls, built on trust, sealed in loyalty. We stand at each other's side now by choice."

He paused, breath trembling. "And I choose this," he said, voice rough with an emotion Elysia had rarely heard from him. "I choose you, Elysia."

Her ears rang with the force of those words. A deep flush spread across her cheeks, yet she did not look away. She was vaguely aware that her father shifted in the crowd, that Lady Devia's expression had gone very still, that the baron stood solemnly, and that distant watchers clutched at one another in near disbelief. Perhaps they had never expected this final wedding to ring with genuine emotion. But it did.

The clergyman, a stout, gray-haired man, stepped forward at a gesture from the baron, bearing a small cushion upon which lay the tokens they would exchange. Elysia recognized the silver band etched with Valecrest's crest. Her eyes flicked to the matching pendant engraved with subtle Kallendore runes. They had crafted these items quietly in the past days; she had spent hours working alongside a Kallendore cousin to ensure the runes were correct, and Lorand had personally supervised the forging of the band with a Valecrest swordsmith.

The clergyman cleared his throat. "These tokens," he intoned, "embody the union of two houses. Lady Elysia, you will offer the pendant, a gift that infuses Valecrest steel with Kallendore sorcery in the runes. Lord Lorand, you will offer the ring, marked with Valecrest's crest. May these tokens ever remind you, and all of Highdale, that from two traditions comes one pledge."

Elysia brushed her fingertips over the pendant, feeling its faint warmth. She watched Lorand lift the slim silver band, his eyes never leaving hers. Then, carefully, he slipped it onto her finger. Another wave of hush rippled through the courtyard while Elysia's heart hammered. The band was cool at first, then warmed almost instantly against her skin. A subtle engraving of Valecrest's crest—a small, stylized sword—rested on the outer surface, glinting in the afternoon sun.

She swallowed, her eyes shining. Then, softly, she lifted the pendant from the cushion, stepping forward. Lorand bowed his head so she could slip the slender chain around his neck. She felt the faint press of runic markings beneath her fingertips, the delicate glow of the magic etched into the metal. Though she had woven only a mild ward—a symbolic flourish—she sensed it hum faintly in resonance with the orchard wards she had cast days earlier. The chain settled against his tunic, and he raised his head, meeting her gaze with a quiet, reverent expression.

For a heartbeat, no one spoke, as though the entire

courtyard held its breath. Then the clergyman looked to the baron, who nodded. The baron's voice carried. "In the name of the Crown, and for the peace of Highdale, I declare these vows witnessed before all. May your partnership stand firm and enduring, guided by both steel and healing."

Stillness, then a swell of relieved applause, building from a few uncertain claps into a heartfelt ovation. Elysia's vision blurred with unshed tears as she and Lorand turned to face the courtyard together. Figures from both houses cheered, though some let out only reserved nods. She spotted a few watchers from Kallendore with proud smiles, even while Valecrest knights raised gauntleted hands in salute. The crowd's wave of applause carried a sense of real celebration, not mere forced compliance. Elysia caught sight of Darius cheering heartily among the knights, while Mira dabbed at her eyes with a handkerchief, her expression shining with warmth.

Sir Remine wore a look of professional satisfaction, offering a small but distinct nod as if acknowledging that the king's demands had grown from forced duty into something deeper than anyone had anticipated. Beside him, a scribe scrawled notes, face creased in wonder.

The baron stepped aside, indicating that Elysia and Lorand might conclude as they saw fit. Lorand squeezed her hand. He dipped his head, leaning in. She caught her breath. Part of her remembered the stiff, awkward brush of lips forced on them at the original betrothal, when tension had clung to them like a chain. This time, she raised her chin and met him willingly.

TWENTY-FIVE

The kiss was soft and unhurried, a gentle melding that seemed to release months of pent-up worry in a single exhalation. A sweetness—in the hush of her own heartbeat—filled Elysia. Applause rose again, and she felt Lorand draw her closer, a protective arm sliding around her waist without any hint of reluctance. She let herself savor the moment, let the crowd's presence blur, reaffirming that they had moved beyond the monarchy's decree and into their own choice.

When the kiss ended, she heard scattered cheers ripple again. The baron coughed lightly, though amusement tugged at the corners of his mouth, and the clergyman beamed like a proud grandfather. Elysia, cheeks glowing, took an unsteady breath, glancing sideways at Lorand. His own cheeks were faintly flushed, a half-smile lurking on his lips. She read in his expression that same sense of relief and promise.

They stepped down from the dais together. Lord

Daryon approached first, face set in its usual stern lines, but his eyes gleaming with uncertain pride. He bent, pressing a formal fatherly kiss to Elysia's brow. "My daughter," he said gruffly, adjusting the emerald-edged robe at his shoulders. He darted a look at Lorand, gave a small, measured bow, then stepped aside. She recognized the tension in her father's posture, but also recognized it was the first time he had bowed in any sense to a Valecrest. A step forward, but in its own quiet way, momentous.

Lady Devia stepped forward as well, regal in her bearing. She inclined her head to Elysia, then let her gaze settle on Lorand with a flicker of maternal tenderness. A faint smile softened her mouth. "My son," she murmured, "and Lady Elysia. You have proven more than I expected." Though her voice was subdued, Elysia sensed a measure of acceptance in her tone—a willingness to see that Kallendore's "witch powers" were not the threat she had once believed.

Then the throng pressed in. In a swirl of color and movement, local villagers and minor nobles formed a winding line to offer their respects, well wishes, and a flurry of small gifts—bundles of orchard fruit or woven charms for good fortune. Elysia found herself half-laughing, half-breathless as she thanked them. Her mind spun with the realization that they had truly done it. The final wedding vow was spoken, not shackled by dread but bright with promise.

She glanced up to see the sun sliding toward midafternoon, golden rays painting the courtyard with a warm glow. In one corner, a few Kallendore watchers opened a hamper of fresh flowers, distributing them to the younger children bounding in excitement. Across the courtyard, Valecrest knights poured out small cups of spiced wine from an ornate pitcher they'd brought for the festival. If someone had told her months ago that these two groups would stand amicably beneath the same arch, celebrating a union they once despised, she would have scoffed.

Yet here they were.

The baron, wiping sweat from his brow, found Elysia amid the bustle and offered the slightest wink of encouragement. Then he signaled for a handful of attendants to bring forward two large tables loaded with fruit tarts, honey bread, and roasted meats for an informal feast. Today, apparently, he was determined that the wedding would be more than a rigid ceremony. Laughter broke out among the crowd as the baron's staff hurried to set up a small array of benches. Some local fiddlers stepped forward at the baron's prompting, adjusting their instruments with shy grins.

Lorand guided Elysia toward the table, his hand settling at the small of her back. She felt a tingle of awareness at that casual intimacy, recalling how once his mere nearness had spurred defiant tension in her. No longer. She drew in a steady breath, letting the hum of the day settle around her. Couples or small groups began drifting over from the dais area, forming a loose circle around the fiddlers. The first notes of a lively tune filled the courtyard, and children squealed, grabbing each other's hands to dance in clumsy circles on the uneven cobblestones.

"Are you all right?" Lorand murmured, a voice low near her ear.

She turned. A grin tugged at her lips. "Overwhelmed," she admitted. "But—happy." She flexed her fingers, letting the sunshine play over the new silver band on her hand. "I never imagined this day ending in anything but stiff politesse."

Lorand's mouth curved gently. "Nor did I. But it seems we've made a real celebration of it." He gave a slight tilt of his head, scanning the courtyard. "The baron has outdone himself," he observed, "and so have half the villagers. Did you see the orchard workers bring crates of fruit?"

Elysia nodded, feeling a surge of affection for the people of Highdale. They had endured sabotage and rumor, yet many had chosen to trust in this new alliance. She spotted old Salander, one of the orchard's caretakers whose farmland she had personally warded, now beaming as he offered pears to a knight in Valecrest colors. The sight sparked a warm ache in her chest. This was exactly what she'd hoped for from the start: not forced truce, but actual cooperation.

A cluster of well-wishers paused near them, inclining their heads in shy greetings. Elysia recognized one, a local caretaker named Bren, who had once glowered at her for "witch meddling" in his orchard. Today, his posture radiated contrition and awe. He presented her with a small cloth-wrapped bundle. "Lady Elysia, my family humbly thanks you for all you've done," he said, voice wavering. "A gift from our orchard—the best apples I could pick."

Touched, Elysia parted the cloth, revealing rosy apples

that gave off a sweet, earthy scent. "Thank you, Bren," she replied gently, remembering how reluctant he'd been to let her set wards among his trees. "I'm so glad to see your orchard thriving again."

He bobbed his head, then turned to Lorand. "And, my lord Valecrest, we... we appreciate your knights protecting us when traveling merchants came through. We never expected to see Kallendore watchers and Valecrest knights side by side. It... it heartens us all."

Lorand accepted the gratitude with a subdued nod. "We do what we must to keep Highdale safe," he said, though Elysia caught the flicker of genuine humility in his eyes. Bren withdrew, smiling at them both.

As the man departed, a group of youngsters raced past, squealing and weaving through the crowd, clutching ribbons. Elysia exhaled a quiet laugh, stepping aside to let them swirl around the dais. Lorand shifted closer, a protective reflex. The fiddlers launched into a quicker tune, and the baron beckoned people to partake in the newly arranged food.

Elysia cast a sidelong glance at Lorand, considering whether to slip away from the immediate throng for a moment's peace. But then she noticed one more figure cutting through the crowd: Sir Balin, the older knight who had practically raised Lorand. The scar at Balin's temple gleamed faintly in the sun, and his posture was typically stiff. Elysia braced herself; she remembered how strongly he had resisted the forced union earlier.

Sir Balin came to a stop before them, helmet tucked beneath his arm. His expression was guarded, but not hostile. At last, he offered a short, formal nod. "My lord Lorand, Lady Elysia…" He cleared his throat. "I won't pretend I didn't doubt this union. But I see now that you stand together by true choice, not merely for the monarchy's sake. Today's vow… it cements a new future for House Valecrest."

Elysia inclined her head. "Your acceptance means much," she said softly. She could see how much it pained him to relinquish old prejudices.

Sir Balin's gaze flicked from Elysia to Lorand, lingering on the faint glow of the runic pendant at Lorand's chest. "You wear Kallendore's magic so openly," he commented, voice subdued. "If you find it beneficial… well, I must trust your judgment, Lorand. The realm changes, and I must change with it."

Lorand's expression softened. "Balin, you taught me half of what I know. I value your presence here. This union doesn't erase Valecrest's proud history—it builds upon it."

Sir Balin studied them, mouth pressed in a thin line, then gave another curt nod. "Then I shall do my part to ensure it thrives." With that, he withdrew, posture carefully neutral. Elysia watched him depart, suspecting that was as close to an open blessing as he might offer. Still, it felt like a small but significant victory, a sign that even Valecrest's staunchest defenders could move forward.

A light tap on Elysia's shoulder made her turn. Mira stood there, eyes shining. "They're setting up those benches near the orchard gate," she said, pointing a short distance off. "Seems the baron wants to extend the festivities past the courtyard. Would you two like a moment to breathe? There's a smaller path behind the orchard if you need quiet."

Elysia looked at Lorand, who raised an eyebrow. "Shall we?"

She nodded gratefully. They padded away from the immediate throng, weaving between chattering well-wishers, and stepped beyond the courtyard's edge. A small gate in the woven fence led out to a strip of grass that skirted the orchard behind the keep. The orchard's crooked apple trees, their branches heavy with early summer fruit, formed a quiet canopy that offered a welcome respite. Only the faint notes of fiddles drifted after them, muffled by the gentle rustle of orchard leaves.

Once they'd gone far enough that the bustle lay behind them, Elysia released a soft exhale. She turned to Lorand. "I never thought it would feel like this," she admitted, voice catching. "The orchard, the vow... everything is so different now. A few months ago, I could barely look at you without remembering the forced ceremonial vow and how it chafed at my pride."

He slipped his hand into hers, a gesture increasingly natural. "I know," he said quietly. "I remember how furious I felt, believing Kallendore wards threatened Valecrest farmland, believing your magic overshadowed my training. But the more we fought side by side, the more I realized how hollow those beliefs were."

They reached a spot where gnarled branches formed a low arch overhead. Dappled sunlight slipped through the green leaves, casting playful shadows on the grass. Elysia leaned against a sturdy trunk, a gentle hum of living energy drifting in her senses—less a formal magical ward than the orchard's natural vigor. Lorand stepped close, his new pendant glinting. She couldn't resist touching it lightly with her fingertips, feeling the faint thrumming presence of runic lines.

"How does it feel?" she asked softly, eyes drifting up to his.

He gave a small, almost self-conscious shrug. "Oddly comforting," he admitted. "I know it's just a symbolic ward you inscribed, but… it reminds me that you're here, that we protect each other. And I don't fear it, not anymore."

Her heart squeezed with affection. She recalled the day he'd first looked upon her wards with suspicion, muttering under his breath about illusions and curses. Now, he wore Kallendore runes on his chest. Carefully, Elysia slid her hands up to rest on his shoulders. "I'll never forget that you accepted me, and my magic," she said, voice quiet. "Truly accepted it, not just tolerated it. That's how I know we can help build a better life for Highdale."

A quiet hush settled. He bent his head, letting their foreheads touch. The orchard air felt warm against her cheeks. "And your father?" he asked after a moment. "Do you think he'll remain at peace with all this?"

Elysia took a thoughtful breath. "Father is stubborn," she replied. "But he also loves me, and he's seen that my healing caught no trick from Valecrest. He can't deny that I stand here by choice. House Kallendore needs acceptance, not isolation, if it's to endure." She nodded gently. "He'll find a way to reconcile with it, I believe. Over time."

Lorand's arms slipped around her waist, the orchard's hush wrapping them in a bubble of closeness. Elysia felt the comforting press of his breath near her temple, the subtle shift of muscles beneath his tunic as he eased his posture. The sense of quiet intimacy, away from the humming courtyard, made her heart flutter.

Her mind skimmed over the last days: preparing this final vow, ensuring they included gestures from both houses' traditions, not merely staging a theatrical show. She remembered drafting parchment with the baron, ensuring no mention of the monarchy's threat overshadowed the actual ceremony. She remembered the hush of the library as she carefully lettered runes onto Lorand's pendant. Each recollection brimming with the knowledge that their wedding, at last, was truly theirs.

"When you said you choose this," Ephona said softly, slipping on a playful note to her voice, "did you imagine we'd be waltzing around orchard trees moments after?"

Lorand's quiet laugh warmed her ear. "I never pictured an orchard waltz, no," he said. "But I find I'm not opposed to it." He lifted his head, a teasing glimmer in his gray eyes. "We look quite official in these clothes, though. I'm not sure orchard grass and wedding finery mix well."

Elysia snorted softly. "We endured far harsher terrain in road-weary garments. I'll risk the orchard grass for a moment of peace if it means we can savor this." She clasped his hands, stepping into a gentle sway. Far off, faint music from the fiddlers carried on the breeze— enough for them to form an approximation of a slow dance.

They moved in unhurried circles, the orchard's soft light illuminating the shifting expression on Lorand's face. Elysia felt a fluttery mix of contentment and disbelief. Here they were, in a swirl of orchard hush and celebration, forging a quiet dance that no one else might see. The final wedding vow might have ended, but for her, the deeper vow persisted in each breath she took alongside him.

Soon, the music's echo wavered, the courtyard hush reminding them a festival still beckoned behind the orchard. Reluctantly, Elysia slowed her steps, letting her hands slide down from Lorand's shoulders. He bracketed her waist gently.

"We should head back," she murmured. "The baron might worry we've vanished. And we do have a feast to attend. People will line up to speak with us for hours, I suspect."

Lorand's mouth quirked in a rueful smile. "True. Let's not be wholly antisocial on our wedding day." He lingered one more moment, brushing a tender kiss to the edge of her neck. The sweetness of it sent a current of warmth through her body, almost enough to coax her into ignoring all the well-wishers. But an upsurge of faint cheering from the courtyard reminded her that half of Highdale was waiting. With a final shared smile, they turned and meandered back the way they had come.

By the time they reached the courtyard gate, the atmosphere had evolved into a bustling mix of laughter and informal chatter. A few bold souls had formed a dancing circle near the fiddlers, stomping clapping rhythms on the cobblestones. The baron presided over the tables with an air of triumphant relief, urging passersby to fill a plate and enjoy the day. Elysia caught glimpses of Valecrest knights sampling honey bread, Kallendore watchers sipping spiced wine, and villagers weaving through them all without fear.

TWENTY-SIX

As she and Lorand stepped back into the throng, a small wave of renewed cheers and polite nods rippled around them. Many parted to make way. She felt her cheeks warm under so many gazes, though her heart brimmed with gratitude. Part of her recognized that this final wedding was, in a sense, the entire barony's healing, not merely her own union. Kallendore and Valecrest standing together in unguarded fellowship—imperfect, but undeniably hopeful.

Darius appeared, a broad grin slanting across his face as he stepped close. "My lord, my lady," he greeted them in an audibly teasing tone. "We missed you at the table. The baron is making an impromptu toast soon. Are you prepared?"

Elysia exchanged a glance with Lorand, who inclined his head. "We are," she said, summoning a lighthearted smile. "Lead on, Darius. Let's hear the baron's words."

Darius nodded, gesturing for them to follow. They

traced a path around the edge of the courtyard, passing clusters of lesser nobles. Some watchers' eyes flicked uncertainly, but Elysia recognized a hint of softening in their expressions. More than once, someone pulled Lorand aside to offer a hearty clap on the shoulder or paused Elysia with a respectful half-bow. The mood was neither stiff nor forced. She caught a swirl of orchard-scented air in the breeze, and the sun gleamed off the polished silver ring on her finger.

They reached the table where the baron, perspiring from the heat yet smiling, cleared his throat. The baron raised a modest cup of spiced wine, calling for attention. He beckoned Elysia and Lorand to stand with him so the onlookers could see. Lord Daryon and Lady Devia edged nearer, each wearing carefully composed expressions, though Elysia detected hesitant approval in her father's stance.

The baron's voice carried easily, shaped by years of corralling feuding nobles in Highdale's halls. "People of Highdale," he said. "Our realm has known strife—but today, we celebrate a vow spoken freely: the union of Elysia Kallendore and Lorand Valecrest. We have witnessed how they overcame sabotage and rumor. How they risked themselves for each other and for our farmland, orchard, and common folk. Let none say this union is mere ceremony."

A brief cheer rose. Nearby, Elysia glimpsed Mira clapping enthusiastically. The baron nodded, acknowledging the applause. "May this final wedding," he continued, "remind us of all that old grudges need not define the future. May we learn to harness Kallendore magic for healing, Valecrest might for defense, and so preserve Highdale's prosperity. Raise your cups, if you will, to the newlywed heirs who have shown us the better path."

Cups lifted all around. Elysia's throat tightened at the wave of applause that followed, heartfelt and warm. The baron winked at her, then stepped aside as the cheering continued. She felt Lorand's hand brush against hers in a gentle show of solidarity. The crowd parted slightly, allowing them to step up to the table.

Before Elysia could muster a reply, she heard her father's voice behind her. "Elysia," he said, subdued. She turned and saw that Lord Daryon stood there with his arms clasped behind his back. "And Lorand," he added, inclining his head toward his new son-in-law. "You... have given the barony a moment of calm I did not believe possible. My hopes—" He paused, words catching. "May you be happy. Truly."

Elysia felt a wave of emotion rise. She reached out, gently resting a hand on her father's forearm. It was the most vulnerable she'd seen him in a long time. "Thank you, Father," she said quietly. "I hope House Kallendore can find new ways to flourish with Valecrest, not in spite of it."

Lord Daryon looked at Lorand a beat longer, lips pressed tight, then exhaled. "I stand by my daughter," he said. "And so, I pledge to stand by Valecrest—for as long as you keep her safe and respect our traditions. Let there be no more talk of grudges."

Lorand bowed respectfully. "Her safety is my promise.

And together, we'll ensure Kallendore's healing arts thrive. You have that from me."

A flicker of acceptance crossed Daryon's features before he turned with measured dignity and wove back through the crowd. Elysia let out her breath, looking up at Lorand with a small, relieved smile. Another thread in the tapestry of centuries-old distrust had just been cut free. One by one, these gestures set the stage for real reconciliation.

Lady Devia approached next, capturing Lorand's hand and analyzing the new pendant he wore. She brushed her thumb over the runic lines, then looked to Elysia. "I never thought I'd see my son wearing such a piece," she commented in a soft tone. "But it suits him." She lifted her gaze to Lorand's. "You do seem... content, my son."

Lorand nodded, the corners of his mouth curving into a faint but genuine smile. "I am, Mother," he said. "Thank you. And for allowing House Valecrest to stand with Kallendore, even after all we believed."

A moment of stillness passed. Then Lady Devia released Lorand's hand and inclined her head to Elysia— an unspoken acceptance. She, too, slipped away into the swirl of well-wishers, leaving Elysia and Lorand to breathe in this moment as the newly recognized heads of a single alliance.

The baron's staff pressed cups of chilled cider into their hands, encouraging them to partake. Elysia sipped, letting the sweet tang roll over her tongue, her pulse gradually settling. She watched the swirl of music, the drifting conversation, the genuine fellowship bridging two houses that once stood at sword's length. Something about it felt surreal and perfect, an ending and a beginning.

Lorand leaned in, murmuring near her ear above the chatter, "Would you like to sit? I know you used a little magic earlier to keep your wards on the orchard. You mustn't tire yourself too much."

Her heart melted at his concern. "I'm a bit tired, but we'll see. Let's greet a few more people first." She turned, hooking her arm in his. He accompanied her, weaving them into the crowd, exchanging words with lesser nobles who offered carefully worded blessings. Others approached shyly, hoping to catch a moment with the famed "healer-lady" and the "steadfast knight." Their praises blended together, leaving Elysia slightly dizzy with gratitude.

At some point, a young orchard girl with braids, no older than eight, tugged at Elysia's gown, face alight. "Is it true you can cure blight in one wave of your hand, Lady Elysia?" she whispered in awe.

Elysia knelt, ignoring the protest of her formal skirts, and said softly, "A wave of my hand, plus a bit of help from the orchard's own strength—and a bit of time. Magic can't do everything alone."

The girl beamed. "That's still amazing," she said, hugging a small sprig of blossoms to her chest. "I like your wedding." Then she darted off, joining another child. Elysia rose, feeling her eyes sting with tears that threatened to overflow. She hadn't realized how dearly she longed for acceptance in the eyes of the young, of future generations unburdened by centuries of feud.

Time slipped onward. The fiddlers took turns with a traveling harpist, weaving melodies that lulled the crowd into an easygoing celebration. Trays of food were passed, wine and cider poured, and Elysia found herself frequently near Lorand's side, exchanging small touches and private smiles. Each contact underscored that they were no longer forced to maintain distance or stoic formality. Even the monarchy's envoy was satisfied, which meant they could move freely and openly as newlyweds in their own right.

Finally, the day's glow softened toward a gentler light. Purple shadows began to stretch across the courtyard, a hint that evening lay in wait, though the festival still showed no sign of stopping. The baron, flushed with success, was cajoling a handful of watchers to attempt a dance with the Valecrest knights. Elysia spied Mira, laughing as she coaxed a reluctant cousin to try a short reel. The orchard caretaker Bren hovered at the edge of the dancing circle, looking uncertain but cheerful.

Lorand glanced at Elysia. "It's going to continue well into the night," he observed, voice warm with contentment. "But we can slip away soon if you need rest."

She eyed him teasingly. "You're always concerned with my rest. I might not be as fragile as you believe, my lord Valecrest." But the affection in her tone softened any rebuke. Truth be told, she did feel the stirrings of magical fatigue at the edges of her consciousness—and an even stronger desire for quiet time alone with him, away from so many eyes.

"Not fragile," Lorand conceded, brushing a playful kiss

against her temple. "Strong. Braver than I ever imagined. But everyone needs respite after a day like this."

She smiled. "One last dance," she murmured. "Then maybe we can vanish—for a short while, at least. We can always rejoin them if we like."

Lorand's gaze grew heated in a gentle way, and he took her hand. A new tune began, a lilting melody that Elysia recognized as an old festival dance. This time, she did not hesitate. They stepped onto the courtyard's makeshift dance floor, joining a swirl of couples forming sets around them. If there was any remaining tension in the watchers, it was lost amid laughter and swirling skirts. Elysia surrendered to the music's rhythm. Lorand guided her deftly, an arm around her waist, steps measured but fluid.

With each turn, Elysia felt more certain that from this day forward, the old feud truly lay behind them. She saw it reflected in the eyes of onlookers, in the unguarded way Valecrest and Kallendore officers mingled, in the orchard caretaker dancing near a Valecrest knight. The sense of blossoming unity was deeper than any forced truce. It was real.

When the dance ended, Elysia's lungs fluttered with exhilaration. Laughing softly, she leaned into Lorand's side. He led her clear of the circle, giving a polite nod to those who turned to congratulate them. Then, with Elysia's hand tucked in his, they slipped quietly through a side archway that led to a corridor connecting the courtyard to the living quarters of the keep. No guard tried to stop them, and no one in the courtyard seemed to mind that the newlyweds were taking a moment away.

At last, the stone corridor enveloped them in cool shadows. The echoes of music dimmed, replaced by the gentle hush of footsteps on old flagstones. Torch brackets lined the walls, though most were unlit in the midday-into-evening glow. Lorand paused near a tall, arched window. A hint of orchard-scented breeze floated in, rustling the hem of Elysia's gown.

Silence stretched. She turned to Lorand, letting the swirling tension of the day's formalities seep away. Her gaze dipped to the silver band on her finger. She touched it lightly with her other hand, marveling at how naturally it fit. Then she looked at the runic pendant at his chest, glimmering faintly in the dusk.

"One union, shared by both houses," she said softly. "And no monarchy forced it this time."

He answered with a quiet laugh, yet his eyes shone with sincerity. "No. We forced ourselves, in a manner," he teased gently, "by realizing we stand stronger together."

She smiled, sliding her arms up around his shoulders. "We do." The corridor hush felt intimate, her heart thudding at the nearness of him. She recalled their orchard dance, the words they'd shared. She recalled the vow he'd spoken, how it resonated with her deeper than any formal pledge. "I'm yours," she whispered, pressing her forehead to his. "By choice."

His breath caught. "And I'm yours," he echoed. Then he cradled her cheeks, tilting her face up, and kissed her— a slow, lingering seal upon a promise they had already made in the courtyard. Elysia closed her eyes, letting the sun-warmed hush cradle her. The swirl of orchard leaves, and festival music lingered in the distance, but here in this quiet corridor, the only reality was the soft press of his lips, the heat of his palms at her jaw, and the gentle spark of magic that flared inside her chest.

When they parted, she let out a trembling breath. "Ready to face the rest of them?" she murmured. "Or do we vanish entirely?"

A wry smile twisted at Lorand's lips. "I think we owe them some presence," he said, "but not all day. The barony will soon realize we need a private moment. A wedding feast can last hours—maybe we'll slip back to greet the others, partake in a final toast, and then vanish. We have a lifetime to accomplish great things, but for now, it might be enough to share a quiet evening."

She couldn't agree more. Together, they strolled back to the threshold connecting the keep's corridor to the courtyard. Through the arch, the music soared. People danced, drank, and laughed, forging new bonds across the previous rift. Elysia felt a kinship with them all: for they, too, were part of this transformation, forging a barony no longer shackled by old grudges. The orchard's sweet tang beckoned, reminding her that seeds of unity, once scattered, could flourish into something strong and enduring.

Stepping through the arch, Elysia and Lorand returned to the swirl of festival joy. A small circle of watchers greeted them with raised cups. She glimpsed her father, standing near Lady Devia, both of them wearing reserved but unmistakable expressions of acceptance. She caught

Mira's shining grin, the baron's hearty wave, and the flicker of relief in Sir Remine's stance. Everything converged into a single, resounding thought: This vow was truly theirs.

And so, they stepped into the gentle roar of applause, hand in hand, forging onward. The final chords of the wedding day drifted around them, each note echoing brightly with promise. After so much tension, so many forced steps, this moment felt like the first breath of open air. And with the orchard's rustling leaves, the swirl of bright banners overhead, and the press of Lorand's steady arm at her side, Elysia Kallendore Valecrest—she realized she should start thinking of it that way—smiled with her entire being, knowing that from this day forward, she walked into a future shaped by mutual trust, abiding love, and a vow that no foe or old feud could ever tear apart.

CHAPTER

TWENTY-SEVEN

Elysia Kallendore Valecrest stirred the coals in the makeshift brazier, the warmth crackling just enough to illuminate the old barn's interior. Winter had not yet arrived, but the nights were growing cooler. She could feel the temperature shift in her bones—a subtle reminder that the harvest season was ending and that Highdale's villagers would soon hunker down for colder months. A few oil lanterns cast gentle, dancing lights across the array of wooden tables inside the barn. Each table was lined with a handful of neatly folded cloths, pestles, glass jars, and small pouches of herbs, all set out for her first official training session with the local volunteers.

Outside, twilight lay across the farmland like a woolen cloak, the fading amber sky streaked with purple and gray. In the distance, she could hear laughter from the baron's courtyard, echoing across the crisp air. The orchard behind the keep was in the midst of another mild celebration—though in truth, it felt like Highdale had been celebrating for weeks. From the day she and Lorand Valecrest had spoken their final vows before a gathered crowd, a renewed sense of hope had taken root in the barony. Some townsfolk called the optimism a reflection of "Highdale's new dawn," but Elysia tried not to let the flattery overwhelm her. After all, she and Lorand were hardly miracle workers. They were just two heirs who had chosen to end a pointless feud.

A swirl of satisfaction nudged at her heart as she spied Mira stepping into the barn, arms full of fresh linen. Mira's eyes danced with excitement, her mousy-brown hair slipping from her pinned style. She was no longer just a watching presence; she had become Elysia's frequent partner, assisting with the new clinic they had set up in this once-abandoned barn.

"Just in time," Elysia called softly, setting aside the long spoon she used to stir the hot coals. "We'll need those for bandages, or for warming compresses if any travelers arrive late tonight."

Mira brushed a stray lock from her face. "The orchard festivities show no sign of slowing," she remarked with a conspiratorial grin. "I saw at least a dozen Valecrest knights and half as many Kallendore watchers improvising some sort of dance under the lanterns. If you'd asked me months ago whether I could imagine that I'd have called you mad."

A smile lifted Elysia's lips. "I would have agreed. Seems we are all somewhat mad together, then."

She moved along the central table, double-checking

each mortar and pestle. The new clinic aimed to unify local knowledge with Kallendore healing spells that Elysia quietly taught her volunteers—men and women from both Kallendore and Valecrest lineages, and even a few from other minor families scattered across Highdale. She had spent the last few days walking them through the basics: identifying common medicinal roots, combining them with arcane wards safely, and learning small, simple incantations that would not threaten or scare people. Some watchers—a little uncertain about openly sharing Kallendore's magical methods—had raised questions at first. But Elysia reminded them that knowledge saved lives. Stubborn pride saved no one.

"In an hour or so, I expect them to wander in," Elysia said, glancing at the empty barn door. "We have half a dozen farmers who said they'd volunteer. And perhaps two Valecrest knights from the night shift. If they can learn a few basic healing teas or poultices, it'll spare them from traveling all the way to the keep whenever someone bruises a shoulder in training."

Mira nodded. "I'll set these cloths near the washing basin, then. Darius was by earlier—he mentioned some returning patrol might come in with mild scrapes. They ran into brambles clearing a trail."

"I'll be ready," Elysia promised. "Thank you, Mira."

She watched as Mira darted away; arms loaded with linens. The barn's wide interior smelled faintly of straw and old wood, a comforting scent that reminded Elysia of all the farmland she had striven to protect. She recalled how, only a few months past, these fields were threatened by sabotage and swirling rumor. But the crowning moment—exposing Lord Kester's machinations and forging a true bond with Lorand—had changed everything. Now, a hush of relative peace blanketed Highdale, giving Elysia and her newly formed watchers' group the chance to do genuine good.

The memory sparked a soft glow in her chest. Several weeks had passed since her final wedding vows to Lorand. The monarchy, in the end, had given its full endorsement, courtesy of Sir Remine's favorable report. In a single dispatch, the king reaffirmed House Kallendore and House Valecrest's noble status, praising their "example of unity." So, the monarchy was, for the time being, satisfied. More importantly, the people of Highdale had begun to accept that Kallendore wards and Valecrest swords could genuinely be allies.

A gentle breeze drifted through the barn door, and Elysia stilled at the sound of footsteps approaching. A familiar shape appeared in the threshold—tall, broad-shouldered, wearing a slightly dusty tunic of crimson with gold trim. Lorand Valecrest. He had evidently come straight from the training yard or an evening patrol; a streak of dust grazed one forearm, and his hair was slightly mussed from the wind. Elysia's pulse gave a subtle leap. Even now, after weeks of calling him husband, she found she was not immune to that little jolt whenever their gazes locked.

"Hard at work again," he greeted, stepping inside. His voice was pitched low, laced with an understated warmth she'd grown to recognize. "I expected to find you at the orchard, celebrating with our neighbors. Instead, you're cooped up here, making sure these pestles are aligned perfectly."

She let out a slight laugh. "Hardly perfect. But with the new volunteer healers, I want everything prepared. I suspect at least half of them have never ground an herb properly, let alone combined it with arcane wards."

Lorand came closer, leaning a hip against the central table. The lantern flame highlighted the faint lines of fatigue around his eyes, but also the soft curve his mouth made whenever he was near her. "You never rest, do you?" he teased gently. "Might be better if you took at least one evening to enjoy the orchard's music or the baron's hospitality."

"I suppose I learned from Valecrest discipline," she shot back with a playful edge. "Never letting my guard down, always forging ahead." Then she paused, glancing at him with genuine concern. "Though I might say the same about you. Have you eaten? I heard you were out at the far border."

He exhaled, mouth twisting ruefully. "Darius and I led a small patrol near the footbridge. We discovered a collapsed cart that belonged to wandering peddlers. Nothing sinister—just a broken axle. We helped them fix it. One of the peddlers recognized me from the festival, gave me a carved trinket as thanks." He lifted a small wooden token from his belt pouch—a rustic carving shaped like a stylized orchard tree. "He said it was 'for luck.'"

The sincerity in Lorand's tone made Elysia's heart tug.

She remembered how, before, villagers would have glared at a Valecrest soldier or at a Kallendore mage with equal amounts of distrust. Now they offered tokens of gratitude. The shift felt surreal. She rubbed her palms together for a moment, as if brushing away the memory of those more hostile times. "We'll need all the luck we can get," she remarked softly. "Despite all the progress, I still hear stray rumors in the market—some hush that Valecrest's swords might eventually turn on us, or that Kallendore wards are controlling the farmland. Bare pockets of distrust, maybe, but it lingers."

Lorand's eyes flickered. "Yes, there will always be a few who cling to old grudges. But each day, fewer people listen to them. We're proving that real unity is possible."

She studied his expression. The lines of his face bore that subtle determination that had once intimidated her, back when everything between them was mandated by the monarchy. Now, though, she knew that same determination shielded a protective heart and a calm sense of leadership. "I'm grateful," she said quietly, "that we have the chance to show them, day by day."

He reached out and brushed his hand over her arm, a casual, gentle contact that still sent a flicker of warmth through her body. The day's efforts weighed on both of them, but she could sense his devotion bolstering her, urging her to keep forging ahead.

"How is the orchard tonight?" she asked, changing the subject. "Still lively?"

Lorand let out a short laugh. "More than lively. The baron has three fiddlers, a drummer, and a small choir from one of the hamlets. I think they intend to keep the party going well into the night. I nearly had to dodge a young Kallendore mage who insisted on teaching me some rustic dance steps."

She huffed, amused at the mental image. "I'm sure you handled it with all the Valecrest grace you could muster."

He gave a light shrug. "Crowds or dancing are not my favorite things. But" his tone softened, "I am learning."

The corner of her mouth curved. "Yes. We both are."

A distant rumble of laughter drifted through the open barn door, no doubt from the orchard festivities. Elysia felt a momentary pull to join them—to see the orchard's lanterns shimmering overhead, to observe watchers and knights mingle, to soak in the fruit of their labor. But then her gaze traveled to the supplies on the table. She was keenly aware that the baron's orchard gatherings were hardly the end goal. She wanted a real chance to integrate watchers and knights, not just in guard rotations but in aspects of healing and farmland stewardship. Merging everyday herbal knowledge with subtle wards would ensure that no sabotage—for instance, leftover illusions or tainted fields—could fester unnoticed.

"Lorand," she said, more quietly, "would you stay a moment? Barring any new upheaval, that is. I could use your help with something."

He nodded. "Certainly. Anything."

She motioned him to follow her to a smaller side door that led to a lean-to storage area. Out there, she had organized bundles of dried herbs and jars of salves donated by villagers. "I've arranged what we have so far," she explained, lighting another small lantern. "But we need safe storage for a few more potent items that watchers use in wards. They're not strictly dangerous, but in the wrong hands, someone might claim we're hoarding some 'witch brew.' I'd like a locked chest or trunk—something with combined wards. Perhaps your knights can craft something with sturdy metal bands, or a hidden latch?"

Lorand took in the mismatched crates and sacks. "Yes, Darius might know a carpenter or blacksmith who can reinforce a storage trunk. But if we want wards on it, I'll need to coordinate with one of your watchers. Or you, if you have time."

"I'll do it," she said firmly. "But we'll need a knight's presence for the forging. The whole point is to create a trunk both sides trust. And maybe we'll officially declare it a joint resource for farmland solutions. If we label it as 'Kallendore only,' that inflames suspicion." She paused, memories of the old prejudice swirling in her mind. People had once believed she would hex them at a whim. "No sense letting those rumors rise again."

"You've learned how Valecrest minds work, haven't you?" Lorand said softly, a trace of wry humor in his tone. "Transparency. Let them see the trunk, see the wards, so no illusions can be spun."

Elysia closed the small door behind them, stepping back into the main barn. "Precisely." She set the lantern on the long table. "So, yes, if you'd do me the favor of gathering your best craftsman. Or share input yourself. But enough shop talk," she added, turning to fix him with a curious glance. "You said you nearly got roped into dancing. Did you manage to escape entirely?"

His mouth curved into a faint, wry grin. "I might have promised them I'd return with you." A mild flush touched his cheekbones. "They insisted that we, the newlyweds, should share at least one dance under the orchard lights to bless the harvest season. Apparently, we're responsible for all manner of good luck now."

Elysia's heart gave a twinge at the notion. "They're probably waiting for us, then."

He gave a half-shrug. "We can always slip in, do a polite dance, slip out. Unless you'd rather stay here. I understand the volunteer session starts soon."

She cast a look around the barn, noticing again how quiet it was. "We can spare a bit of time. If the volunteers arrive, I suspect Mira can entertain them with a primer on each herbal station. She's quite capable of explaining the basics until we return."

Lorand offered his arm—an old-fashioned gesture. She laid her hand lightly on it, letting him guide her toward the barn's front exit. As they crossed the threshold, a hush of night air welcomed them, along with the distant glow of lanterns from the orchard behind the keep. Now that the sun had fully set, the sky was a tapestry of navy-blue lit by pinpricks of stars. The hush enveloped them as they walked the short distance from barn to orchard, enclosed by the faint chirp of crickets and the crunch of gravel underfoot.

TWENTY-EIGHT

When they neared the orchard, the murmur of voices grew. Lanterns hung from low boughs, each offering a soft circle of golden light. Dozens of men and women—some in Valecrest armor minus the helmets, some in Kallendore's green-hued attire—mingled in a half-formed circle near a musician's makeshift stage. The swirling notes of a fiddle drifted, joined by a lively drum. The orchard's sweet perfume hung in the air, reminiscent of blooming flowers and fruit-laden branches. It felt both festive and peaceful, a combination Elysia had rarely seen in Highdale's gatherings before now.

A cheer went up from a cluster of watchers when they spotted Elysia and Lorand approach. A few knights joined the cheer, ushering them forward. The fiddler caught sight and launched into a new tune, more playful than the last.

"Dance, newlyweds!" someone near the front called. Elysia caught Mira's grin amid the crowd, and she had the fleeting urge to scold her friend for such well-meaning meddling. But laughter welled in her chest, mingled with the gentle pressure of Lorand's arm around her waist.

"Seems our presence was indeed requested," Lorand murmured, leaning close so only she could hear. "Shall we?"

She took a breath, scanning the orchard to see her father, Lord Daryon, standing a little way off, a neutral if faintly bemused expression on his features. Lady Devia Valecrest, Lorand's mother, was not far from him, looking more composed. Together, they formed the older generation whose acceptance had long been uncertain. But they did not protest. Elysia saw a subtle nod from her father, as though acknowledging that perhaps all these orchard festivities and swirling dances weren't as frivolous as he once believed them to be. A surprising softness in his gaze glimmered for an instant before he turned to speak with someone else.

Finally, Elysia returned her attention to Lorand. "Yes," she said with a small smile. "We shall."

He guided her into the circle of dancers, an area left clear among the orchard's roots and scattered blossoms. The fiddler played a lilting melody with a steady beat, a reel that required easy, swaying steps. At first, it felt slightly awkward—Elysia was more accustomed to formal steps in a keep's great hall. But the orchard's atmosphere was more rustic, full of laughter and improvised twirls. Knights and watchers alike took up partners. Lorand placed one hand on her waist, the other holding her hand, and they began to move.

She let out a breath she hadn't realized she was holding. Surrounded by warm lamplight, the hum of good spirits, and the faint aroma of crushed grass, she found herself swept up in the moment. Lorand's footwork was careful but surprisingly graceful—a far cry from the stiff soldier's posture he used to carry when forced to stand at attention. Elysia felt her heart flutter. He guided her gently in a series of turns, the orchard's branches overhead forming a canopy that flickered with each lantern's glow.

At a pivotal crescendo in the music, they spun in place. Elysia's laughter escaped, blending with Lorand's low chuckle. Every swirl of her skirts, every subtle shift, echoed the synergy they had discovered in so many battles. Only this time, it was not to parry or cast wards, but to celebrate. She felt the orchard's soil beneath her slippers, nearly bursting with gratitude that such peace had even become possible.

The tune slowed after a minute, merging into a calmer sequence of notes. Dancers parted or switched partners, but Lorand drew Elysia closer, ignoring any unspoken social norm. She let him hold her in a gentle sway, content to remain. The orchard's silence pressed around them, the rest of the crowd momentarily distant. She spotted the baron across the clearing, leaning on a staff reminiscent of a conductor's baton, just observing with an almost fatherly grin. The baron's exhaustion from months of tension seemed to have lifted, replaced by relief that the monarchy had recognized Highdale's progress.

As the final notes of the fiddle trailed off, a smattering of applause rippled through the orchard. Elysia and

Lorand stepped apart, though he kept her hand in his, the warmth of his palm steady. Valecrest knights in the crowd gave a few hearty cheers, while a couple watchers chimed in. Panting lightly from the dance, Elysia cast a grateful nod toward them, feeling her cheeks glow.

One of the watchers, a woman who had recently volunteered for farmland ward duty, beckoned them over. "Lady Elysia, Lord Lorand—please, try some of the orchard's cider," she called, holding out a wooden mug. "It's from apples your father's orchard staff saved last season, now expertly pressed."

"Thank you," Elysia replied, stepping forward to accept the mug. She took a measured sip. A crisp sweetness spread across her tongue. She offered it to Lorand, who also sampled it. Then he passed it back, letting out a contented sigh. Around them, the orchard glowed with the promise of a new season, unspoiled by sabotage or secrets.

Soon, the crowd returned to dancing, the fiddler launching another lively tune. Elysia stepped away from the center, moving to the orchard's edge, near a row of softly glowing lanterns. Lorand stayed with her, watching the swirl of dancers. It was mesmerizing—Kallendore watchers and Valecrest soldiers, noble cousins and farmhands, all weaving in a shared circle. The faint stamp of feet on grass replaced old tensions with a single communal rhythm.

She leaned toward Lorand, voice low. "If someone had shown me a vision of this orchard half a year ago—

knights and watchers dancing under the same lanterns—I would have laughed. Or maybe believed it an illusion."

He grunted quietly in agreement. "I likely would have assumed it was a trick of your wards," he admitted, lips quirking in wry humor. "Yet here we are."

They drifted a bit farther, stepping out of the main ring of torchlight, passing a few orchard trees that offered privacy. Elysia could still hear the music, but it was more subdued here, the chatter of the crowd muffled. Overhead, the sky gleamed with bright starlight. She came to a stop near a trunk laden with nearly ripe apples. Leaning a hand against the bark, she breathed in the orchard's cool air.

Lorand stood beside her, his expression gentle in the moonlit hush. "You look tired," he observed softly. "But not in an unhappy way."

She sighed, half-smiling at his perceptiveness. "I am tired—there's so much to do each day. Coordinating watchers and knights, training local volunteers in basic wards, receiving reports of farmland improvements. Yet I feel alive in a way I never did before." She glanced up at him. "My father used to say that a Kallendore must always carry a weight of duty. But it doesn't feel like a burden now, not with you there to share it."

He reached out, brushing his knuckles softly across her cheek, the tenderness of the gesture igniting warmth in her chest. "I never thought I'd be grateful for a forced marriage," he murmured. "Yet I can't regret anything that led to this."

Their gazes locked, and for a moment, the orchard's

distant music and laughter faded. Elysia's pulse throbbed with quiet intensity, the memory of the dance still swirling in her veins. After everything they had endured—open hostility, sabotage, doubters demanding proof—this sense of closeness felt almost miraculous. Gently, he bent his head, and she rose onto her toes, meeting him halfway in a soft, unhurried kiss. The orchard air pressed around them as they lingered in that sweetness, the hush broken only by the faint hum of fiddles in the distance.

Eventually, they eased apart, and Elysia's cheeks warmed, though not from embarrassment. She savored the moment, letting out a small breath. "Shall we get back? The barn volunteers might think we've abandoned them."

He nodded, but a flicker of reluctance glinted in his gray eyes. "Yes, we probably should." Then he captured her hand in his. "But if they complain—tell them your husband demanded a single dance first. They can blame me."

She let out a soft laugh. "Oh, they'll likely just be thrilled to see us both. People seem enthralled by the notion of the 'healer-lady' and her 'resolute knight-lord' working together. I can't say I'll ever grow used to that sort of attention."

Lorand led her back toward the orchard's center, weaving through the crowd. Another wave of music rose as the fiddler changed tunes once again, but Elysia only gave a nod of greeting to a few watchers, quickly explaining that she needed to return to her tasks. The orchard dwellers didn't protest. Instead, a wave of friendly smiles and "thank you for everything" followed them. That alone was enough to twine a sensation of warmth in her chest.

They skirted past the keep's courtyard. The baron beckoned them with a raised cup, but Elysia gestured apologetically that she had to go. The baron offered a good-natured shrug and raised the cup in salute. From the dais behind him, she noticed Lady Devia Valecrest standing with her back straight, possibly discussing the day's farmland updates with Lord Daryon. They, too, merited a cordial wave—though Elysia suspected it would take time before either house's older generation felt entirely comfortable. Still, at least they all shared these orchard festivities without flinging barbed remarks.

Soon, Elysia and Lorand were walking back across the dirt path to the barn, the breeze carrying faint echoes of fiddles behind them. She breathed in the cooler air, grateful for the respite from the orchard's press of bodies. Overhead, a few errant clouds drifted across the moon, painting fleeting shadows on the ground.

They stepped inside the barn to find it much busier than before. Lanthorns had been lit along the makeshift wooden racks, illuminating the group of volunteers ranging from a handful of watchful Valecrest knights to a few Kallendore watchers in green sashes to local villagers in simple homespun clothes. Mira stood near the center table, describing the differences between lavender buds for salves and mug wort to ward off mild illusions. To

Elysia's relief, the newly arrived volunteers seemed engaged—she could see them carefully leaning in to examine each herb. At the far edge, a few had begun rummaging through the mortar and pestle sets.

Their arrival caught Mira's eye. "Ah, here they are!" she announced, waving Elysia and Lorand over. "Everyone, you already know Lady Elysia—she's the reason this barn is a real clinic now. And Lord Lorand, who ensures we keep it well-stocked and well-protected."

A ripple of polite greetings passed through the volunteers, though Elysia sensed that many of them looked at Lorand with faint awe. Valecrest knights who, a few months ago, would have eyed her warily now nodded in respect. Meanwhile, watchers who once bristled at Valecrest "brute force" studied Lorand with open curiosity. This was precisely the synergy Elysia had dreamed of: a space where no one panicked if an incantation was mentioned, nor scowled if a knight's sword clinked in the corner.

Mira turned to Elysia. "I was just finishing the overview of basic herbs. Perhaps you can demonstrate a small healing rune? Then these folks can see how wards might be embedded in ordinary salves."

With Lorand at her side, Elysia stepped to the table. "Of course." She drew a round piece of thin cloth from one of the jars. "For those who haven't seen it yet, this is the simplest example of Kallendore's layering technique. We take a pinch of dried herb—let's use comfrey for minor bruises—and place it here." She sprinkled a little ground comfrey onto the cloth. "Then we speak a focusing phrase.

Not a grand incantation—just a whisper that channels the healing aura. If you're not a Kallendore mage, don't worry. You might not produce the same glow, but your intention can still help."

She glanced up, noticing that a few volunteers were following with rapt attention. In the corner, a Valecrest knight with a bandage around his forearm seemed especially interested. Possibly he had fought bandits years back and never once considered that a "witch's method" could help him. Elysia suppressed a smile. How the world changed.

Repeating a soft phrase, she moved her fingertips over the comfrey-laced cloth. The hum of her healing magic stirred in her chest, flowing nestled at the edges of her consciousness. The cloth glowed faintly gold for a heartbeat, a shimmer so subtle that it might be dismissed as a trick of lantern light. Then she pressed the cloth to her own wrist, pantomiming how one would secure it with a bandage. "If you secure this for about an hour, the swelling reduces, the bruising alleviates faster. No illusions, no traps—just a gentle healing impetus."

A murmur spread around the group. One older woman —whom Elysia recognized as a farmer's wife from near the orchard—ventured forward. "Could you show me that phrase again, my lady? I'm no mage, but my child gets scrapes all the time."

"I'd be happy to," Elysia answered, guiding the woman in pronouncing the short phrase. She explained that the power was minimal, far less strenuous than the advanced spells that once took a toll on her life force. "Even if you can't conjure the glow, your mindful focus can help direct the herb's natural efficacy," she emphasized. "It's not the same as a full Kallendore ward, but it's a start."

Lorand observed from the side, arms folded in a relaxed posture, occasionally offering quiet remarks. Whenever one of the Valecrest knights asked if it was "truly safe," Lorand chimed in with reassurance that he'd relied on Elysia's spells himself during raids, living proof that no one was enthralled or cursed. A subdued wave of relief seemed to pass through those assembled. At times, the evening's lessons felt almost surreal to Elysia—teaching watchers, knights, and farmers side by side. If only the monarchy could see this real integration.

They spent nearly an hour walking the volunteers through basic herb preparation. Elysia assigned them tasks: some practiced measuring proper amounts of crushed leaves, others repeated the short focusing phrase while bandaging a volunteer's arm. Meanwhile, Lorand tested small shifts in the barn's layout, ensuring the table positions allowed enough space for a wounded visitor to lie comfortably. Occasionally, he teased that Elysia's perfectionist streak rivaled even Valecrest discipline, to which she mock-glared.

At one point, a Valecrest knight approached Lorand, murmuring about a separate supply wagon that might bring more bandages next week. Elysia let them speak quietly, moving on to help a young watcher measure thyme. She heard snatches of Lorand's conversation: a calm, practical discussion about inventory and guard rotation. Yet the lightning rod of old tensions was nowhere to be found. The Valecrest knight, who once might have ridiculed Elysia's "witch paraphernalia," now spoke of how best to store it safely. Her heart glowed with cautious pride.

By the time the training session wound down, the barn was aglow with lamplight, the brazier's coals burned low, and the orchard music had become a distant echo. A half moon hung high, casting silver stripes through the barn's rafters. Elysia dismissed the volunteers with quiet thanks, encouraging them to practice carefully on small bruises or mild aches in the coming days. They left in twos or threes, some discussing how they might replicate the short focusing phrase at home, others swapping suggestions for storing herbs. The sense of camaraderie was unmistakable.

Finally, only Elysia, Lorand, and Mira remained. Mira yawned dramatically. "Effective session, I'd say," she said, rearranging the leftover supplies. "Though it's well past full dark. Tomorrow, we can restock these herb bundles. Elysia, would you let me copy your notes on comfrey proportions? I think a few volunteers want them in writing."

"In the morning," Elysia promised, stifling her own yawn. "Thank you, Mira."

Offering them both a bright smile, Mira excused herself, no doubt returning to the orchard or perhaps the keep's guest chambers. The barn door swung shut behind her, leaving Elysia and Lorand in the warm hush. The coals in the brazier glowed faintly red, accompanied by the faint smell of heated metal and herbs.

"What an evening," Lorand commented. "You taught a crowd of people to harness arcs of healing, answered every question calmly, and even found time to dance in the orchard. Your father would be proud."

She gave a soft hum. "He's shifting, isn't he? Slowly letting go of centuries of prejudice." Her gaze drifted over the now-empty barn. "I never would have believed we could accomplish all this so soon. There's still so much to do, but... it no longer feels impossible."

Lorand nodded, stepping closer. "Agreed. And you do realize you're an inspiration to them? Each time you show how these wards are safe, how your gifts help the common folk, the old rumors fade faster."

His closeness made her heart skip. In the barn's dim glow, the planes of his face looked both strong and gentle. She reached out to trace a faint smudge of dust on his tunic. "After what you did—leading joint patrols, forging alliances at the border—my watchers see you as an exemplar too. Some of them told me you're the first Valecrest knight they ever trusted with farmland watch schedules."

He brushed a soft kiss against her forehead, an unhurried gesture. "That means more to me than they know," he murmured. "I spent years believing I had to mistrust Kallendore wards. Seeing watchers accept me as an ally is... unexpected and welcome."

She closed her eyes briefly, letting the warmth of his presence soothe the weariness of the day. "Together," she whispered, "we'll keep building. This clinic, these lessons, the farmland checks—it's not just for show. It's for Highdale's future."

"Indeed." He tightened his arms around her, gently tucking her head under his chin. They stood for a moment in that shared silence, the hush filled with the barn's subtle crackles. Elysia felt the strong beat of his heart against her cheek, a steady rhythm that banished any lingering tension.

TWENTY-NINE

Before long, they separated, tidying up the last bits of the evening's work. Elysia stored away the leftover comfrey and thyme, while Lorand ensured the brazier's flame was banked safely. Then they left, stepping outside into the cool night. The orchard lights had dimmed, indicating the festival's main dancing had winded down. Overhead, the moon glowed, painting the farmland in gentle silver.

They strolled side by side up the path toward the keep's main courtyard. Along the way, they passed a pair of knights posted near the gate, who saluted Lorand with genuine respect. He nodded in return, and Elysia added a polite goodnight. The keep loomed ahead; its tall stone walls lit by a few torches. No longer did the sight of Valecrest and Kallendore colors side by side feel forced or jarring. Thin ribbons of green and crimson fluttered softly in the breeze, signifying their union—something that used to bring Elysia pangs of indignation.

Now, she allowed herself a small, peaceful smile at the sight.

When they finally reached the keep's interior corridor, the hush intensified. Most guests were gone or asleep, leaving only a handful of staff quietly moving about. The baron must have retired. A wave of tiredness hit Elysia, heavier than before. She realized she craved a moment of solitude with Lorand, away from the orchard crowd and the barn's volunteer bustle.

He must have sensed her fatigue, because he took her hand and guided her wordlessly down a side corridor. A single wall sconce flickered, revealing a modest wooden door: the suite they shared. For the first few weeks after their official wedding, they had navigated the strangeness of living together in the keep, sorting out daily tasks and personal boundaries. Yet the transition no longer felt awkward. They had outgrown that sense of forced arrangement.

Stepping inside, Elysia closed the door behind them, the stillness welcome after so many hours. The modest suite held a small table, a tall wardrobe, and a simple fireplace that was currently dark. Lorand moved to set aside the scabbard at his waist, propping his heirloom sword carefully near the wall. She let out a soft sigh, loosening the ties of her bodice. A wave of relief spread through her shoulders. The day had been a long one, filled with the orchard events, the training session, and countless small tasks.

Lorand shrugged off his tunic, revealing the simple undershirt beneath. He turned, meeting her gaze in the soft light of the single candle. "You realize we're nearly at the end of harvest season," he said, voice low. "After that, the nights grow colder. Perhaps we can slow down—just a little."

She laughed softly, though warmth pooled in her chest at the image of quieter winter evenings. "I'd like that. Look at us," she added gently, stepping close, "laying out plans for orchard clinics and farmland ward updates as though we've been doing this for years."

He lifted a hand to cup her cheek. "Maybe it's a sign we'll handle the winter just fine," he murmured. "We're forging a new tradition, Elysia. One that belongs to both of us."

She raised her eyes to his, letting the sincerity of his words wash over her. Yes, a new tradition—somewhere between swords and spells, orchard fruit and farmland wards. She could imagine in the coming months, the orchard trees stripped of leaves yet protected by the wards they had combined. Valecrest knights traveling with watchers, ensuring roads were safe from any leftover sabotage that might try to exploit the gloom of winter. And throughout it all, she and Lorand were at the center, not merely fulfilling a royal edict but shaping a brighter barony. The monarchy, in the end, had only started this. They had chosen to continue it.

A tender hush spread through the suite. Her breath slowed as Lorand eased nearer, his closeness magnetizing. Gently, he bent his head and captured her mouth in a soft, lingering kiss. She responded kindly, fingers drifting up to get entangled in his hair. The day's tension slipped away, replaced by an undercurrent of sweet relief. Here, in the privacy of their suite, the burdens of watch rosters and warding demonstrations dissolved into simple closeness.

When the kiss ended, he held her gaze. "We've come far," he said quietly. "And there's no one else I'd rather share the rest of the journey with."

Emotion swelled in her chest. She pressed her palm lightly over his heart. "And there's no one else I trust to watch my back. The monarchy forced us onto this path—but our choice to continue it was always ours. No regrets."

His expression shone with unspoken understanding. Then he guided her gently toward the side table, insisting she sit while he fetched a small pitcher of water from a shelf. He poured two cups in a calm, routine gesture that hinted at how comfortable they'd grown in each other's presence. Passing one cup to Elysia, he took a seat beside her. The single candle flame danced, illuminating the subtle curves of his face as he sipped.

They lingered in that hush, sipping water, letting themselves bask in the day's successes. Elysia felt her muscles relax. The orchard, the barn clinic, the orchard dance—each memory glimmered with the promise of what Highdale could become. Once, everything about Lorand had represented the forced betrothal she despised. Now, he was her partner in every sense.

"How about tomorrow?" he asked softly, after a moment. "Shall we ride together to that farmland near the orchard? I heard rumors of a traveler with an injured horse. Maybe your healing wards can help. I can see if the farmland garrison needs any reorganization. You can do a quick demonstration of wards, and maybe, if we have time, we can slip back to the orchard for lunch."

It sounded so simple, so... domestic. Elysia's heart lifted. "Yes. I'd like that," she said. "We'll see if the traveler needs more thorough healing, and we can keep an eye on the orchard perimeters." Her smile widened. "Though you might find you prefer orchard dancing to orchard patrolling after tonight's experience."

He gave a low chuckle. "Doubtful. Twirling among apple trees isn't quite in my nature. But for you, I make exceptions."

A glow of affection spread through her. She finished her water, placed the cup aside, and rose. He rose as well, taking her hand with a quiet devotion that matched her own. A wave of contentment pulsed between them as they began to prepare for rest, removing shoes and setting aside belts. The single candle flickered, casting dancing shadows along the stone walls.

At last, Elysia slipped under the light blanket, Lorand settling beside her. The day's exhaustion pressed around her eyelids, but in the serene hush of the suite, she felt safe. For weeks, they had worked tirelessly to transform the forced union into a genuine alliance for Highdale. And now...

Her thoughts drifted to the orchard's starlit canopy, the sounds of fiddles, the hum of combined watch stations. So much had changed since that first edict. She turned her head slightly on the pillow, seeing Lorand's silhouette in the candlelight. "Goodnight," she whispered.

"Goodnight, Elysia," he murmured, leaning over to press a final, featherlight kiss against her temple.

She closed her eyes, letting the day's triumphs and small, tender intimacies lull her into rest. The orchard festivities might continue outside, but in their humble suite, the hush of unity echoed more strongly than any forced vow. Here, as they settled into a quiet darkness, Elysia felt certain that Highdale's future shone brighter than ever. The sweetheart orchard where watchers and knights danced, the barn full of potential healers, the farmland rosters Lorand maintained—each piece was forging a new legacy, one based on trust rather than fear.

Tomorrow, they would rise to carry on their tasks. Next week, next month, new challenges would surface— she had no doubt. But tonight, contented warmth filled her, and she let sleep take hold with the certainty that her marriage had become an unbreakable bond, her old enemy a treasured ally, and the land they both guarded brimming with promise.

THE NEXT MORNING broke as gently as a sigh. Pale sunlight roused Elysia from restful dreams, painting their suite in a soft glow. She stretched, blinking away from the haze of sleep, aware of Lorand's steady presence. Outside, the keep stirred with morning bustle: the clang of servants fetching water, the call of a stablehand guiding horses out for grooming, and the faint ring of a blacksmith's hammer from a distant corner.

Elysia rose, dressed quickly in a simple gown of practical green, then slipped on comfortable boots for farmland travel. Lorand, too, donned his more unassuming attire: a snug tunic and riding trousers, though he belted on his sword. She didn't protest. Valecrest knights, after all, rarely went unarmed. Just as watchers rarely ventured out without a small supply of wards. Their synergy was something she'd grown used to, a comforting mirror of each other's devotion.

They emerged into the corridor to find Mira waiting with a bright grin. "You must be heading to the farmland," she guessed, refusing to let them pass without a hush of excitement. "I'll look after the barn. If any volunteers show up, I'll keep them busy sorting herbs until you return. But please come back by midday if you can. People still want your direct guidance."

"We'll do our best," Elysia promised. "Thank you, Mira."

Lorand nodded, thanking her as well, and the two of them departed down the keep's main staircase. The baron's staff had prepared a modest breakfast—fresh bread, cheese, fruit—and they ate quickly in a corner of the hall. The baron was evidently still abed after last night's late festivities. Elysia felt a little pang of guilt for not saying goodbye, but they would be back soon enough.

After breakfast, they strolled to the stables. The stablemaster, an older man who had once complained bitterly about "witches meddling," now greeted Elysia with genuine respect. He offered them two horses, each brushed and saddled. Lorand's mount was a sturdy bay with a Valecrest-embroidered bridle. Elysia's was a gentle palomino she'd grown fond of during the goodwill tour. With the stablemaster's help, they mounted up and set off, riding out the keep's gate into the bright morning.

Highdale's farmland greeted them with lush fields bearing the last remnants of the harvest. Swaying golden stalks of grain, patches of root vegetables ready for picking, and orchard groves that had begun shedding leaves. They passed a newly formed orchard guard station where a Valecrest soldier and a Kallendore mage shared a vigilant watch. The soldier recognized Lorand, saluting promptly, and Elysia found herself exchanging a friendly wave with the mage. Two worlds once divided, now entirely comfortable working side by side.

Heading southwest along a winding dirt track, they soon reached the farmland rumored to house the wounded traveler's horse. A small cluster of farm buildings lay ahead, and as they approached, Elysia spotted a figure waving at them. They slowed their horses near a fence where a gaunt man in a patched tunic hurried over.

"My lord and lady," he panted, ducking his head respectfully. "You're come about that traveler? She's in yonder barn, her mare too lame to travel further. We tried splinting the leg, but we're only farmers, not healers. She nearly fainted from worry last night."

Elysia dismounted quickly, passing her reins to Lorand. "I'll look." She motioned for the farmer to guide her to the barn. Lorand followed, stationing the horses near a post. Inside, the barn smelled of hay and old timber. A dark-haired woman crouched at the side of a trembling gray mare. The animal's left foreleg was heavily bandaged, and the woman's eyes were rimmed red from lack of sleep.

Seeing Elysia, she made a strangled sound. "Please, can you help? I feared the leg might be broken, and I've no coin to pay for advanced remedies. A kind farmer here let me stay, but—"

"It's all right," Elysia assured her, kneeling beside the mare. Slowly, she unwrapped the bandage to examine the leg. The mare whickered softly, eyes rolling with pain. Elysia gently ran her fingers along the limb, feeling for breaks. "Seems more like a severe sprain or hairline fracture, not a complete break," she said after a moment. "I can attempt a healing infusion that should mend the bone quickly, if her body responds well. We won't let her suffer."

Tears streaked down the traveler's face. "Bless you, my lady."

Elysia slipped into silent concentration. She retrieved a small pouch from her belt—a portion of dried comfrey, plus a bit of goldenseal to soothe inflammation. Murmuring a soft Kallendore invocation, she pressed her palms along the horse's leg. Warmth grew under her touch. She felt the faint pulse of her magic bridging the boundary between muscle and bone, knitting each fiber with careful coaxing. The cost was not trivial; healing an animal's fracture required energy, but Elysia had grown more adept at rationing her life force. Over the last few weeks, she had refined her technique to avoid the draining extremes of the past.

Gradually, the mare's trembling lessened. Elysia finished the infusion by sprinkling the herb mixture over the leg and whispering the focusing phrase. A golden shimmer flickered, then faded. The horse let out a calmer whinny, the tension seeping from her posture.

"Wrap it lightly," Elysia instructed, turning to the traveler. "I wouldn't mount her again for a day or two, but she'll heal stronger now. Let her rest in a safe space if possible or lead her gently if you must move on."

The traveler's gratitude poured out in a tumble of words, tears shining in her eyes. "I—I've heard such rumors of Kallendore magic, that it was fearsome or dangerous, but you've saved her, my lady, and asked nothing in return... I don't know how to repay you."

Elysia offered a humble smile. "Just treat her well. And if you pass others in need, share that we rely on healing powers for good, not harm." She rose, pressing a hand lightly to her lower back, feeling a mild ache from kneeling. Lorand appeared at her side, concern in his expression.

"You all right?" he asked, voice low.

She nodded. "Yes, just a bit of exertion. It was a small fracture. She'll be fine with a day's rest."

Relief flickered in Lorand's eyes. He helped her step away, leaving the traveler to dote on her newly relieved mare. As they exited the barn, a faint breeze ruffled the farmland. The farmer who had greeted them thanked her profusely, expressing awe that "once, I'd have guessed only knights could help, but that's nonsense now, clearly."

Elysia suppressed a quiet laugh at how quickly perspectives shifted when real need arose.

Lorand's posture remained watchful as they returned to their horses, scanning the farmland for any sign of leftover sabotage or trouble. But the fields lay quiet. Nearby, a small cluster of sprouts had begun to bud—proof that the farmland wards were stable. Elysia smiled to see it. The orchard's influence had spread, mending farmland that once might have fallen to blight.

They mounted again, turning their horses back toward the orchard path. The morning sun lifted higher, bathing the fields in a golden light. Elysia felt contentment settle in her bones. Here they were: two heirs once forced together, now choosing to ride side by side, healing the land and strengthening the watch. She cast a glance at Lorand, struck once more by how his presence no longer felt like an intrusion on her life, but rather a steadfast complement to it.

He caught her look and arched her brow. "Something on your mind?"

A warm grin curled her lips. "Just thinking how different life is now."

Lorand's mouth quirked with quiet humor. "Yes, I suppose if someone had told me a year ago, I'd be trotting across farmland with a Kallendore mage to heal a horse, I'd have drawn my sword in disbelief. But I'm glad for it."

She nodded, urging her palomino forward. The breeze carried the tang of freshly tilled earth, a reminder that each day brought new tasks but also new possibilities for growth. As they rode, Elysia felt a surge of gratitude for the orchard behind the keep, for the baron's unwavering over-sight, for the monarchy's final acceptance, and above all, for the bond she and Lorand had forged. Their union had guided Highdale from an abyss of fear into a hopeful dawn.

They soon approached a gentle hill that sloped in the orchard's direction. From the crest, one could see the keep's stone walls and the orchard's canopy. In the mid-morning brightness, the orchard's autumn leaves glowed in shades of yellow and orange. Elysia inhaled the crisp air. "Let's pause here," she suggested, reining in her mare. "Just a moment. It's beautiful."

Lorand guided his horse alongside hers, both animals snorting softly. Together, they looked out at Highdale spread before them—rolling farmland, orchard, keep, and the distant roads that connected them to the rest of the kingdom. A hush of unity enveloped the scene, as if the land itself recognized the feud was over, replaced by coop-eration. Elysia felt Lorand's hand brush hers where the horses stood side by side. The contact was fleeting but enough to make her heart quicken.

"I can't quite believe it," she whispered. "We've done it, at least for now."

Lorand's voice was steady, a soft rumble in the quiet. "And we'll keep doing it, day by day."

She turned, meeting his gaze. The orchard breeze ruffled his dark hair, and his eyes shone with the promise of all they had yet to achieve. The monarchy's decree might have begun this journey but love and hard work had carried them through. Each challenge had strengthened their resolve, forging a bond unbreakable by any sabotage or rumor.

Elysia lifted her free hand and let it rest lightly over Lorand's fingers. The warmth of his skin grounded her, reminding her that beyond all the farmland wards and orchard festivals, this was the heart of it: their shared choice to protect Highdale, to stand by each other through every season. With a slow exhale, she offered him a small smile. The orchard's leaves fluttered downhill, brightening the horizon like a tapestry of gold.

"Shall we head back?" she asked, voice tinged with gentle affection. "I promised Mira we'd return by midday."

Lorand nodded, returning her smile. "Yes. Let's climb that next hill and see if the orchard is still spinning with leftover festivities from last night. I suspect we'll find a new surprise waiting for us." His tone carried a hint of fond exasperation—no doubt referencing the baron's endless dedication to communal feasting.

Elysia laughed under her breath. "Probably so." She clicked her tongue, urging her mare forward. "Onward, then, to see what new joys or tasks greet us."

They rode side by side, descending the slope toward the orchard path. The rustling leaves overhead accompanied them, and with each step, Elysia felt the tapestry of Highdale's future unwinding before them. If caretaker mages, farmland watchers, orchard knights, and traveling healers all bonded under the synergy she and Lorand fostered, there was no telling how bright the region might shine.

Glancing at Lorand, Elysia's heart lifted. As they

pressed on through the orchard's dappled light, she thought of evenings yet to come: more orchard dances, more barn clinics, shared triumphs, and the tangible product of their love, their future children.

They disappeared among the orchard's golden branches, two figures united in purpose and affection, ushering Highdale's tomorrow with every breath. And in the hush between heartbeats, Elysia smiled, certain that the future of this land—and the promise she and Lorand carried—would blossom more vividly than any orchard fruit ever could.

SORCERY AND SECRETS

Book One, *SABOTAGE,* coming soon to Amazon.

Her magic could save him - or destroy them both.

Cassandra thought her exile was permanent. As a witch cast out from Baron Ulric's keep, she carved out a life among the forest's outcasts, learning to survive on her own terms.

But she's been summoned back.

The baron's son, Taron, is losing control of his volatile magic. His dangerous surges threaten to reduce the entire keep to ash - and Cassandra is the only one whose wards can contain his power.

Returning means facing old wounds and bitter betrayals. The keep seethes with suspicion, treating her as both savior and saboteur. Taron, the man who once meant everything to her, stands at the center of a web of political manipulation that threatens to destroy them both.

With evidence of sabotage mounting and deadly accusations swirling, Cassandra must uncover who is really behind the keep's magical disturbances.

Every step closer to the truth draws her deeper into a dangerous game of power, passion, and revenge.

Will Cassandra and Taron's rekindled connection be strong enough to overcome years of heartbreak and mistrust? Or will the dark forces conspiring against them finally tear apart the last threads of their shared destiny?

OTHER FLORID ROMANCE BOOKS

To be notified of new releases and special promotions from Florid Romance, please join our email list:

https://floridromance.lmbpn.com/about/sign-up-for-our-newsletter/

For a complete list of books published by Florid Romance please visit our website:

https://floridromance.lmbpn.com/

BOOKS BY RIVER TATUM

The Dating Diary
One Is Too Many BF's (Book 1)
Two Many Choices (Book 2)
Three is A Crowd (Book 3)
Four Is a Disaster (Book 4)

<u>The Firebrand Chronicles</u>
Forged in Flame (Book 1)
Bound By Flame and Illusion (Book 2)
Crowned in Flame and Oath (Book 3)

<u>Vows in Magic and Steel</u>
Duty Bound (Book 1)
Hearts in Conflict (Book 2)
Unbreakable Vows (Book 3)

BOOKS BY MICHAEL ANDERLE

Sign up for the LMBPN email list to be notified of new releases
and special deals!

https://lmbpn.com/email/

For a complete list of books by Michael Anderle, please visit:

www.lmbpn.com/ma-books/

CONNECT WITH MICHAEL ANDERLE

Connect with Michael Anderle

Website: http://lmbpn.com

Email List: https://michael.beehiiv.com/

https://www.facebook.com/LMBPNPublishing

https://twitter.com/MichaelAnderle

https://www.instagram.com/lmbpn_publishing/

https://www.bookbub.com/authors/michael-anderle

www.ingramcontent.com/pod-product-compliance
Lightning Source LLC
Chambersburg PA
CBHW020245010826
48973CB00006B/1664